Robert E. Strahorn

**The Hand-Book of Wyoming**

and guide to the Black Hills and Big Horn regions - for citizen, emigrant and tourist

Robert E. Strahorn

**The Hand-Book of Wyoming**
*and guide to the Black Hills and Big Horn regions - for citizen, emigrant and tourist*

ISBN/EAN: 9783337190804

Printed in Europe, USA, Canada, Australia, Japan

Cover: Foto ©Andreas Hilbeck / pixelio.de

More available books at **www.hansebooks.com**

THE

# HAND-BOOK OF WYOMING

AND GUIDE TO THE

# 𝕭𝖑𝖆𝖈𝖐 𝕳𝖎𝖑𝖑𝖘 𝖆𝖓𝖉 𝕭𝖎𝖌 𝕳𝖔𝖗𝖓 𝕽𝖊𝖌𝖎𝖔𝖓𝖘

FOR

CITIZEN, EMIGRANT AND TOURIST.

BY ROBERT E. STRAHORN ("ALTER EGO"),

OF THE WESTERN PRESS.

CHEYENNE, WYOMING.

# PREFACE.

A LITTLE more than sixty days ago the writer announced his intention of producing this work, and commenced the task of gathering statistics and placing them into the form now presented. A few promises were made in the prospectus first issued, and the kind-hearted and enterprising citizens who have assisted upon the strength of such collateral are respectfully asked to compare the result with the "good intentions." Inspection and criticism are not invited, however, in the belief that the volume is devoid of errors or incongruities. In a field possessed of such grandeur and wonderfully varied interests as that presented by Wyoming a year might well have been devoted to the creation of such a work; and in stating that only one-sixth of that time has been applied, it will hardly be wondered that imperfection may be admitted. In collecting, sifting and tabulating these statistics the writer has endeavored to be thoroughly conscientious, and to accept only that from other hands which has been deemed thoroughly reliable. When the reader remembers that there has been no similar work published here, that official statistics in so young a commonwealth are few and almost valueless, and that every department of our industry and resource is at least briefly touched upon, he can, in a measure, realize the amount of labor which has been bestowed.

The writer cannot lose the opportunity here presented for thanking the Wyoming public generally — and a few of the Territory's best citizens more particularly — for the substantial favors and unvarying kindness extended him. For most valuable personal favors received from Mr. E. A. Slack, of the Cheyenne *Daily Sun*; Dr. George W. Corey and Judge D. McLaughlin, of Cheyenne; Col. Stephen W. Downey and Dr. J. A. Hayford, of Laramie City; A. McIntosh, Esq., of Green River City, and Homer Merrell, Esq., of Rawlins, he is deeply grateful.

CHEYENNE, WYOMING, July 20, 1877.

# ILLUSTRATIONS.

—

# CONTENTS.

## PART FIRST.

### The Resources of Wyoming.

## PART SECOND.

### COUNTIES, CITIES AND MISCELLANEOUS INFORMATION.

## PART THIRD.

### THE BIG HORN AND BLACK HILLS REGIONS.

# PART FIRST.

# THE RESOURCES OF WYOMING

## AND PRESENT DEVELOPMENT.

# WYOMING.

## CHAPTER I.

### A BIT OF EARLY HISTORY.

SINCE the time when Isabella pawned her jewels to procure an outfit for Columbus, the desire to discover the golden sands of the west has not lessened; and to recount the disappointments and disasters that have resulted therefrom would be no easy life-time task. Although the Genoese navigator had no idea of enriching himself by his perilous launch, in 1492, he at least hoped that the coffers of Ferdinand and his queen would be replenished by the wealth of new possessions. But most of his companions were adventurers in quest of gold and glory, reckless and oftentimes cruel to brutality. The missionaries who accompanied him were Franciscan friars, whose zeal for the conversion of the savages was only surpassed by the thirst of their companions in bucklers for gold. Thus a religious zeal, which teaches its votaries to despise riches on earth and lay up treasures elsewhere, and a most avaricious desire for wealth on the part of these adventurers, went hand in hand exploring the southern part of North America more than three centuries ago.

Four survivors of the ill-fated Spanish expedition to Florida, in 1528, bravely made their way westward across the Mississippi, traversed those sections now known as the commonwealths of Texas, New Mexico and Arizona, and finally reached the Gulf of California. Reappearing among former friends after several years of absence, they occasioned no little astonishment. Their glowing accounts of the kingdoms, cities and towns they had passed through, and the barbaric wealth and splendor they had witnessed excited and fascinated their listeners to such a degree that an Italian friar, named Mark, determined to visit the country. He induced one of these four men, a negro named Stephen, to return, and boldly penetrated the wilderness until he came within sight of the city of Cibola, a location not made plain by early chroniclers. Here the venturesome friar and his companion were attacked by natives, and in the fight the negro was killed, leaving the isolated explorer only the alternative of swiftly retracing his steps.

Friar Mark did not abandon his project, however, and in 1540 he induced the chieftain Coronado to head an expedition to Cibola, stimulating the new adventurers by richly-colored tales of the vast riches and entrancing beauty of the place. Other Franciscans accompanied the expedition. Finally Cibola was reached, but not so the reputed wealth, for the place proved a barren prize. The friar was overwhelmed with reproaches, and, returning to the coast, soon died.

But enchanting tradition whispered that there were other cities of untold wealth farther in the interior, and Coronado pushed on. He crossed the Rio Grande near the present town of Santa Fe and pushed northward to the Arkansas, but still failed to find the golden cities. True, he encountered numbers of small Indian villages, but fortune was no nearer than when he started from the sunny shores of the southwestern gulf. Growing thoroughly discouraged, after a two years' search, Coronado returned, leaving two zealous friars, however, at Indian villages along the Rio Grande.

The fame of the supposed rich cities had now reached the City of Mexico and Tampico, and an expedition in quest of them started from the latter place in 1542. During the march northward an Indian village on the east side of the Rio Grande was named Santa Fé (holy faith), and became the base of future explorations. The two missionaries left behind in this vicinity by Coronado had already suffered death at the hands of the Indians. From this time forward there were alternate successes upon the part of the Spaniards in establishing missions in New Mexico and of the savages in destroying them. The rich cities to the northward were yet undiscovered, although little doubt prevailed as to their existence.

During the progress of the Mexican war, in 1846, a highly educated Mexican padre, named Ortiz, was captured near El Paso

in the act of bearing dispatches to his countrymen south of the
Rio Grande. While a prisoner in the hands of General Stephen
W. Kearney's followers, he volunteered the statement to different
American army officers that the Spanish had early in the seventeenth century obtained a footing in the mountainous region
some seven or eight hundred miles north of Santa Fé, but still
south of the great muddy river (the Missouri); that they had
built stone houses and arastras, and for nearly a quarter of a
century had sent trains to the south laden with gold and rich
furs. About 1650, however, the savages of the region commenced
a wholesale massacre of these pioneers, and all were swept away
as far south as Santa Fé. Ortiz had in his possession an old
Spanish book, written late in the seventeenth century, describing
all of the country between the Rio Grande and the Missouri, and
also containing statements verifying those volunteered by himself, to the effect that the ruins of these settlements existed in
the northwest, and that great canals and other auxiliaries to
mining had been there constructed.

At intervals of many years following, reckless adventurers
risked their lives to reach the northern land of promise, but these
never returned after crossing the Arkansas. As late as 1781, a
small expedition, accompanied by Jesuit missionaries, left Santa
Fé and penetrated the great northwestern plains, but there is no
account of the return of any of the party.

These facts become especially interesting in connection with
the developments of American explorers in our own time. Members of General Connor's Big Horn expedition of 1865, now residing in Cheyenne, vouch for the statement then made that ruins
of stone houses, evidently more than a century old, were found
near the shores of the beautiful Lake de Smet, at the eastern base
of the Big Horn Mountains. In 1866, the remains of an old
Spanish arastra — a quartz-crushing implement — were found in
the same region, at a point about fifty miles southwest of Fort
Phil Kearney. Ruins of stone houses and fortifications were
also discovered by Colonel Mills' expedition in the Big Horn
country as late as the fall of 1874. Montana miners who were
driven by the Indians from the Rosebud Mountains, east of Fort
C. F. Smith, where they were prospecting in 1866, reported that
there was evidence that mining had been extensively carried on,
on some of the bars there, a long time previous to their visit.

They found traces of iron tools which had been devoured by rust, the line of a former ditch to convey water upon the bars, and some other indications which lead to the conclusion that the Spanish adventurers alluded to had not only obtained a footing in the region, but had also perished there while in the realization of their wildest dreams.

It is stated as a fact, capable of verification, that there is now a map in the archives of Paris, prepared by Jesuits as early as 1792, which contains a correct topographical sketch of the Black Hills and Big Horn Mountains, and that both are marked as auriferous regions; but from whence the information was derived is more than can be definitely ascertained. Certain it is, however, that missionaries and gold-seekers visited portions of the present Territories of Wyoming and Montana, in search of souls and the royal metals, during the last century.

*Father De Smet.*—No doubt one of these indomitable missionaries, Father Peter John De Smet, became thoroughly acquainted with the country now embraced in Wyoming upward of thirty years ago. This intrepid disciple of Loyola emigrated from Belgium to America in 1823, and, proceeding to St. Louis, soon founded the St. Louis University. His abilities as a naturalist, botanist, metallurgist and geologist were very marked. His love for these studies, and a genuine desire to elevate our savage races, soon led him to follow a resolution made before he left his native land — to become a missionary among the Indians. Accordingly, in 1838, he commenced the career which has since given him so much prominence, and in 1839, with two companions, drifted fearlessly northward, destined for the fur-trading post of Fort Benton. In June of that year the trio camped at the present site of Cheyenne — a fact that the venerable missionary cited when here in 1868 with Generals Sherman and Sheridan.

"How long have you lived in Cheyenne?" asked the Father of a gentleman with whom he was conversing.

"Since last November, Father. I suppose I may consider myself one of the oldest settlers of the place."

"If I were so minded," remarked the missionary, "I could justly lay claim to being an older settler than you, for I camped here one night in June, 1839, on the banks of Crow creek, near the railroad bridge."

After leaving Crow creek the missionaries crossed the country to the Yellowstone, and from there to Fort Benton. They had many interesting adventures with Indians during the trip; were often delayed by the savages, their movements suspiciously watched, and their motives in visiting the country carefully inquired into. But the gentle manners and sincerity of De Smet soon won for him their confidence and esteem. For about ten years his travels and explorations among the northern tribes were practically unrestricted — he was free to go and come, and met with hearty welcomes from the same savages who have since carried on a bitter warfare, and who have just succumbed to the military under General Crook and other officers. In 1849 the " Black Gowns " (as these missionaries were styled among the Indians) were prohibited from coming out on their missions at the trading posts, because the small-pox had been communicated to some of the bands by whites, and swept with fearful fatality to others. This was the only obstacle ever placed in the way of the self-sacrificing priests, and this was again soon removed. During these years of pilgrimage Father De Smet became well acquainted with the geological formation of the country, as well as with its geography and topography. From the forks of the Cheyenne on the east to Great Salt Lake on the west, and from the head waters of the Columbia river on the north to the Platte on the south, he was quite generally " at home." On his return to St. Louis from one of his long trips, just as the discovery of gold in California was made known, he heard some acquaintances expressing doubt as to the wonderful stories from the west. Turning to them, he said: " I do not doubt it. I am sure there is gold in California;" and after a moment's pause he quietly added: " I know where gold exists in the Rocky Mountains in such abundance that, if made known, it would astonish the world. *It is even richer than California!*" Among those who knew him best his statements were taken for literal truth, and when asked to corroborate the assertion quoted he would make no explanation, merely adhering to it and saying that he had promised the Indians never to describe the location of this wealth.

Rev. Toussaint Mesphlie, now a Catholic chaplain in the United States army, is authority for the story, already quite generally known, in which De Smet told of the Indians showing

him handsful of nuggets which they proposed manufacturing
into bullets for an old pistol which the Father had given to a
prominent chief. De Smet was really taken to the spot from
whence the nuggets were obtained, and found it to be immensely
rich. But he taught the savages the value of it, told them their
beautiful country would soon be desecrated by white miners if
the facts became known, and in return was compelled to promise
never to reveal the secret of its location. To the question once
asked him by a bishop of his church at Omaha, "Are those
mines on the Pacific coast the ones you have told about?" the
Father answered in the negative, and then sorrowfully added,
"but I fear it will not be many years until they are discovered,
and then what will become of my poor Indians?" To army
officers and others he has often admitted his knowledge of those
mines in the northwest, when closely pressed to do so, and many
persons are now living who have tried in various ways to extract
more definite knowledge from him. Most of these believe that
a careful prospecting of the Big Horn and Wind river regions
will certainly reveal the terra incognito, because it is understood
that the old Montana mines were not meant, and that no spot
yet discovered in the Black Hills answers to his glowing description.

While in Cheyenne, in 1868, he visited the home of a well-
known citizen, and during his stay gave a most interesting and
satisfactory account of northern Wyoming and the Yellowstone
region. Among other things, he said: "There are a great many
lovely valleys in that section, capable of sustaining a large population. The mountain scenery is truly grand, and the vast
forests of timber wonderful and invaluable. Often have I seen
evidences of mineral wealth in this wonderful country at different
places. The whole range of the Rocky mountains, from New
Mexico to British America, is mineral bearing. In many places
the streams are stocked with trout, and game was abundant
wherever I went. The climate is delightful, often reminding
me of the climate in the south of France, near the Pyrenees. I
have ridden through some of these rich valleys where the grass
was so rank and tall that my head was not visible above its top
when seated on horseback."

Among the many literary works of Father De Smet were a
series of letters which were continued for nearly thirty years and

"FATHER DE SMET AND THE ABORIGINAL MINER."

were published in a French periodical. These letters no doubt contain a fund of information concerning our Territory, which some future historian will gladly avail himself of. His death at St. Louis in 1873 was a matter of universal regret. It can never be said that the thought of gain on earth was the secret of his labor, and the pure unselfishness which so strongly characterized his missionary work gave him the confidence of our savage races to an extent never before, and probably never again, to be gained by one man. To-day his name is reverentially used by young and old of the agency Indians. The sacred emblem of his faith — the cross — is worn universally, by hostile and peace Indian alike, and it is the principal design for ornament on their weapons and garments. His name is inseparably connected with the history of Wyoming.

*Other Explorers.*—Granting that our old-time friend, Jim Bridger, was here when, as he expressed it, "Laramie Peak hadn't commenced to grow and was a hole in the ground," we are compelled to divide honors about equally between officers of the American army and representatives of the great fur companies for first following in the wake of Spanish and Jesuit adventurers and missionaries. These later explorations, which resulted in a permanent occupancy of the country, dated from the first years of the present century. Besides the gallant achievements of Lieutenants Lewis and Clarke, Captain Bonneville and General Fremont, the latest nearly half a century ago, we have it from reliable authority that the hardy spirits of the northwestern fur companies had trapped no less than 3,000,000 beavers along the northern range of mountains previous to 1825 — a statement which tells the whole story of early pioneering, with its train of thrilling episodes and soul-trying emergencies.

*Organization.*—After the creation of Dakota Territory, the greater portion of the region now embraced within the limits of Wyoming belonged to our sister commonwealth first named. To Dakota, therefore, our earliest pioneers looked for what little law and justice was given them; and it was the rule, rather than the exception, that citizens at this long distance from the capital waited either very long or else hopelessly for even such little satisfaction. It is a fact well known that more revenue was gained by the territorial treasury from this isolated section than from all of eastern Dakota, while the taxation here laid by the

United States aggregated very handsome amounts. But with the completion of the transcontinental railway a new era was inaugurated, and the enterprising settlers who laid the foundation for our new State, that is to be, made vigorous efforts to secure an organization nearer home. These were baffled until July 25, 1868, when the act to provide a temporary government for the Territory of Wyoming became a law. The boundaries designated for the foundling were the forty-first and forty-fifth degrees of north latitude and the twenty-seventh and thirty-fourth meridians of longitude west from Washington. This gave the Territory the generous dimensions of 355 miles in length by 276 miles in breadth, and, besides taking a large proportion of Dakota's domain, carved smaller areas from Colorado and Utah.

Federal appointments for nearly all offices were made during April, 1869, and on the 10th of May following the new government was in complete working order, with Cheyenne as the capital. The gentlemen who first filled positions of trust were: J. A. Campbell, Governor; Edward M. Lee, Secretary: Church Howe, Marshal; J. M. Carey, United States Attorney; John M. Howe, Chief Justice; J. W. Bingham and W. S. Jones, Associate Justices; C. D. Ruger, Surveyor General: Frank Walcott, Receiver Public Land Office.

The first legislative assembly in Wyoming was organized at Cheyenne October 12, 1869, with Wm. H. Bright as President of the Council, and S. M. Curran, Speaker of the House. The legislature adjourned *sine die* on the 10th of December, after having given the first laws that were considered really binding by the people of this section. Succeeding sessions have been held biennially, meeting, according to enactment, one month later than the first.

The present Territorial government consists of the following: Governor, John M. Thayer; Secretary, Geo. W. French; Marshal, W. F. Sweezy; District Attorney, E. P. Johnson; Surveyor General, E. C. David; Treasurer, A. R. Converse; Auditor, Orlando North; Collector, E. P. Snow; Justices of the Supreme Court, J. W. Fisher, Wm. W. Peck, J. B. Blair; Superintendent of Instruction, John Slaughter; U. S. Commissioner, J. W. Bruner; Register U. S. Land Office, G. R. Thomas; Receiver of Public Moneys, I. C. Whipple; Librarian, John Slaughter.

The following is the official count of the elections for delegate to Congress in Wyoming since the organization:

| COUNTIES. | 1869. | | 1870. | | 1872. | | 1874. | | 1876. | |
|---|---|---|---|---|---|---|---|---|---|---|
| | Corbett. Rep. | Nuckolls. Dem. | Jones. Rep. | Wanless. Dem. | Jones. Rep. | Steele. Dem. | Carey. Rep. | Steele. Dem. | Corbett. Rep. | Steele. Dem. |
| Albany .......... | 320 | 515 | 428 | 369 | 359 | 563 | 555 | 699 | 1,010 | 533 |
| Carbon .......... | 190 | 389 | 150 | 183 | 79 | 261 | 282 | 363 | 529 | 407 |
| Laramie ......... | 722 | 886 | 398 | 380 | 518 | 572 | 677 | 881 | 1,242 | 940 |
| Sweetwater ...... | 593 | 862 | 363 | 279 | 399 | 186 | 306 | 406 | 496 | 423 |
| Uintah .......... | 138 | 679 | 327 | 228 | 116 | 160 | 584 | 657 | 587 | 457 |
| Totals......... | 1,963 | 3,331 | 1,666 | 1,439 | 1,471 | 1,742 | 2,404 | 3,006 | 3,864 | 2,760 |
| Majority ...... | .... | 1,368 | 227 | .... | .... | 271 | .... | 606 | 1,104 | .... |
| Whole vote (including scattering).. | 5,266 | | 3,202 | | 3,213 | | 5,404 | | 6,626 | |

It should be mentioned that the vote of 1869 was greatly out of proportion to the permanent population, as the new railroad towns and mining camps were filled with a large floating population, which disappeared with the flush times of the earliest days.

# CHAPTER II.

WHILE perusing the pages which follow, the reader should ever keep in mind two very important facts: First — that the field reviewed has until the present been almost wholly recognized as the sacred and impenetrable stronghold of the most powerful of America's savage nations; that the Indian has held possession of nearly all of the domain which could be rendered productive and has greatly retarded the development of the remaining and most undesirable portion by systematically plundering its pioneers. Second — that while more accessible commonwealths have always held out great inducements for speedy settlement, and have thus in a single decade quadrupled their population and productions, Wyoming has really made no earnest effort to attain such an end. It was plain that protection could not be afforded the emigrant except along the southern line of the Territory, where desirable locations are limited, and the legislature which abolished all efforts tending to secure miscellaneous immigration was wise and judicious — even if its humane spirit was wondered at by rival Territories.

But the Wyoming of to-day glows with a new life. Peace has dawned so suddenly that the long-fettered frontier has scarce awakened from its ten years of darkened dreaming. To realize that her grand area of nearly 100,000 square miles, crowded with all the bountiful resources of a coveted empire, is at once and forever emancipated from savage sway, may be easy in quiet New England, but not so where the keys of development have always been carried at the girdle of a hostile possessor. To define the thrill which permeates the frame of the first herdsman who pushes his flocks northward across the Platte river at staunch old Fort Fetterman, and sets his feet firmly upon "Indian ground," might also be a prosy task in the east, but in the valleys of Wyoming it will meet an echoing tingle never to be forgotten. And now, while celebrating such an epoch, let us not forget to whom its bright inception is due, but with our rejoicing mingle thanks to the gallant, hard-worked and faithful military of the Department, directed by General George Crook, and to the new zeal manifested in our welfare by an awakened administration.

The natural capabilities of few regions are so generously and favorably diversified as in that embraced within the limits of Wyoming. Forest and plain, mountain and valley, water-course and upland alternate and unite to furnish the most accessible field for the speedy creation of a large and prosperous commonwealth. Her grazing area proper aggregates 55,000 square miles, while much of the mountain surface omitted in this estimate is thickly carpeted during summer and fall with her most succulent and nutritious grasses. That portion of the surface susceptible of cultivation comprises nearly 20,000 square miles of bottom and uplands. The timber area, less the many extensive patches along water-courses in the lower valleys, is fully 30,000 square miles — a portion of this covering the best grazing lands. Including the latest discoveries in the northern part of her domain, Wyoming possesses 24,000 square miles of coal lands, with vast deposits of rich iron ores alternating in different sections. The regions in which precious metals are known to exist present an area of 40,000 square miles, all underlying the forest region already noted. Among other important natural auxiliaries are immense deposits of marble, soda, plumbago, oil-bearing shale, petroleum and red oxide of iron, all adjacent to the line of the Union Pacific Railway, and some of them already commencing to swell the wealth of the Territory's productions.

To more strikingly present the extent of these natural features and their capabilities, let us indulge in a few comparisons. Wyoming's grazing area is greater than the entire area of Kentucky, a State which in 1870 owned 1,639,092 head of sheep and cattle, beside over a million head of other live stock. Her agricultural area of virgin and fertile soil is greater than that of the States of Massachusetts and Connecticut combined, which on their artificially fertilized soil produced in 1870 5,857,239 bushels of grain. Wyoming's forests cover more territory than those of the great lumbering State of Michigan, whose product in this line reaches a value of $40,000,000 per annum. And her surface underlaid with strata after strata of coal, exceeds that of the coal lands of Pennsylvania, whose product reaches $50,000,000 or more annually.

The eleven principal rivers of the Territory — the Yellowstone, North Platte, Big Horn, Green, Bear, Snake, Tongue, Laramie, Cheyenne, Powder and Sweetwater — have a total length within her limits of 4,000 miles, and with their numberless tributaries afford her a more complete and better distributed water system than any of the trans-Missouri States or Territories can boast. These facts are all enlarged upon in succeeding pages, and are merely thus outlined to give the reader an idea of the wealth lying latent in the new northwest. And now let us see hastily what progress the pioneer, in his trammeled state, has made in the utilization of these princely resources.

The following table, exhibiting the assessed valuation and population of the Territory in 1870 and 1877, is compiled from the official returns and includes the reports of the present year.*

| COUNTIES. | EST. POPULATION. | | ASSESSED VALUATION. | | Rate of Taxation Total. | NAME OF COUNTY SEAT. |
|---|---|---|---|---|---|---|
| | 1870. | 1877. | 1870. | 1877. | 1876. | |
| Albany ........ | 2,500 | 8,500 | $593,547 | $2,500,000 | Mills. | Laramie City. |
| Carbon ........ | 2,000 | 2,500 | 1,731.418 | 1,900,000 | | Rawlins. |
| Laramie ...... | 4,000 | 9,540 | 1,397,771 | 3,000,000 | 21 | Cheyenne. |
| Sweetwater ... | 4,500 | 3,500 | 1,840,120 | 1,918,449 | 15 | Gre'n Riv.Cy. |
| Uintah ........ | 1,750 | 4,500 | 1,900,000 | 2,500,000 | 28 | Evanston. |
| Totals...... | 14,750 | 28,540 | $5,516,748 | 11,818,449 | | |

Basing this estimate upon the opinions of numerous well informed citizens in different sections of the Territory, the writer places the true present valuation of all property at $15,500,000.

Wyoming is in a most healthy and gratifying financial condition. There is no territorial indebtedness, but the handsome surplus of $13,000 remains in her treasury. The valuation of property, according to assessment returns just noted, has increased from $5,500,000 in 1870 to $9,000,000 in 1876, and $11,818,449 in 1877. The Territorial tax of three mills for this year will place the treasury in even better condition than it is at present, notwithstanding the fact that the meeting of the legislature during the coming autumn will cause a large drain upon its funds. A majority of the counties can present the same proportionate financial prosperity.

* Returns from Carbon and Uintah counties could not be obtained, and are therefore estimated from best data at hand.

A careful summing up of Wyoming's productions for the year 1876 results as follows:

Coal, 524,000 tons at average of $4 per ton ....................$2,096,000
Gold, dust and bullion..........................................  815,000
Hay and other farm products.....................................  485,000
Live stock and wool ..........................................  ..  990,000
Manufactured articles, including lumber, stone, etc............. 3,918,120

Total ..............................................$8,304,120

Internal revenue collections for the past five years, as reported by Collector E. P. Snow, will give readers an idea of the steady and rapid increase of Wyoming's returns to the home government. They are as follows:

1872 ..................................................... $6,727 27
1873..................................................... 10,652 94
1874..................................................... 11,233 38
1875..................................................... 11,942 11
1876..................................................... 15,063 37

Total....... ................................$55,619 07

For a Territory so young and hitherto harassed by savages, Wyoming deserves no little credit for her fine system of rail, stage and telegraph. The following figures again strongly illustrate what inducements her great natural wealth has held out to capitalists:

The Territory contains 2 railways aggregating a length of ...... 500 miles.
"               "      6 telegraph lines aggregating a length of 1,401  "
"               "      4 daily mail routes    "          "       908   "

A third railway is in course of construction, and a fourth, to penetrate the Big Horn, Black Hills and Yellowstone regions, will be well under way within the coming year. Excellent wagon roads reach from the Union Pacific Railway to even the most remote and newest mining districts.

There are those who are ever ready to assert that as the Indian troubles are settled and military posts are abandoned, much government patronage will cease, prominent industries will wane, and our now thriving cities will absolutely suffer. The writer grants that the entire loss of government patronage will amount to a few millions annually, should that very improbable loss occur within a quarter of a century. But, judging the future by the unmistakable past, let us see how, with peace

3

within our borders, old channels of production are widened and
new ones created. And, further, let us carefully note the proportion of gain, by a perfect peace, to that of loss under the old
superficial stimulus of government expenditure in times of
disquiet.

In 1870, with a population nearly as large as at present — but
limited in its range to comparatively unproductive centers —
and with a larger number of military posts and agencies, our
productions of every nature amounted to less than $1,000,000 in
value, according to official estimates. In 1877, with a greater
safety in the operation of mines, a determined occupation of
productive territory and a greater freedom in the investment of
capital, our various industries will yield a product of not less
than $8,200,000. With little more than the same amount of
population and our productions already twice quadrupled, it is
self-evident that our scope for securing revenue has widened
just so much. Within the past ten years Nebraska has enjoyed
comparative peace and has increased her population from 50,000
to 300,000. Kansas, with her wild tribes subdued, has in the
same period grown from a population of 175,000 to 475,000 and
has more than quadrupled her productions; while Colorado,
with no greater natural resources than those of our own Wyoming, has increased her 30,000 people to 130,000, and rivals some
of the older States in the diversity and value of her productions.

In none of these States has the limit of prosperity been half
approached. Wyoming excels any of them in pastoral resources
and equals any for the value of mineral deposits or forest lands.
With these grand capabilities will not the hour soon come when
the enthusiastic writers of to-day will be proven even modest in
their now apparent extravagance? The time draws near when
the emerald plains and the metal-ribbed mountains of Wyoming
will enable her to take exalted place among her sister States,
holding deeply hidden in her rocky defiles a nation's wealth and
bearing in her sheltered valleys the keys which unlock those
wondrous treasures.

# CHAPTER III.

## STOCK-RAISING AND DAIRYING.

HOWEVER much we may theorize upon our vast wealth lying hidden beneath the soil, all speculation ceases when we consider the industries which flourish upon and above it. The riches of mountains and gulches may often be glowing and fascinating uncertainties, but the treasures, latent and developed, in our broad pastures and thousand nestling valleys are facts as certain as our existence. At this late day no argument is necessary to show that the world pays its greatest tribute to food — to bread and beef — and that the demand ever keeps its proportion beyond the supply. Then, being assured of a market always stimulated by deficit, the question only remains where in the new west these industries can be most profitably pursued.

After weighing the many facts and observations bearing upon the climate of this region, so ably presented by Dr. Corey in another chapter, the reader will not be surprised at the statements so long thrown broadcast that beneficent Nature cures our grasses and herbs, and that not one out of ten thousand of our cattle has ever consumed an ounce of other food. A striking illustration of this grand advantage in stock-raising was the answer received by the writer from a prominent stockman in regard to the latter's preference for cattle over sheep — " because cattle take care of themselves and sheep don't!" This assertion, while not literally true, is far nearer the mark than novices can realize. It is true that ranch sites are improved and herders employed, but to feed, water, shelter or salt the steer of the period would be a sad innovation upon the all-prevailing custom of letting said steer shift for himself.

A brief outline of the several systems employed by cattle-growers of Wyoming will give readers a more correct idea of our advantages than can be given by presenting volumes of generalities. A quite popular mode of handling cattle is that in which breeding is given little attention, and buying and selling steers

season after season takes the preference. Two and three-year-old
steers are purchased in Texas in the early summer at say $12 and
$16 per head delivered at Cheyenne. With them are often pur-
chased a few heifers and cows, which, upon being located on the
range, are kept as a nucleus to assist in holding the strange animals bought each year within the limits of the range. A desirable ranch site is chosen, and as a rule the improvements made
are much less expensive than those on regular breeding ranches.
The cattle are kept upon our rich cured grasses during the winter, and during the summer following (one year from the date of
their entry) the best three and four-year-olds are sold to local
dealers or are consigned to eastern commission men. These
well-conditioned Texans sell at an average of $28 per head at
any of our stations, while the few not fit for sale are left with
the nucleus already referred to and held over for another season.
The profits are at once reinvested in the manner first described,
and the buying, pasturing and selling thus continued year after
year.

Following is a tabulated statement of the industry as thus
carried on. It is taken from the books of an experienced and
thoroughly reliable stock-dealer of Cheyenne, and while the
profits are very moderately figured the percentage of loss is admitted by the gentleman in question to be an exaggerated estimate:

### STOCK INVESTMENT, No. 1.

Result of investment in 750 head of Texas steers made July, 1874, and profits
reinvested yearly, and kept in operation without closing account for three
years:

#### FIRST INVESTMENT.

| | |
|---|---:|
| Bought July, 1874, 350 head 3-year-old steers at $16 | $5,600 |
| Bought July, 1874, 400 head 2-year-old steers at $12 | 4,800 |
| | |
| Sold from July to December, 1875 — | |
| 450 head 4 and 3-year-olds at $28 | $12,600 |
| Bought from July to December, 1875 — | |
| 450 head 3-year-old steers at $16 | 7,200 |
| 450 head 2-year-old steers at $12 | 5,400 |
| | 12,600 |
| Carry over old stock not fit for market — | |
| 300 head 4 and 3-year-olds at $20 | 6,000 |
| | |
| 1,200 head on hand end of first year; value | $18,600 |

## SECOND YEAR.

Sold from July to December, 1876 —

| | |
|---|---|
| 250 head 4 and 5-year-old steers at $30 | $7,500 |
| 550 head 4 and 5-year-old steers at $28 | 15,400 |
| | $22,900 |

| | | |
|---|---|---|
| Bought 800 head 3-year-olds at $16 | $12,800 | |
| Bought 800 head 2-year-olds at $12 | 9,600 | |
| | | 22,400 |

Carry forward old stock —

| | | |
|---|---|---|
| 50 head 4 and 5-year-olds at $30 | $1,500 | |
| 350 head 4 and 5-year-olds at $20 | 7,000 | |
| | | 8,500 |

| | |
|---|---|
| 2,000 head on hand; value | $30,900 |
| Balance, cash on hand not reinvested | 500 |
| Assets at end of second year | $31,400 |

## THIRD YEAR.

Sales from July to December, 1877 —

| | |
|---|---|
| 350 head 4 and 5-year-olds at $30 | $10,500 |
| 1,000 head 4 and 3-year-olds at $28 | 28,000 |

On hand from last year, not fat, or otherwise unmarketable —

| | |
|---|---|
| 50 head 5 and 6-year-olds at $30 | 1,500 |
| 650 head 3 and 4-year-olds at $20 | 13,000 |
| Amount of assets at end of third year | $53,000 |

Total cattle bought 3,200 head.

Deduct for losses of three years at 10 per cent —

| | | |
|---|---|---|
| 320 head at $20 | $6,400 | |
| Original investment | 10,400 | |
| | | 16,800 |

| | |
|---|---|
| Net profit | $36,200 |

The next account presents the results of breeding cattle exclusively. The estimates are made from actual experience, and the profits are as entirely free from exaggeration as in the previous showing:

### STOCK INVESTMENT, No. 2.

Nucleus of 1,000 Texas cows and necessary Short-Horn bulls, requiring a capital of $15,000. The account runs for a period of five years, during which time the amounts realized from sales are not reinvested, except those necessary for the purchase of bulls:

### 1877.

```
1,000 cows @ $12 .............................$12,000
   40 bulls @ $75 .............................  3,000
                                         ——————  $15,000
```

### 1878.

| | |
|---|---|
| 1,000 cows. | Sell 50 dry cows @ $20.... $1,000 |
| 250 heifer calves ⎰ 50 per cent | Buy 6 bulls for use July, |
| 250 steer calves ⎱ first year. | 1879, @ $75 .........   450 |
| ——— | |
| 1,500 | Cash balance.........   550 |
| 46 bulls, less deaths. | |

### 1879.

| | |
|---|---|
| 950 cows. | Sell 50 cows @ $20....... $1,000 |
| 250 heifers, 1 yr. old. | Balance from 1878........   550 |
| 250 steers, 1 yr. old. | ——— |
| 350 heifer calves ⎰ 70 per cent. | 1,550 |
| 350 steer calves ⎱ | Buy 12 bulls for use July, |
| ——— | 1880, @ $75 .........   900 |
| 2,150 | ——— |
| 58 bulls, less deaths. | Balance ............   650 |

### 1880.

| | |
|---|---|
| 900 cows (70 per cent calves). | Cash balance............ $650 |
| 250 heifers, 2 yrs. (40 per cent | Sell 50 cows @ $20....... 1,000 |
| calves). | Buy 15 bulls for use July, |
| 250 steers, 2 yrs. | 1881, @ $75 .........  1,125 |
| 350 heifers, 1 yr. | ——— |
| 350 steers, 1 yr. | Balance ............   525 |
| 380 heifer calves. | |
| 350 steer calves. | |
| ——— | |
| 2,830 | |
| 73 bulls, less deaths. | |

### 1881.

| | |
|---|---|
| 850 cows. | Cash balance............ $525 |
| 250 " (half-breeds). | Sell 50 cows at $20....... 1,000 |
| 350 heifers, " 2 yrs. | Sell 200 steers, 3 yrs., @ |
| 380 " " 1 yr. | $30 ................  6,000 |
| 250 steers, " 3 yrs. | ——— |
| 350 " " 2 yrs. | Cash balance .........  7,525 |
| 350 " " 1 yr. | No bulls allowed for last |
| 460 heifers " calves. | year. Those bought in 1880 |
| 450 steers " " | do service in 1881, and the |
| ——— | party buying or keeping the |
| 3,690 | heifer stock should provide |
| 73 bulls, less deaths. | for service of 1882. |

1882.

| | |
|---|---|
| 800 cows (old). | Cash balance............ $7,525 |
| 600 " (half-breeds) 3 & 4 yrs. | Sell 100 cows @ $20...... 2,000 |
| 380 heifers " 2 yrs. | Sell 50 steers, 4 yrs., @ $35 1,750 |
| 460 " " 1 yr. | Sell 250 " 3 yrs., @ $30 7,500 |
| 50 steers " 4 yrs. | |
| 350 " " 3 yrs. | Cash proceeds, end of fifth |
| 350 " " 2 yrs. | year................. 18,775 |
| 450 " " 1 yr. | Net over purchase of bulls. |
| 575 heifers " calves. | |
| 575 steers " " | |

4,590
60 bulls—say 13 dead.

4,650 head, total end of fifth year, July, 1882.

### VALUE OF STOCK ON HAND.

| | | | |
|---|---|---|---|
| 1,300 cows @ $20........$26,000 | Cash balance............$18,775 |
| 100 steers, 3 yrs., @ $30. 3,000 | Stock .................. 65,140 |
| 730 heifers and steers, 2 | |
| yrs., @ $18...... 13,140 | 83,915 |
| 910 heifers and steers, 1 | Deduct capital .......... 15,000 |
| yr., @ $12.50.... 11,375 | |
| 1,150 heifers and steers, | Profit .............. 68,915 |
| calves, @ $7.50.. 8,625 | |
| 60 bulls @ $50 ........ 3,000 | |

4,250 head total, deducting
sales. 65,140

There are also many stock men who prefer to combine these systems, and who claim that the business is more profitable and satisfactory in every way when thus conducted. For parties who do not desire to continue in the industry more than a few years the first plan presents the strong inducement of not requiring so much preparation and expense in starting; while the rather "gipsy" fashion of conducting the enterprise admits of the settlement and termination of it without inconvenience at almost any time. The last plan can only be appreciated, and its grand possibilities realized by its being followed for a series of years. Made a permanent industry, it is undoubtedly a surer, and possibly as short a road to wealth as is offered by any legitimate enterprise under the sun.

Texas yearlings, either sex, can be bought at almost any railroad point in eastern Wyoming at $7.50 per head; two-year-olds, $12; cows, $13. A good ranch site, with necessary buildings and corrals, located within two days' drive of the railroad, can be secured for $1,500. First-class herders (and others are dear at any price) can be readily obtained at an average of $32.50 per month and board. Texas cattle are taxed at an average valuation of $10 per head, the rate being twenty-eight mills on the dollar. Very close calculations, made by several competent informers, make the total expenses of keeping cattle each year, after the necessary permanent ranch improvements have been made, as follows: In herds of 1,000, per head, $1.75; in herds of 5,000, $1.40; in herds of 10,000, $1. It is also reliably stated that such stock growers as J. W. Iliff, who graze over 25,000 head, figure their expenses down to from sixty-five to seventy-five cents per head per annum.

Think of our average cattle man raising a steer and putting him on the market, a three-year-old, at a total expense of *four dollars and fifty cents.* The same animal in Illinois, be he scrub or thorough-bred, would cost his owner two-thirds of his selling price for feed alone. It may be remarked by the critical reader that the Illinois bullock sells for two-thirds more than the one native to Wyoming. We need only answer that it will not cost five cents more to raise the sleek, high-grade animal on the plains than the Texan steer now costs. It is a mere matter of choice upon the part of the breeder whether he continues raising the scrawny Texan, year after year, and sells him at $28, or by introducing better blood into his herds soon produces a grade which brings him $45.

Two per cent. is considered a liberal estimate of losses from all causes in this northwestern region, although it would be too low on the plains of Kansas, or even portions of Colorado, for the reason that the humidity of the atmosphere during storms, and the almost inevitable partial melting of snows immediately after their fall in those sections are most fatal to weakened animals. While snows in those regions are moist and soon badly encrusted, our nutritious grasses are at once laid bare for grazing by the almost unceasing winds which sweep the light dry snows from the broad level plateaux, and pile them in narrow gulches.

Early in the summer of each year the great "round-ups" occur. All herders, and frequently owners of stock, gather

together in certain localities, and, with the most experienced and skillful stockmen for leaders, inaugurate a short season of the herdsmen's wildest revelry. Mounted upon their best ponies, the herders swiftly scatter out across the range, gathering in every animal, and finally concentrating the property of perhaps a dozen prominent stock growers in one immense, excited herd. Passing near the ranches of respective owners, the animals are halted in a convenient location, and part of the cow-boys hold the mass while others ride through it, single out the "brand," or animal, belonging to the adjacent range or ranch, and separate it from the main body of cattle until none of that description are to be found. Moving along to the next man's range, the scene is repeated, and so continued until the cattle are divided. Then young stock is branded, marketable stock sometimes disposed of, and the cattle are again allowed their freedom. Five or ten thousand head are thus frequently gathered together, and during the round-up season men "camp out," wagons following the herd with provisions, blankets, etc. Our artist has given a very fair representation of the "cutting out" scene on another page.

In regard to the wonderful and often exaggerated results placed upon paper in relation to this industry, a few words may not be amiss. A steady profit of twenty-five per cent. per annum is really a common result. Forty and fifty per cent. have been realized, but the writer who lays down such figures as an average is very liable to get his reputation involved. It is not uncommon for experienced stockmen, who know how to utilize every advantage, and to guard against nearly all discouragements, to do business for a time on capital borrowed at two per cent. per month, and to make a small margin on the investment. The writer has in mind a gentleman whose large herds roam in southern Wyoming, who for five years has made the very handsome profit of forty per cent. per annum. He has been especially judicious in his purchases and sales, exercised great care and judgment in the selection of a range, and in his system of ranch improvements, and has been so fortunate as to secure some of the best men on the plains to carry out the practical workings of his business. Constant supervision and study upon the part of the *owner* of stock is a grand point. There are practical cattle men who will do as well for the investor as they would do for themselves, but these are never looking for work; and one of the

secrets of the few failures that have been made is the fact that
men of no experience in the business put their money and property into the hands of total strangers, in the belief that the latter
would set at defiance every law of human nature, and look out
purely for the interest of the novice.

The assessment returns of the present year place the total
number of cattle and sheep in Wyoming as follows: cattle, 90,005
head; sheep, 67,871 head. Following are the reports returned,
together with the total area of each county, the estimated area
thus far appropriated, and the estimated wool clip:

| COUNTIES. | Total area in square miles. | Area appropriated. sq. miles. | No. cattle. | No. sheep. | Wool clip, pounds. |
|---|---|---|---|---|---|
| Albany | 10,488 | 3,000 | 9,895 | 24,604 | 125,000 |
| Carbon | 22,080 | 4,000 | 8,000 | 1,500 | 8,000 |
| Laramie | 16,836 | 6,500 | 53,233 | 35,602 | 175,000 |
| Sweetwater | 29,532 | 9,000 | 11,377 | 1,965 | 9,000 |
| Uintah | 17,064 | 3,500 | 7,500 | 4,200 | 18,000 |
| Totals | 96,000 | 26,000 | 90,005 | 67,871 | 335,000 |

These reports do not include this season's increase, and are
certainly twenty-five per cent under the real figures, without
taking the increase into consideration. From many estimates
made by reliable stockmen we would therefore credit the Territory with 150,000 cattle and 100,000 sheep at this writing. The
drive of cattle from Texas into Wyoming this year is estimated
at from 50,000 to 65,000 head. The demand is still brisk, and
at least 20,000 more would have been taken by our dealers and
cattle-growers but for the falling off of the supply at southern
points. Over 26,000 head are to be sold and shipped from
Wyoming stations this season, representing a value of nearly
$800,000. There is a reliable home market for 10,000 head per
annum in the Territory and Black Hills camps at the present
rate of consumption. Beef steers here average $32 per head;
cows, $22.50; calves, $8.

*Mutton and Wool.*— Much that is said of the adaptability of
the Wyoming climate and grasses to cattle-raising applies equally
well to the production of sheep. But, as has already been intimated, sheep require a little extra attention in herding, feeding,
sheltering, etc., during occasional storms. A comparative statement will exhibit the extra expense, and also the advantage here

obtained over flock-masters in the older States. In the official reports of 1862, before the inflation of prices, it was estimated, from many communications from all the northern States, that the average cost of keeping sheep was $2.65 per head per annum. Taking this as a basis, the comparative cost of keeping sheep in the States and on the plains would be as follows:

```
3,000 sheep in the States, at $2.65 per head... .....................$7,950
3,000 sheep in Wyoming, herding and shearing ...............$800
100 tons of hay, fed during severe storms, at $6............... 600
                                                              ____
  Total............................................... 1,400
                                                              ____
Difference in favor of Wyoming...................................$6,550
```

In ordinary winters not one-fourth of the hay would be needed. Flock-masters in the crowded east, can you afford to pasture sheep on land worth from $50 to $100 per acre, when such facilities as free pasturage, the most nutritious grasses, a climate naturally adapted to wool-bearing animals, and a never-failing market for mutton and wool, are presented by Wyoming and Montana? Mark the difference and place the balance in favor of this section in even the most discouraging light possible, and you will yet see enough left that is sufficiently encouraging to persuade you to make a change.

There are points in this industry, bearing upon absolute success or failure, which must not be overlooked. Experience, study and watchful care over the flocks is an absolute and undeniable necessity. As well might an unlearned journeyman blacksmith attempt to conduct a great daily newspaper as might a man from the business centers of the east, with no semblance of practical knowledge, expect to achieve almost instant success as a wool-grower on our great plains. To show that this animadversion is really called for, the writer need only quote an actual occurrence. A firm came from London, a few years ago, upon the strength of representations that in this blessed pastoral country sheep could be turned loose to care for themselves; they would require neither herding, shelter nor feed from one year's end to another, and in the small space of three years a flock of a few thousand would make their owners immensely wealthy. The sheep were bought, "turned loose" upon a good range, and the flock-masters spent most of their time at a convenient railroad station. During the fall the wolves disposed of large numbers of the helpless ani-

mals, and in the course of an unusually severe winter, hundreds
were "bunched up" in gulches by heavy storms and frozen or
starved to death. The same firm are to-day numbered among
our model wool-growers, but mark the cost of the experience.

If, during the late and trying winter months, a severe storm
arises, the sheep are at once driven to shelter, and should the
storms continue longer than is their usual wont, hay is at hand
to bridge over the period during which grazing is prevented.
The flocks are visited daily by either the owner or a capable
overseer, and herders either rendered trustworthy or discharged.
Shearing is delayed until danger of late spring storms is at an
end. Employes are well paid, well fed, and made to feel an
interest in the employer and his business. The ranch is located
where shelter and suitable buildings can be cheaply erected and
repaired, and where hay sufficient for all possible demands can
be economically put up. Then wool and mutton markets are
carefully studied. These are a few of the points watched by
successful wool-growers, and among those who are managing
their business thus systematically there is as much enthusiasm
and as much success, as a rule, as among the best cattle-growers.
Successes have been recorded without these precautions, but one
failure made in this way retards the development of our grazing
resources to a greater extent than two triumphs encourage it.

The writer cannot forego mentioning one other and vital
point bearing upon the realization of *all* the possibilities within
range of the careful flock-master — that of improving the quality
of both mutton and wool.

Let Wyoming flock-masters — let all the brave pioneers who
are engaged in the great work of founding the grand trans-Missouri empire, which the world shall yet look upon and admire
—remember this fundamental maxim: "Whatsoever is worth
doing at all is worth doing well." It is true, as we believe, that
the most advanced and intelligent of Wyoming's wool-growers
do already recognize and act upon this axiomatic and golden
truth. The evidence is found in the existence of many flocks of
superior sheep in the Territory, young as she is in her civilized
pastoral life.

Showing the advantages of the improved system of sheep
husbandry over the old, shiftless, improgressive system, is like
attempting to prove the truth of an axiom — it is almost a work

of supererogation; yet these advantages cannot too often be held up to public view, for not all sheep breeders are thinking, progressive men. For example, take a band composed of native Mexican ewes and bucks, and with them conduct operations during a term of, say, five years. Then take a band of the breed and quality of ewes (*i. e.*, common Mexican), cross them with pure Merino or Cotswold bucks, and conduct operations in breeding and wool-growing during a similar period of time: the result will strikingly illustrate the practical advantages of the improved system. Thus: One thousand Mexican ewes (with twenty common bucks to start with) will, with reasonable care, skill and judgment on the part of the flock-master, yield the results shown in the first of the following tables, which were prepared and published by the writer several years since, but which he feels justified in bringing forward again at this time. The calculation, as will be seen, is based on the low annual increase of seventy-five per cent., an average yield of two pounds of wool per head sold at twenty cents per pound, and an annual expense of fifty cents per head for every animal (including original flock and all increase), during the five years.

The estimated yield in numbers and fleece is moderate, while the margin allowed for expense is ample to cover usual outlay for that purpose, as well as mortality and all reasonable contingencies. On this basis, then, the yield in wool alone of one thousand ewes would be in five years as given in the table, counting no fleece from lambs the first year:

STATEMENT

Showing the yield in five years of 1,000 common Mexican ewes and bucks.

| YEARS. | Sheep. No. of wool-bearers, each year. | Wool. Amount at 2 lbs. per head. | Value of wool at 20 cents per lb. |
|---|---|---|---|
| First............. | 1,000 | 2,000 | $400 00 |
| Second.......... | 2,030 | 4,060 | 812 00 |
| Third ........... | 2,416 | 4,832 | 966 40 |
| Fourth .......... | 2,948 | 5,896 | 1,179 20 |
| Fifth............. | 3,679 | 7,358 | 1,471 60 |
| Totals........ | | 24,146 | $4,829 20 |

The increase of the 1,000 ewes, at 75 per cent annually, would number 7,823 in five years, worth, at $2.25 per head, $17,601.75. Add this to the value of wool produced, $4,829.20, and the aggregate is $22,430.95 — not including the value of the original band. From this deduct expense of keeping and tending (averaged, as above stated, at 50 cents per head), $6,411.50, and there is left, as the net profit for the five years' operations, $16,019.45. Even this is a splendid result, showing, as the ancient Spanish proverb runs, that " Wherever the foot of the sheep touches, the land turns to gold."

But let the operation be conducted with the same number, breed and quality of ewes, under the better system of elevating the stock by crossing with fine bucks, and then see how much greater results will be realized, in a like period, on same basis. In the next calculation, the original 1,000 ewes are estimated as fleecing two pounds per head each year, and their increase (grades) three pounds each. (This is a reasonable estimate; the second, third and fourth crosses would fleece from three and one-half to four pounds.) The price of the common fleece is counted at 20 cents per pound, as before, and of the grade fleece at 25 cents. The value of the 7,823 head (increase) of improved sheep is estimated at $3 each, instead of $2.25, the price of the common animal. Everything else being equal, the results would show as follows:

STATEMENT

Showing the yield in five years of 1,000 common Mexican ewes, crossed with pure Merino or Cotswold bucks.

| YEARS. | Sheep. No. of wool-bearers, each year. | Wool. Amount at 2 and 3 lbs. per head. | Value of wool at 20 and 25 cts. per lb. |
|---|---|---|---|
| First | 1,000 | 2,000 | $400 00 |
| Second | 2,030 | 5,040 | 1,172 50 |
| Third | 2,416 | 6,248 | 1,462 00 |
| Fourth | 2,948 | 7,841 | 1,861 00 |
| Fifth | 3,679 | 10,037 | 2,409 25 |
| Totals | | 31,219 | $7,304 75 |

To the above $7,304.75, add value of the increase (7,823 head at $3), $23,469, and we have $30,773.25 as the gross result in five years, without including the value of the original band, still on hand (less ordinary mortality, of course), or value of the bucks. From this $30,773.25 deduct expenses, as in first operation, $6,411.50, and $1,000 to cover difference in cost between common and pure-bred or high-grade bucks — total, $7,411.50 — and there is left, as a net profit on five years' operations, under the improved system, $23,361.75, showing a difference in its favor (over the old system) of $7,342.30 — *seven thousand three hundred and forty-two dollars and thirty cents.* The writer has in mind an instance in which one ranchman clipped 18,000 pounds of wool from 2,000 improved sheep, while a neighbor thought he was doing well in getting 8,000 pounds from the same number of low grades. "Blood will tell."

Of course, improved sheep-husbandry involves something more than high breeding alone. If the flocks of the western plains have heretofore made fortunes for their owners when left to almost shift for themselves from one year's end to another, without the benefit of sufficient prepared food or the shelter of a first-class hay-rick, they may be made to do better with extra provisions in these respects during severe winters. For every dollar expended in this direction by the master, the bounteous flock will return him two dollars in increased yield of wool, lambs and weight. In fact, no owner of good sheep can *afford* to neglect them. The best flocks of the future are to figure largely, not in mere numbers, like those of the principal New Mexican flock-masters, but in *results* — in superiority of their blood, giving weight of carcass, weight, fineness and luster of fleece, enhanced individual excellence, and consequent aggregate value. Smaller flocks, better care, larger returns, will be the rule of the future on the plains, as it already is among the best wool-growers of the east.

To commence with a herd of 1,000 sheep — which is about the average number started with — will require an investment of $4,000, as follows: 1,000 Mexican sheep, $2,000; 20 Merino rams, $300; corrals, cabins, etc., $500; leaving $1,200 for carrying on the herd until some income from the flock can be obtained. Mexican ewes are delivered at Cheyenne at from $1.75 to $2.25. Grade sheep, from fifty to seventy-five per cent higher, are rarely on the market. Mutton lambs sell in Cheyenne at $2.50 to $3; mutton sheep, $2.50 to $2.75. A home market for 15,000 sheep and lambs per annum is afforded by the Wyoming and Black Hills settlements. Wool is selling the present year at from 18 to 20 cents per pound, or about two cents per pound higher than wool from the same sheep in southern Colorado and New Mexico commands. It is noticed that a much thicker and better quality

4

of wool is produced from the Mexican sheep a year after the
animal has reached our Wyoming pasture-lands than was clipped
two or three hundred miles farther south, the hair disappearing
almost entirely and being supplanted by a clean, long and heavy
coat of excellent fibre.

*Dairying.*— In all official reports on the dairy interest in
States east of the Missouri, we find that the great drawback mentioned is the heat at just the season when the product is greatest.
Along the base of our mountain ranges and among our sheltering
foot-hills the extreme of heat is seldom known, and no matter
how glaring may be the sun's rays, let the shade be sought, or let
night approach, and a cool, refreshing temperature is at once enjoyed. It therefore follows that artificial auxiliaries, so necessary in the east, are of secondary importance where climate and
grasses so nearly fill all conditions as they do here. As these
artificial auxiliaries are always burdensome items of expense, it
also follows that in dispensing with them, without sacrificing the
quality or quantity of a product, an immense advantage is gained.

Connoisseurs pronounce the first quality Wyoming ranch
butter of as delicate flavoring and tint and as perfect an article
in every way as the choicest eastern grades. Mark the difference
in manufacture : The eastern product is the result of expensive
scientific "petting" and unnatural forcing from beginning to
end. Delicate grasses are carefully nurtured for pasturage ;
months are spent in putting up just the right kind of feed for
winter sustenance ; fine breeds of cattle are stabled and cared for
as though the effect of a zephyr was feared ; and the milk and
butter is manipulated in costly houses with iced temperatures,
and then the "gilt-edged" product, turned out by professional
dairymen, sells in our markets at from five to ten cents per
pound less than the article daily made at our mountain ranches,
where the crystal stream, the native grasses and a delicious
atmosphere are about the only auxiliaries asked by our modest
ranchman, with his band of native cattle, his log cabin and his
unsheltered corral.

Following is an account of the operations of a Wyoming
dairyman for a period of one year :

### INVESTMENT AND EXPENSE.

| | |
|---|---|
| Ranch site, buildings and corral . . . . . . . . . . . . . . . . . . . . . . . . . . . . . . . . . . . . . . . . | $1,200 |
| Fifty American cows at $40, and two sires at $75 . . . . . . . . . . . . . . . . . . . | 2,150 |
| Two assistants — wages and board . . . . . . . . . . . . . . . . . . . . . . . . . . . . . . . | 960 |
| Fifty tons of hay for winter feed at $6 . . . . . . . . . . . . . . . . . . . . . . . . . . . . | 300 |
| Conveying product to market, and minor expenses . . . . . . . . . . . . . . . . . . | 200 |
| Total . . . . . . . . . . . . . . . . . . . . . . . . . . . . . . . . . . . . . . . . . . . . . . . . . . . . . . . . . . | 4,810 |

### PRODUCT.

| | |
|---|---|
| 14,000 pounds of butter, sold at 40c . . . . . . . . . . . . . . . . . . . . . . . . . . . . . . . . | $5,600 |
| 2,000 gallons of milk, sold at 30c . . . . . . . . . . . . . . . . . . . . . . . . . . . . . . . . . . | 600 |
| Increase 34 calves, sold at $10 . . . . . . . . . . . . . . . . . . . . . . . . . . . . . . . . . . . . | 340 |
| Total . . . . . . . . . . . . . . . . . . . . . . . . . . . . . . . . . . . . . . . . . . . . . . . . . . . . . . . . . . | 6,540 |
| Less investment and expense . . . . . . . . . . . . . . . . . . . . . . . . . . . . . . . . . . . . | 4,810 |
| | 1,730 |

The dairyman in question had the advantage of mining and lumbering camps for his market, otherwise he would have realized a few cents per pound less for his butter. To more than double capital, the first year may strike the reader as an exceptional venture, but this experience is duplicated by hundreds of thrifty dairymen along the eastern base of the Rocky Mountains. Hundreds more will duplicate it in the near future, when these plain facts become more widely promulgated, and the underpaid husbandmen on worn-out soils beyond the Mississippi can be aroused by the knowledge of the golden opportunities lying unappropriated in the new west. We have in mind another Wyoming dairyman who has realized a net profit of $2,600 in one season from the yield of eighty cows.

Nearly 300,000 pounds of butter have been consumed in Cheyenne alone during the past year. Of this amount it is estimated that three-fourths, or about 225,000 pounds, have been shipped from beyond Wyoming's borders — much of it a distance of a thousand miles. At an average price of thirty cents per pound we find that one Wyoming city alone is sending out of the Territory to eastern dairymen a tribute of nearly $70,000 annually. A leading hotel keeper has assured the writer that ranch or home-made butter is always in demand at from five to ten cents per pound more than is asked for the foreign article. If eastern dairymen can manufacture butter at a profit, on land worth $50 per acre, where cattle must be fed and sheltered six months in the year, and ship it a distance of 1,000 miles to our market for thirty cents per pound, what may not the coming butter-maker of Wyoming look forward to, when, producing the same article at half the expense, he can sell it at home for thirty-five or forty cents per pound?

*Eminent Authority.*—Hon. Wm. D. Kelley, of Pennsylvania, in referring to our grazing resources in a letter to Dr. Latham, several years ago, said: "Your natural grasses and aromatic herbage are identical with those of the great sheep fields of Asia and Australia." Hon. William Lawrence has said: "I saw at Laramie, in Wyoming Territory, a herd of 4,000 cattle and some 3,000 sheep grazing in Laramie valley, in healthy condition and good order. Laramie valley is covered mainly with a short but very nutritious grass, well adapted to grazing cattle and sheep. The climate is generally cool, with a healthful, bracing atmosphere, with nothing to produce disease either in men or stock. Sheep can be raised at no expense except herding, and in some places the cost of cutting grass along the streams for hay to feed a short time in winter; while in much of this vast region, as I learn, sheep can be kept the year round in good order, without hay or grain, simply by grazing. Already the prospect of sheep growing in this great central region is having its effects. It is, in my judgment, only a question of time, and that a few years at most, when sheep growing for wool will be transferred to this great central section." Hon. S. F. Nuckolls, a former Wyoming delegate to Congress, wrote in 1871: "As to my opinion of the character and capacity of Wyoming Territory for pastoral purposes, I would say, briefly, that the soil, grasses and climate render it eminently superior, especially for sheep. The soil absorbs the falling rain rapidly, while its lighter particles refuse to attach permanently to the fleece, affording a clip as clean without washing as in other countries with washing. The grasses are highly nutritious, cure on the ground, remain as permanent food during the entire winter, and have better fattening properties than the prairie grasses in the more eastern and northern States. The position is elevated, the air pure, and the ground seldom muddy or soft. In addition to all this there are no burrs of any kind, which are such pests in other regions. Sheep are, therefore, healthy and free from foot rot and other distempers common to low, moist lands and rank, coarse food. They have been kept for the past twelve years about the military posts without trouble, and last winter some thirty thousand went through without shelter or food other than the grass on the ground. Cattle in large numbers are kept in the same way, and the cattle worked poor in freighting turned out in the fall are fat and ready for the yoke or the butcher when spring comes." Alexander Majors, so long known as a stockman and freighter on the plains, expressed himself thus emphatically eight years ago: "I have been grazing cattle on the plains and in the mountains for twenty years. I have during that time never had less than five hundred head of work cattle, and for two winters — those of 1857 and 1858 — I wintered fifteen thousand head of heavy work oxen on the plains each winter. My experience extends from El Paso, on the Rio Grande, to one hundred miles north of Fort Benton, Montana. Our stock is worked hard during the summer, and come to the winter herding range thin. Then it is grazed without shelter, hay and grain being unknown. By spring the cattle are all in good working order, and many of them fat enough for beef. During these twenty years the firm with which I was connected wintered many cattle in Missouri and Arkansas on hay and corn, and I am sure the per cent. of loss of those wintered in all the valleys of the trans-Missouri country is less than it was in those States with food and shelter. All the country west of the Missouri river is one vast pasture, affording unequaled summer and winter pasturage, where sheep, cattle and horses can be raised with only the cost of herding."

Wyoming contains 55,000 square miles of all-the-year pasture lands, with an additional area of 25,000 square miles of unexcelled summer grazing lands. Her 150,000 head of cattle and 100,000 sheep have appropriated less than one-third of this gathered treasure of mountain and plain, and even in that liberal estimate have never fully utilized their range. Luxuriant carpets of gramma, bunch and blue grass, with many other varieties, nearly everywhere cover bluff, plain and valley, while in numerous localities the diminutive species of white and black sage, so eagerly sought by stock in winter, are added to the great variety of nutritious native shrubs. Sheltered and wooded valleys are usually so conveniently interspersed that in time of storm the animals are enabled to avail themselves of much comfort and good browsing by a few miles' travel.

There are millions of dollars of capital rusting in the vaults
of the east which might as surely be earning their twenty-four
per cent per annum by investment in any of these branches of
stock-raising as that we have mouths to feed and bodies to
clothe.   The requisites are, in a nutshell, careful study of the
business, personal direction, and the same attention given that
would be bestowed upon any legitimate business venture of equal
magnitude.   When men dispossess themselves of the notion of
tarrying in the Far West only for a year or two, until they can
make their fortunes, and then turn ungratefully from the land
which has made them all they are; when they finally determine
to live here, to create homes here, and add their means and
influence permanently to the development of the country, then
will the golden era of our prosperity be unmistakably ushered.

# CHAPTER IV.

## AGRICULTURE—THE POSSIBILITIES.

THE great inducements offered by Wyoming to the agriculturist have always been apparent to those who have cared to inquire. But the tempting attraction of mines, the large profits realized in stock-raising, and the field for speculation generally offered in such new regions, have, until quite recently, claimed the greatest attention. As well can the country produce its bread as it produces its beef, and in the matter of markets the farmer is here more favored than the stock-grower, for the simple reason that the former has always a home demand, while the latter depends largely upon a foreign market.

Experiments have been made with the different cereals, vegetables and small fruits in the different localities and under all ordinary conditions, with perfect success in almost every case. Near the western outskirts of Cheyenne, an old soldier, Major John Talbot, is showing what the upland soils at an altitude of over 6,000 feet will produce under good ordinary treatment. Fourteen acres are under cultivation, and on the well-kept plat may be seen every variety of the hardy vegetables, thousands of young shade and fruit trees and the tame grasses, flourishing as well as they could be made to do elsewhere. Wheat, oats and rye succeed admirably, and such small fruits as currants, cherries, gooseberries and strawberries have been bearing nicely for two seasons. Of the ten thousand young trees growing upon the grounds, such varieties as white ash, elm, soft maple, walnut, poplar and box-elder seem perfectly at home in their transplanted state. Over 70,000 pounds of potatoes were marketed from one third of the patch last season, and, with other vegetables sold, yielded the proprietor $2,000. Potatoes sold at two and one-half cents per pound, and other vegetables from three to five cents per pound. Cabbage, averaging twelve pounds per head, and turnips weighing from ten to eighteen pounds each, were marketed. The soil is a dark, sandy loam, very friable and mellow, and usually requires irrigating only twice during the season. One man has done all the work, with plenty of time to spare.

In the valleys of Crow Creek, Chugwater, Laramie, North Platte and Hat Creek, in the eastern part of the Territory, such results as the above have been attained in different instances. The growing seasons have been favorable and long enough to mature all crops save corn, and in a few cases the early, small-eared varieties have also been raised. In the central and western portions of the Territory, where the agricultural area is largest, more pronounced successes have been recorded, and much more progress has been made in the cultivation of the rich valley soils than elsewhere. In the Wind River valley and its tributaries, and in the Bear River valley, hundreds of ranchmen have been producing vegetables for their own consumption and the home markets for several years. Where wheat, rye, oats and barley have been experimented with the yield has equaled that obtained from the best farming lands of Utah or Colorado, and the almost entire absence of milling facilities alone prevents a very general production. The value of hay, vegetables and other strictly farm products marketed by Wyoming ranchmen this year will closely approximate half a million dollars.

The valley and bench lands of Wyoming, capable of producing crops common to this latitude, have a total area of 20,000 square miles or aggregate nearly 13,000,000 acres. With unlimited natural facilities for irrigation, fencing and building material always convenient and unexcelled fertility of soil, there is no reason why a strictly agricultural population of 50,000 people should not flourish within our borders and supply to the mineral-producing residents and non-producing population the food which otherwise must come from abroad. The soils are largely the washes and wear of the great mountain ranges. For ages our valleys and plains have been gathering their present accumulation of valuable decomposed and pulverized organic matter, which is so largely drawn upon by vegetable growth. Those qualities which eastern farmers try to replace by plaster of paris, bone-dust, ashes, lime, etc., exist in lasting quantities in our alkaline earths. This fact and the dry, pure atmosphere account for the great superiority in all elements of nutrition of our grasses, grains and vegetable products over those of the States.

From careful estimates made by grain merchants of Wyoming,

we find that 28,800,000 pounds of grain have been shipped into the Territory from Nebraska, Utah and Kansas during the past twelve months, not counting the immense quantities shipped hither by the government and used at military posts. At the average price of two cents per pound this costs us nearly $600,000, and taken from us about that amount of currency which never returns. This may seem a small matter, but the loss will be doubled in a year and quadrupled in two years if our non-producing population continues to increase in such a proportion over the little band of producers. It is only one item, and it alone is thirty times greater than the entire amount paid for the maintenance of our public schools, more than three times as great as the amount of taxes we collect from our 500 miles of railway, and four times as great as the amount invested in all the public improvements of Wyoming. One-thirtieth of the arable soil of our hundreds of fertile valleys would easily produce this simple item and stop the serious leakage.

Vegetables brought from the east or west, though far inferior to those raised here, sell at enormous prices, and the money sent out of the Territory for them runs up into the hundreds of thousands annually. Even along the line of railroads potatoes are commanding an average of two cents per pound the year round, turnips one to three cents, onions three to six cents, cabbage three to seven cents, and other garden produce in proportion. In the mining districts such products are from 200 to 300 per cent. higher. During the month of June, of this year, potatoes sold in Deadwood, by the wagon load, for from twelve to fourteen cents per pound, and turnips at ten cents. Small fruits, which coming half-ripened and often unfit to eat, from distant States, command prices that would insure competence to whoever would engage in their production. The freight is often far more than the cost of production on all of these articles, and the inquiring agriculturist can easily see that such an increase in the selling price of produce must always allow ample margin for profit to local producers.

Irrigation has always seemed a stumbling-block to those who do not understand its advantages. But when once acquainted with the system few farmers would exchange it for the uncertain rains of moister climates. The first expense need not be greater than that of breaking up wild lands in the east, and the labor of

irrigating being light and simple, crops can be watered at an
expense not to exceed the percentage of loss on eastern farms by
long continued rains or drouths.  There is not half the trouble
encountered in keeping out weeds by this system, and loss need
never occur through storms after grain has been harvested and
placed in shocks.  In the early settlement of other sections of
the west, before the art of irrigation was understood, farmers
were laughed at for their attempts to raise anything in the "barren sands."  Yet today those faithful few are the wealthiest and
most respected citizens of Colorado, Utah and Montana.  While
the thousands were risking everything on the richness of mines
and were often losing, these tillers of the soil gathered up the
waste and in the end received the tribute which must be paid to
the producer of bread.

An important drawback to the more rapid development of
our agricultural and pastoral resources is the fact that our principal railroad traverses the most uninviting portion of the Territory.  Thus the great throngs of tourists and emigrants hastily
passing through receive the impression that other portions are
probably identical.  From descriptive articles which follow, it
will be seen that the now almost unknown and unappreciated
Big Horn, Wind River and Yellowstone regions are to furnish
the bulk of arable lands for the sustenance of new communities
in the northwest.  They furnish the most beautiful and productive valleys in the Rocky Mountain region, with millions of
broad and fertile acres unclaimed, and to be had for the simple
taking.  After an attentive reading of our article on climatology,
it cannot be said that an extreme northern latitude renders our
claims untenable.  The few occupied valleys of Montana, all
lying north of Wyoming's agricultural belts, and depending upon
irrigation, produce nearly a million bushels of grain and potatoes
annually, which, with other farm productions, sell at home for
over two million dollars.

# CHAPTER V.

## MINES AND MINING.

AN entire volume like this could be judiciously devoted to the description of a mineral region so extensive and varied as that embraced within the limits of Wyoming. Therefore, being confined to one short chapter, we can promise little more than a hasty tour and a glimpse of different districts and products.

*The Coal Fields.*—The importance of the coal interest, either in a general or local way, was never more strikingly portrayed than in these words of Daddow: "If you would see what coal can do for a people who turn it to full account, look at Pittsburgh, a city, with its environs, of 300,000 inhabitants, built up by its mines of coal. There are no drones in its hive—heads and hands are busy. It lost $30,000,000 by the rebellion without shaking its credit. Possessing in its coal the creative power, it stretches out its mighty arms and gathers the wealth of half a continent into its lap. It brings to its furnaces and forges the iron and copper of Lake Superior, glass-sand from New England, Missouri and Illinois, lead from Wisconsin and Missouri, zinc, brass and tin from beyond the seas. You pass through its gigantic establishments and are amazed at the variety and extent of their perfected productions. Yet all these, from the most delicate fabric of glass to the ponderous cannon and steam engine, are in the coal which underlies the smoky hills of Pittsburgh." It is said by statisticians that the power developed by coal imported into Massachusetts accomplishes more for industry than could be done if all the millions of men, women and children in the United States should devote themselves to manual labor. In Great Britain, says a reliable writer, machinery moved by coal equals the man power of all the inhabitants of the globe.

However, the coal measures of Wyoming are given the precedence, not especially because of a belief that they will always lead the deposits of precious metals in importance, but because of their present advantages in the way of development and yield. As already stated, our known area underlaid by coal reaches 24,000 square miles in extent. Drawing a line across the Territory from east to west, one hundred miles from the southern boundary, then drawing another in a similar manner one hundred miles from the northern boundary, the reader can at once locate the principal portions of our coal-bearing belts. In different sections of this southern belt of one hundred miles in breadth by three hundred and fifty in length are located the largest bodies of coal yet discovered in the Union. Crossing northward over the central belt, of less than one hundred miles in width, we find the generally rougher region, in which fewer deposits of coal, but more of the precious metals, have been discovered. Then, reaching the extreme northern belt of one hundred miles in width, the natural coal-bearing formation is again very frequently encountered, and vast outcroppings of bituminous and semi-bituminous coals are noticed.

We will first briefly review the southern belt, already extensively developed, beginning at the eastern end. Commencing at Cooper Lake, near the center of the Laramie plains and twenty-six miles northwest of Laramie city, a vein of soft coal, fifteen feet in thickness, has been discovered adjacent to the Union Pacific Railroad. The deposit is not worked at present, but its accessibility, extent and fair quality must combine to render it of paramount value in the near future.

Proceeding fifty miles westward to Carbon, we find the first mines worked. Although inferior to the product of mines farther west, the coal is a fair sample of the tertiary brown kind, very compact and pure, and excellent for locomotive use. It is mined and used quite extensively by the coal department of the Union Pacific Railway, and is consumed to a limited extent by residents along the road. The average thickness of the deposit is ten feet. An analysis gives water 6.80, ash 8.00, volatile 35.48, fixed carbon 49.72. About 80,000 tons of coal have been produced here during the past year. Other important but undeveloped deposits are found at numerous points along the road to the westward. At Separation, Rawlins and St. Mary's the outcroppings are especially noticeable.

At Rock Springs, 314 miles west of Cheyenne, are the extensive mines operated by the coal department of the Union Pacific

Railroad and the Excelsior Coal Company. The deposit owned by the railroad company consists of several veins from four to nine feet thick and is at present the principal source of supply for all points along the road as far east as Omaha. Owing to its excellent quality this coal is much sought for by adjacent States and Territories. For blacksmithing, smelting and steam-generating purposes the coals of this district compare favorably with the anthracite.

The Excelsior mine, the property of Colonel E. P. Snow, of Cheyenne, and Blair Bros., Rock Springs, which is a part of this same general deposit, has, in years past, been considered more valuable and has been credited with yielding a better quality of semi-bituminous coking coal than is found elsewhere in the trans-Missouri regions. A natural discrimination, however, made against its owners by the railroad authorities, has served to limit yield and profit. The principal vein is ten feet thick and practically exhaustless. The following analysis, made at the Massachusetts Institute of Technology, is far more favorable than can be exhibited by any of the tertiary coals of Colorado or Wyoming that have come to our knowledge:

| | |
|---|---|
| Ash (white) | 1.55 |
| Hydrogen | 4.75 |
| Carbon | 76.00 |
| Sulphur | .07 |
| Phosphorus | .00 |
| Oxygen and Nitrogen | 17.63 |
| | 100.00 dried at 100° C. |
| Coke | 60.00 |
| Specific gravity | 1.26 |

The coke is compact and not easily crushed, and being practically free from sulphur and phosphorus can be especially recommended for iron smelting.

For the year ending June 30, 1877, these mines produced 144,000 tons, or an increase of nearly 25,000 tons over the year preceding. Coal sells by contract on the track at from $1.55 to $2 per ton, and at outside points at an average of $5. One hundred and fifty white men and the same number of Chinamen are employed the year round. Engines, hoisting apparatus and interior arrangements are exceptionally complete and systematic.

Still journeying westward with the glistening coal formation

visible on the face of numberless bluffs, we find in the vicinity of
Carter station, a point on the Union Pacific 388 miles from
Cheyenne, some of the most remarkable coal measures yet discovered. One of these, known as the "Mammoth Sandstone
Mountain Mine," has been traced and prospected for a distance
of four miles. Throughout this length there are some fifteen
veins, one lying above the other, with thin layers of sandstone
intervening. These veins are from five to sixty feet in thickness,
and aggregate nearly four hundred feet of solid bituminous coal.
The veins slope at an angle of about twenty-two degrees. The
coal is free from slate or dirt and with the product of the Mammoth mine, a similar deposit near by, must at some future period,
when the demand for fuel is greater and transportation facilities
are better, effect a revolution in the western coal trade.

In the vicinity of Evanston, at the western boundary of
Wyoming, are the most extensively worked deposits in the Territory, while within a days' ride of the city are a number of other
magnificent veins of the softer coals. Two and one-half miles
from Evanston, at the busy mining town of Almy, the Rocky
Mountain Coal and Iron Company, the Union Pacific Company
and S. H. Winsor, have made great progress in the development
of the measures there found. The strata now worked by the
Rocky Mountain Coal and Iron Company is simply enormous,
being twenty-six to thirty-five feet in thickness and extending far
back from the present openings, which already indicate a length
of deposit of three miles at its face. The mines controlled by
the Union Pacific Company and the Uintah mine owned by S. H.
Winsor, are extensions of the above and produce coal giving the
following analysis: Water 8.58, ash 6.30, volatile 35.22, carbon
49.90. Four hundred men receive regular employment in the
production and shipment of coal at these mines, two-thirds of
them being Chinamen. Nearly 300,000 tons of coal are being
produced the present year. A large percentage of this finds its
way to Utah, Nevada and California, and the deposit is almost
the exclusive supply of the Central Pacific Railroad Company.
From these statements it will be seen that Wyoming not only
supplies her own citizens and railways with fuel, but almost the
entire northern half of the trans-Missouri region as well.

Forty miles north of Evanston is the Twin Creek coal mine,
owned by the Wyoming Coal and Coking Company. This is

claimed to be the best coking coal produced, and that it will yield fifty per cent of coke. Coke being a most important desideratum in the vast mining regions of Utah, Nevada, Wyoming and Montana, this new industry will, without doubt, soon be second only to the production of coal itself. There are yet other deposits worthy of note in this vicinity, but space forbids extended mention, and we must hasten to other topics.

In the northern part of the Territory along the Cheyenne, Powder and Tongue rivers, the indications of vast coal deposits are even more general than in the southern belt just outlined. Bluffs, river banks and water-worn gullies in many localities plainly show the sparkling black seams protruding from between the soft sandstone, slate or other natural formations. Veins are frequently noticed running from four to ten feet in thickness. The quality of some of these coals has been tested in the camp-forges and fires of different military expeditions, with favorable results; and the writer is cognizant of one case in which loosened wagon tires were well set with fragments of the coal taken from the face of one of these deposits. During the occupation of Fort Phil Kearney, at the base of the Big Horn Mountain, in 1866–7, a fine vein of bituminous coal was opened in that vicinity, and used extensively by the garrison.

Estimating from data furnished by the different companies, the amount of coal mined in Wyoming the present year will reach 524,000 tons, and at a low valuation will sell for $2,094,000. Nearly a million dollars are invested in actual improvements on the four principal mines, and the entire number of persons employed in mining, handling and shipping coal exceed 800.

In the important element of fixed carbon, the Wyoming coal is superior to all bituminous or semi-bituminous coals of the Union, and the product of the best mines very closely approaches the anthracite, as the following comparative statement, made from the most careful analysis, will show. Only the best mines in other States are quoted:

| | FIXED CARBON. |
|---|---|
| Excelsior mine, Rock Springs, Wyoming | 76.00 |
| Rock Springs mine, Rock Springs, Wyoming | 54.46 |
| Van Dyke mine, Rock Springs, Wyoming | 53.23 |
| Evanston and Unita mine, Evanston, Wyoming | 49.90 |
| Carbon mine, Carbon, Wyoming | 49.72 |
| Briggs mine, Boulder, Colorado | 47.30 |

Baker mine, Boulder, Colorado .................................... 50.65
Osage mine, Osage, Missouri...................................... 51.16
Monte Diable mine, California .................................... 44.90
Brier Hill mine, Youngstown, Ohio................................ 62.66
Belleville mine, Illinois ........................................ 54.60
Lehigh mine, Pennsylvania (anthracite)........................... 89.15
Beaver Meadow mine, Pennsylvania (anthracite).................... 91.47

*The Precious Metals.* — Concerning the development of these
interests, Colonel Stephen W. Downey, an old-time citizen of
Wyoming, says: "Prior to the organization of the Territory,
discoveries of rich mineral deposits had been made about the
sources of Sweetwater river, in the Wind River Mountains, on
the head-waters of Big Horn river, and on the tributaries of
North Platte, in Medicine Bow Range. From these discoveries
the hope was entertained here, and the opinion prevailed abroad,
that Wyoming was about to take prominent rank as a bullion-
producing Territory. Such hope and opinion received a sharp
check by the unfriendly action of the United States government
in its persistent, though tacit sanction and support of American
savages in their hostile incursions upon the miners in established
camps. These marauders compelled not only the abandonment
of work begun, but also a total cessation of all prospecting through
central and northern Wyoming, between the Black Hills and Big
Horn river. The mining interests of Wyoming have thus been
crippled for nearly a decade. The recent impetus which these
interests have received is due largely to the military expedition
under Custer, made in the year 1875, which gave the public
some glimpses of the rich deposits of gold in the Black Hills.

"Although the Black Hills are the grand central objective
point of treasure-seeking immigration, they are by no means the
only point in or near Wyoming sought, and, within the current
year, to be prospected for gold and silver. Many already, from
the east and from the west, some with capital and some without,
are going into the Medicine Bow mineral districts, on the head
waters of the Laramie and Platte, in the Rock Creek, Elk Mountain, Brush Creek, Centennial, Last Chance and other districts
southward to the borders of Colorado, these all being in the same
mineral belt which, in Colorado, has yielded so much treasure.
Others are seeking, again, the Sweetwater region, from whose
rich mines prospectors and miners were driven by hostile Indians

"BOUND FOR THE MINES—THE FIRST COACH."

in 1869, and from which, by similar causes, they have been kept until the present time. From this very region I hear of companies numbering several hundred each moving northward toward the Big Horn. All indications point to the early discovery and development of the most prominent mineral-producing localities in Wyoming."

We shall, in this chapter, refer more especially to the districts in the southern and central portions of the Territory, leaving the Black Hills and Big Horn regions for special articles. Among the most important gold and silver belts in Wyoming is that in the southern part tributary to Laramie City. The region is almost wholly undeveloped, and consists, first, of the districts in or near the Medicine Bow Mountains, including Rock Creek Placer Mining district, Centennial, Sheep Mountain, Big Laramie and Last Chance, or Douglass districts; and second, of the North Park region, extending across the borders of Colorado to Hahn's Peak and the Rabbit Ear range.

The Rock Creek district is about forty miles northwesterly from Laramie City, on or near the old overland stage road. It was discovered late in 1876 by prospecting the dirt in the old stage road, since which ditches have been constructed to lead water from Rock Creek to one of the bars, and the locators are now prosecuting work with the hydraulic.

The Centennial district, as its name implies, was opened in 1876. One quartz claim in the district yielded about $20,000 during last summer. Several additional ledges have been discovered and promise very fairly, their large deposits of ores assaying an average of $100 per ton, but are thus far only slightly developed. The district is about thirty miles due west of Laramie, by an excellent natural road. No prospecting has been done for placer gold.

Sheep Mountain district is near Centennial. Several silver-bearing lodes have been discovered on this mountain, one of which has a shaft 100 feet in depth, showing very rich ore. Ores assaying as high as 2,000 ounces silver per ton have been taken out at different depths from eighty feet downward. The other claims thus far discovered here are undeveloped and no reduction works are convenient to utilize the large deposits of wonderfully rich ores.

Southeast of Sheep Mountain and also about thirty miles

from Laramie, is the John Mountain and Big Laramie Quartz
and Placer Mining District. Gold was carried largely by the
quartz near the surface, but is being rapidly displaced by silver
as depth is attained. A shaft 100 feet deep on one of the mines
discloses a four-foot vein of "pay rock," averaging nearly 100
ounces silver per ton, with occasional streaks of sulphates of
silver assaying 1,600 ounces. A quartz mill is being located in
this district the present season. Large deposits of copper, assaying $110 per ton, are also found here. Extensive placers are also
found adjacent, which need only a small outlay of capital to
prove exceedingly productive.

Beyond the district last named, and forty miles southwesterly
from Laramie, is the Douglass Creek or Last Chance district,
containing rich gold quartz and placer mines. The placer gold
consists largely of nuggets, and is remarkable for its purity, being
960 to 975 fine. Rich free-gold quartz ledges were discovered
here late last season, on some twenty of which development has
been progressing since, and pay-material has been found on
nearly all from the grass-roots down. Four companies now
operate the principal mines with gratifying success. The first
stamp-mill will here soon be put in operation. Over 300 tons of
ore, assaying nearly $300 per ton, are now on the dump of one
of these mines awaiting treatment. These districts, it should be
remembered, are upon the outskirts of an extensive unprospected
mineral-bearing region.

On the borders of North Park, commencing sixty miles from
Laramie, rich discoveries have been made of auriferous quartz,
argentiferous galena and ruby silver. Some of these give promise
of mineral wealth equal to the best districts of Colorado. Their
remoteness from railroad communication and reduction works,
and lack of capital, have thus far impeded their development.
There is unquestioned foundation for the belief that this vast
region, when once understood, will offer an attractive field for
the investment of capital in exceptionally remunerative mining
enterprises. The most remote of the districts mentioned are
within seventy-five or one hundred miles of Laramie city.

The quartz-mining region tributary to Rawlins, near the
center of the Territory, has in years past attracted considerable
attention, and, with the new impetus now being given the mining
interest, are again materially swelling the yield of bullion. Thirty

miles north of the town are the Ferris and Seminole districts, in which large deposits of gold, silver and copper-bearing ores are found. The ores carrying silver are almost identical in character and accompanying formation with the White Pine mines of Nevada. Over a hundred claims have been located, and about a dozen true fissure veins are now being developed. Selected specimens of ores from some of these have assayed as high as $2,000 per ton, while quantities are raised which yield from $100 to $200 per ton silver. In a dozen of the mines carrying a large percentage of gold, beautiful specimens of free gold quartz have been taken; and in such as the Ernest, Mammoth, Break of Day, and Slattery, gold is disseminated in large proportions through the well-defined veins. Only one stamp-mill has been placed in operation here, and this is a very rudely constructed and incomplete affair. Good wagon roads connect these districts with the railroad, and one of the best routes to the Big Horn Mountains lies across them.

The quartz and placer mines of the Sweetwater and South Pass districts, lying from 100 to 150 miles north of Green River city, have been more thoroughly developed and have furnished a greater yield than those in any other section of Wyoming. In the early discovery of the principal mines, some ten years ago, the outcroppings of quartz for miles were so distinctly visible, and some of the gulches were so extremely rich, that the mining excitement was at fever heat, and thousands of prospectors, who were looking only for grand bonanzas, flocked thither. This mass, with its wild expectations, soon drifted away, disappointed because richer gulches were quickly worked out, and the absence of proper milling facilities rendered quartz mining generally undesirable. Then, constant Indian depredations frightened away both miners and capital until the once noted region was almost unheard of. The mining region proper covers an area of about 2,000 square miles in the Sweetwater mountains and spurs of the Wind River range, and many gulches are yet unworked which will pay from four to seven dollars per day to the man with the hydraulic. From one of the quartz mines $200,000 were taken the first year of its discovery, and six or seven are still yielding large wages to the few who faithfully stand by them. Eight quartz mills, running thirty stamps, are in operation on the free gold ores, and will produce about $125,000 the present year.

Mine owners have been generally poor to start with, and have worked at great disadvantage, both on account of Indian troubles and the total lack of outside capital to assist in development.

For the benefit of those treasure seekers who come west with barely capital enough to reach their supposed Eldorado, it may be well to note that there are thousands of square miles of rich mining area in the southern and central portions of Wyoming practically unappropriated. Lying, as this area does, within easy distance of railway, and rendered less speculative on account of its nearness to varied interests already developed, the prospector of limited means can often find other dependencies to look to. For those who have $250 to $500 and upward, it is believed that no more attractive mineral field can be found. Capitalists looking for investment, and prospectors with means sufficient to outfit and supply them for a season, are especially recommended to visit and explore the fields above specified.

Following is a carefully compiled statement of the mining interest of Wyoming for the present year, compared with the official figures of 1870. In the estimates of both quartz and placer gold about one-half the yield is contributed by quartz and placer mines in the Black Hills known to lie within the limits of Wyoming:

|  | Capital Invested. | | Product. | |
| --- | --- | --- | --- | --- |
|  | 1870. | 1877. | 1870. | 1877. |
| Coal..................... | $250,000 | $650,000 | $800,000 | $2,096,000 |
| Gold, quartz .... ......... | 11,000 | 78,500 | 50,000 | 215,000 |
| Gold, placer... ... ....... | ........ | 130,000 | ........ | 600,000 |
| Totals................. | $261,000 | $858,500 | $850,000 | $2,911,000 |

*Iron.*—Wyoming is no less bountifully supplied with iron ores than with coal for their utilization. These deposits lie in various sections of the Territory, contiguous to railway, coal, water and forest. One of the largest deposits of iron ore in the Union is that found near the headwater of Chugwater Creek, forty miles north of Cheyenne, and twenty-five miles from Laramie City. The ore is a black, crystalline magnetic, yielding as high as sixty-eight per cent of iron, and the deposit is simply a vast mountain, literally inexhaustible. Of this, Prof. Hayden has said: " Near the sources of the Chugwater are some very rich iron mines, which may prove of great value to the country in future. In the winter of 1859–'60, while attached to the exploring expedition of General W. F. Raynolds, I made a trip to the sources of the Chugwater, and found great numbers of these worn masses of iron ore, but not until a comparatively recent period were they traced to their sources in the mountains. The ore is located much like that in the Lake Superior region. . . . The quantity of ore in this locality appears to be unlimited. Thousands of tons have been washed down into the valley of the "Chug," and distributed among the superficial drift. It will be seen by the analysis that the ore is very rich in metallic iron, but it is supposed that it will be reduced with some difficulty. Prof. Silliman is of the opinion that the brown ore or limonite can be employed with it as a flux with favorable results. Should the time ever arrive when this ore is absolutely demanded by the country, it will be easily accessible from numerous points. It is probable, however, that the branch railroad from Cheyenne to Montana will create a demand for these mines, and then the ore can be taken down the valley of the Chugwater with ease." In Stansbury's Report, page 266, the following occurs: "In the bed of the Chugwater, and on the sides of the adjacent hills, were found immense numbers of rounded black nodules of magnetic iron ore, which seemed of unusual richness."

Following is the analysis of this ore, as made by Mr. J. P. Carson at the school of mines, Columbia College. Mr. Carson was an assistant in the Hayden survey in this region of 1868:

| | |
|---|---|
| Sesquioxide of iron | 45.03 |
| Protoxide | 17.96 |
| Silica | .76 |
| Titanic acid | 23.49 |
| Alumina | 3.98 |
| Sesquioxide of chromium | 2.45 |
| Sesquioxide of manganese | 1.53 |
| Lime | 1.11 |
| Oxide of zinc | .47 |
| Magnesia | 1.56 |
| Sulphur | 1.44 |
| Phosphorus | a trace |
| Fe | 45.49  99.78 |

Near Rawlins, on the line of the Union Pacific, are immense deposits of red oxide ores, already becoming extensively utilized in the manufacture of paint. Commencing two and one-half miles north of the city, there are small mountains which are little less than solid masses of the metal, and careful prospecting farther to the north warrants the conclusion that large bodies of the same material extend for miles in that direction. The Rawlins Metallic Paint Company have invested some $25,000 in opening the mines, building paint works and establishing facilities for shipping. Another corporation has also invested quite extensively in an adjoining claim. Over 25,000 tons of the ore have been mined by the company first named, a large proportion of which has been shipped to Utah as a flux for smelting purposes. About 200 tons of metallic paint have been manufactured and found to be of very superior quality, as the following analysis and testimonials will show:

Water......................................................... 0.12
Gangue........................................................ 0.72
Sulphur and lime ............................................. 0.14
Sesquioxide of iron........................................... 9.02
                                                             _____
                                                              10.00

Superintendent Stevens, of the Union Pacific Car and Building Department, says: "Allow us to bear testimony to the value of the Rawlins Metallic Paint manufactured from Rocky Mountain iron ore. We use it exclusively for painting box and flat cars, iron and tin roofs, and buildings on the line of this road; have found it a valuable preservative of wood, and the very thing so long needed for repairs of leaky roofs, for while it is cheap as a paint, it fills up all nail holes and leaks, and becomes virtually an iron-covering — perfectly impenetrable to water. We are satisfied that it will cover more surface, pound for pound, last longer and retain its color better than any paint before the public." The president of the Cooper Engine Company, Mount Vernon, Ohio, writes: "Our painter says the Rawlins paint is the best he ever used. We use it on castings mostly, and are highly pleased with the finish." About a severe test of this paint the master painter of the Chicago, Burlington and Quincy Company's car works says: "I have had your iron paint in test for about six months, and find it one of the best, if not the best, iron paints I have ever seen. I put two coats of it, mixed with boiled oil, on a piece of sheet-iron and buried it in strong brine

A SIMPLE QUESTION OF PRIORITY.

about six months ago, and it has stood the test and does not show any signs of rusting through the paint. I have also used it on locomotive work and find it covers far more surface than any iron paint I have used."

The paint is made dry, is naturally reddish-brown in color, and is sold in car-load quantities at $50 per ton. Thirty-five thousand tons of the ore are now at the track at Rawlins awaiting shipment to Utah. The home company deserves no little credit for thus utilizing so much of our latent wealth as their means and scope will allow.

Other valuable deposits of iron ore are found in the northwestern part of the Territory and in the Laramie range, on Sabille Creek. Hematite ores occur near Cheyenne, Laramie City and other points.

*Soda, Marble, Petroleum, etc.*—Among other interests of a different though somewhat kindred nature, and which give promise of growing within a few years to gigantic proportions, are the remarkable and inexhaustible deposits of native soda, in the forms of sulphates and carbonates, and of marble, in the southern-central part of the Territory, as well as the oil wells and the wonderful mine of sulphur near the western end.

About eleven miles southwesterly from Laramie City is a cluster of lakes exceeding 100 acres in area, consisting of solid beds of pure crystallized sulphate of soda of many feet in thickness. The following carefully prepared document, from the pen of Colonel Stephen W. Downey, of Laramie City, will give readers a thorough appreciation of this grand resource:

LARAMIE CITY, WYOMING, July 5, 1877.

ROBT. E. STRAHORN, ESQ., Cheyenne, Wyoming:

*Dear Sir,*—With reference to the deposits of native soda existing in this Territory, I have the honor to state that attention was especially directed to them by a cube of the material taken from the principal one near this place last year, and exhibited at the Centennial Exposition at Philadelphia, attracting much attention. The cube exhibited contained over two hundred cubic feet of solid crystalline sulphate of soda almost chemically pure, and as it exists in its native state. Its constituent elements, as well as I can ascertain, are, by weight, as follows: 19.4 per cent of soda and 24.8 per cent of sulphuric acid, constituting 44.2 per cent of sulphate of soda, the residue being the water of crystallization (55.8 per cent).

This sulphate fuses in its own water of crystallization at a slightly elevated temperature, and by maintaining a temperature of 91½° Fahrenheit for a short time the material would part with its original water and recrystallize in an almost anhydrous state. The material in the cube, which is as it exists in the deposit, having crystallized below 68° Fahrenheit, contains the maximum of water. In this form it effloresces in the air and its crystals soon fall to powder. Had crystallization taken place at a higher temperature (but under 91½°), a hydrated sulphate would still have been formed, but with less water, and the crystals would have been unalterable in the air. Such being the characteristics of the material, I proceed now to a description of the source of supply.

The deposit whence the sample mentioned was taken covers an area of more than one hundred acres, being a solid bed of crystallized sulphate of soda about nine feet thick. The deposit is supplied from the bottom by springs, whose water holds the salts in solution. The water rising to the surface rapidly evaporates, and the salts with which it is impregnated readily crystallize in the form mentioned. Upon removing any of the material the water rising from the bottom, fills the excavation made, and the salts crystallizing replace, in a few days, the material removed. Hence the deposit is practically inexhaustible, and it now contains about 50,000,000 cubic feet of chemically pure crystallized sulphate of soda ready to be utilized.

Soda is most valuable in the form of carbonate, although its sulphate, also, has its uses. Neutral carbonate of soda is a salt of vast importance, on account of its uses in the arts, and the production of this salt is a desideratum. For a long time it was only obtained from the lixiviation of the ashes of sea-weed — inland plants affording salts of potassa principally, while in marine plants salts of soda preponderate.

Spain formerly produced the greater part of the carbonate used in Europe, called barilla and sometimes Alicant or Malaga soda. It was afterward largely prepared on the coasts of Scotland and Wales and among the Hebrides. In the Peninsula the source of supply was limited, and among the rocky crags of the Western Isles it was a difficult task to gather the sea-weed, principally the algæ and fuci, by whose incineration the lixiviation of the residual ashes and repeated manipulation, four per cent of soda may be obtained. The supply from these sources being so limited, and the cost so excessive, early in the present century, chemists, encouraged by the French government, made many attempts to manufacture the article from other materials. After many unsuccessful attempts and fruitless experiments a process was discovered by Le Blanc for the conversion of chloride of sodium into carbonate of soda, and it is to this process that we mainly owe our present supply.

The soda consumption of the United States amounts to some 250,000,000 pounds a year, all of which is imported at an outlay of about $47 in gold per ton, besides the duty, which is, I believe, about 20 per cent ad valorem. making $56.40 in gold per ton, at sea-board. Here is a staple article which is imported at an outlay of $7,000,000 annually, whereas we have within our borders the material for its production in greater purity and abundance than it exists elsewhere, and there is no reason why we should not supply the domestic demand and also foreign markets.

Le Blanc's process, to which reference has already been had, consists first in converting the chloride of sodium into sulphate of soda by the introduction of carbonic acid, and then in substituting carbonic acid for the sulphuric acid, which is done by heating together, on the brick hearth of a reverberatory furnace to the point of fusion, materials in the following proportions by weight, viz.: 1,000 anhydrous sulphate of soda, 1,040 carbonate of lime, and 530 charcoal. The reaction taking place in such manner that two equivalents of sulphide of calcium, combining with one equivalent of lime, form an oxysulphide of calcium, perfectly insoluble in water, the water dissolving out only the carbonate of soda.

As the material of our native deposit is already sulphate of soda, we may dispense with the first and most expensive part of Le Blanc's process,—the production of sulphate of soda from chloride of sodium and sulphuric acid. All that we have to do is to convert the sulphate of soda into the carbonate, and here the latter part of that process seems precisely adapted to the purpose and could be conveniently adopted here, charcoal and limestone being cheap and abundant in the immediate vicinity. A Marseilles reverberatory furnace, such as is used in England and France for the purpose, with the necessary appliances, buildings, etc., for works with a capacity of one ton per day, of the anhydrous carbonate, would cost not to exceed $10,000, and the capacity might be increased for less than 50 per cent additional for each ton of increased capacity.

Now, by a calculation based upon the atomic weight of the combining elements, it is ascertained that for the production of one ton (2,000 pounds) of anhydrous carbonate of soda there are required,—

2,665 lbs. of anhydrous sulphate of soda.

2,815 lbs. of carbonate of lime.

1,013 lbs. of charcoal.

6,493 lbs. of material, 30$\frac{x}{u}$ per cent of the sum of the combining equivalents being carbonate of soda. The above proportions differ but slightly from those of the Le Blanc process, which has undergone a thorough practical test, so that we have a safe basis upon which to estimate the cost of production. About 56 per cent of the commercial carbonate being the water of crystallization, after making due allowance for waste in manipulation, one ton of the product as above will form two tons in a crystallized state. Hence for the production of one ton of commercial carbonate of soda,—

1,332 lbs. anhydrous sulphate of soda, costing .............. $1 33
1,407 lbs. carbonate of lime .............................. 70
506 lbs. charcoal ....................................... 2 50

3,245 lbs. material, costing ............................. $4 53
besides transportation to works, the average cost of which would be about $1 per ton=$1.62. Manipulation, it is estimated, would cost $10 per ton, and packages, say $3.50. Summing up, we have for

material mined ........................................ $4 53
transportation to works ... .............................. 1 62
manipulation ........................................... 10 00
packages, etc........................................... 3 50

amounting to ......................................... $19 65 per ton of product worth, as hereinbefore stated, $56.40 in gold per ton, assuming that the article would be worth as much here as it is at the seaboard. Making no allowance for the premium on gold, which at current quotations would compensate for the interest on the capital to be invested, we would have a net profit, on the cost of manufacture, of $36.75 per ton, or 187 per cent.

And here it might be well to state that the deposit is convenient to lines of transportation, being only about eleven miles from this point on the great trans-continental railroad, the intervening country being a hard and level plain, affording an excellent natural road-bed, with grass and abundance of good water at convenient intervals. And also, in passing, I might mention that the United States Penitentiary, containing about seventy-five (75) convicts, is located here and at the most convenient point for works. By employing convict labor, which might be obtained for fifty cents per day (a rate as low as the lowest of foreign cheap labor), the cost of production would be reduced far below the estimate given.

Hence, we have a resource here, in addition to our mines of the precious metal, which offers a most promising opportunity for the profitable and safe employment of capital in an immense industry. And as the resource is inexhaustible, the cost of production such as to preclude successful competition by the importers, and other deposits of equal extent, and affording material of equal purity, cannot be found in this country, we may reasonably hope for the establishment of an industry here whose product will supply the entire soda trade of the United States, giving employment to a thousand hands, saving millions to the people and enriching its proprietors.

I remain yours truly,

STEPHEN W. DOWNEY.

Sixty miles north of Rawlins are two soda lakes, almost equally valuable, and now estimated to contain 125,000 tons of carbonate of soda crystallized and held in solution by the waters. Calculating upon the low basis of $45 per ton as the net price of this commodity, these lakes would yield from their present supply of water and crystallizations nearly $6,000,000. By building five miles of wagon road through the Seminole mountains these lakes could be reached in a distance of thirty-five miles from Rawlins.

The marble quarries belonging to the Wyoming Marble Company, located twenty-five miles north of Laramie City and twelve miles from Cooper Lake station, on the Union Pacific railway, are among the wonders of our latent resources. A ledge eighty feet wide has been traced for two miles on its surface and has been prospected to a depth of 100 feet without reaching the bottom. The surface rock is very fine in grain, but naturally discolored by long exposure to the weather. In penetrating successive layers, however, the rock has gradually purified in color until it is a glistening white, and has lost all trace of seams or the partially decomposed texture more common on the top. Specimens now on exhibition at the office of the president of the company, Wm. H. Holliday, Laramie City, have a beautiful crystallized sparkle, and possess all the rich finish of the finest Vermont marble and the solidity and compactness of the best American granite.

Regarding the quality of the marble taken from the surface, when the deposit was first opened, J. Pfeiffer & Son, St. Joseph, Missouri, probably the best authorities in the west on marble, write: "We have dressed the samples of Wyoming marble and are much pleased with their appearance. . . . If the main body of the marble is as good as these samples, we should prefer it to Vermont marble for monumental work. Any of it would be handsome for store or residence fronts. This is the view we take of it while chiseling and polishing it." The superintendent of the Northwestern Marble and Granite Company, Chicago, says: "The sample of stone sent by you is received, and we have worked it down and polished it. We find it to be what is called 'marble limestone'—that is, the stone that comes from the surface, and which generally covers the real marble. We think that by quarrying further down you will strike the 'real thing,' probably as good as they have in Vermont." Henry Wilson, the widely known importer and dealer in marble, St. Louis, has this to say of the surface material: "The specimens are received. . . . The rock takes a faint, greasy, flinty polish, but cuts as nice and clean as statuary marble." Of course it will be remembered that these tests were made from surface layers, and that the specimens by no means represented the quality of the marble as it is found at the bottom of the quarry. A fine vein of richly variegated marble of the delicate bluish tracery, is also found in the deposit.

The proportion of really first-class building stone in the United States is very small, and outside of this deposit no available marble, worthy of the name, is found west of Vermont. Joliet, Illinois, building stone is going into public buildings at Omaha and Lincoln, Nebraska, and has been shipped even farther west. Cincinnati freestone has been similarly used a thousand miles from the quarries, while Maine furnishes granite for the extensive government buildings at St. Louis and elsewhere in the Mississippi Valley States. Vermont marble sells in every city of the Union, and is almost daily shipped across the continent past our inexhaustible quarries — producing as good an article — to the Pacific slope. This trade in marble and fine cut stone in the United States amounts to over $10,000,000 annually, and the production is largely confined to the seven States, Maine, Vermont, Massachusetts, Connecticut, Pennsylvania, Ohio and Illinois. An ordinary grade of Vermont marble sells at any of the Missouri river towns at $6 per cubic foot, while the same quality from our Wyoming quarries could be laid down at similar locations at $3 per cubic foot, at a handsome profit to the producer. We have enough marble in these quarries to build the State-houses of the Union, and enough of the more beautiful grades to share with Vermont and Italy the marble trade of the whole land, reaping as an income therefrom five or six million dollars annually.

The oil-bearing shales and numerous deposits of crude petroleum found in Wyoming are worthy of especial note. Ten miles east of Evanston, at the Bear-river crossing, and at a point known ever since the California stampede as " White's Oil Springs," is an oil-bearing stratum, destined at some day to rival the best similar formation of Pennsylvania. Surface oil in the vicinity has always been draining away in copious quantities, and has been found superior to the best of heavy lubricating oils for stationary machinery or locomotive engines. The well-known shale above and sand-rock stratum below, are identical with the formations of eastern oil regions, and the unmistakable surface indications are traced from northeast to southwest for a distance of twenty miles. Mr. E. L. Pease, of Evanston, formerly for years identified with the oil-producing interest of Pennsylvania, looked this ground over carefully, in 1869, and was so firmly impressed with its value that he at once secured an interest, returned to Pennsylvania, secured the necessary machinery for boring, and soon had his enterprise in working order. At a depth of 175 feet the first layer of sand-rock was penetrated, and a better flow of oil obtained than was ever known at a similar depth in the east.

But on account of large lumbering interests previously acquired, and other calls upon his attention, Mr. Pease was compelled to be away much of the time. The work fell into incapable hands, drills were fastened into the rock and broken off, and other valuable portions of machinery and casing shattered. While reluctantly giving up his favorite project for a few years, this gentleman has always carefully guarded his interest, and is now on the eve of bestowing upon it the attention merited. Improved machinery will soon be introduced upon the scene, and the work will be pushed with the best system and vigor.

Within half a mile of the deposit are inexhaustible quantities of coal and other auxiliaries necessary to refining. Petroleum also exists in Green River Valley, near Red Buttes, Bridger, and at several other points easy of access. Immense quantities of oil-bearing shale near Green River City, are found to yield at the rate of thirty gallons of good merchantable lubricating oil per ton. Oil can be shipped from Wyoming east to the Missouri river, and west to the Pacific Coast and Sandwich Islands in competition with Pennsylvania oils; and to show the importance of such production, even in a local way, it need only be stated that nearly $200,000 worth of refined and crude petroleum are consumed in Wyoming annually. Then it should be remembered that each of the adjoining States and Territories furnish a market for from twice to four times as much more.

On Hayden's Fork, a tributary of Bear river, forty miles southeast of Evanston, is a wonderful mass of sulphur. A vein, forty feet wide, and carrying from fifty to ninety per cent. of sulphur, has been prospected for 300 feet up the side of a large mountain. A United States patent has been secured on the property by a company of enterprising western gentlemen. The deposit can be reached by wagon-road in twenty-three miles from Hilliard, on the Union Pacific.

6

# CHAPTER VI.

## FOREST PRODUCTIONS.

PUBLISHED statements of Wyoming's forest area have varied greatly, and in the case of the estimates sent broadcast by the Department of Agriculture, in its latest annual report, the extent has been sadly underestimated. Instead of 5,000,000 acres, as stated in the report of 1875, the Territory contains more than 15,000,000 acres of forest lands, from nearly every acre of which an average yield of merchantable lumber can be cut. Instead of being placed twenty-ninth, therefore, in the list of timbered States and Territories, Wyoming should be no lower than tenth.

The forests are confined principally to the prominent ranges of mountains in the central and western portions, although quite an extensive area in the northern and northeastern parts of the Territory are bountifully supplied, even on the lower bluffs. Pine, spruce, cedar, fir and hemlock are the varieties predominating in the mountains and bluffs, while along the streams cottonwood, black ash and box-elder are the more prominent species. At present a variety of pine, common in the Rocky Mountain region, furnishes nearly the entire lumber supply. It is as white as the eastern pine, almost as hard as the hardest spruce, and is nearly identical with the Norway pine in size and appearance. By lumbermen from Maine and California it is pronounced far superior in quality to the white pine native to those sea-girt sections, although trees rarely attain great size. While it contains more knots, this native variety is yet finer-grained, more dense and elastic, and takes a much more beautiful finish than the pine growing at lower altitudes either east or west. Six months are required to thoroughly season it in the open air; but by that time, as a Wyoming lumberman expressed it to the writer, "it beats the world for outside work, for flooring, or for other hard usage." It has almost supplanted eastern finishing lumber in the cities of Wyoming.

"GETTING OUT THE LOGS."

The forests most extensively utilized at present are those tributary to Laramie city, along the Laramie and Little Laramie rivers; those along the North Platte and Medicine Bow rivers, adjacent to Fort Steele and Medicine Bow stations; those farther west, along Bear river and its tributaries, in the vicinity of Hilliard and Evanston, and those in the central part of the Territory supplying the mining and stock-raising settlements of the Sweetwater and Wind River regions. The forests within a radius of forty miles of Laramie city are producing 2,000,000 feet of lumber, 2,000,000 shingles, 500,000 lath, 270,000 railroad ties and large quantities of fencing per annum. The lumber is sawed in the forests and hauled to the railroad, while ties, poles, etc., are floated down the streams to booms constructed near the track. Several stations near Laramie city, on either side, are shipping points for a portion of this product. Half a dozen companies, employing from twenty-five to fifty men each, are engaged in the industry in this portion of the Territory. The product is increasing annually.

At Evanston and Hilliard, in the extreme western part of the Territory, three large companies, besides numerous smaller ones, are engaged in the manufacture of lumber and in the production of wood, ties and charcoal. The Evanston Lumbering Company alone produces nearly 2,000,000 feet of lumber per annum, and from a comparatively small beginning in 1869 has grown to such proportions that during the present year seventy-five men are regularly employed, and 2,000,000 feet of logs have already been cut at its logging camps and placed in readiness for the summer's drive down Bear river. The company has improved the river channel to the extent of $10,000. The Hilliard Flume and Lumber Company has constructed a flume twenty-five miles long from its extensive mills in the Uintah mountains to the railroad, at a cost of $200,000. Over 2,000,000 feet of lumber were used in the construction of the flume. This, continually filled with water tapped from Bear river, has proved even more desirable than a railroad for the transportation of lumber to its point of final shipment, as its capacity is all that is required, and it performs its work with speed and rare economy. The business of this company the present year is large in both the production of lumber and of cordwood,—the latter being used principally in the manufacture of charcoal.

At several of the points named, and at other stations along the Union Pacific, the production of charcoal has become a very important interest. Altogether eight or ten firms, operating some fifty kilns or pits, are thus engaged, consuming nearly 50,000 cords of wood and producing 2,000,000 bushels of charcoal per year. The charcoal is used principally in the smelters of Utah, a small amount, however, being appropriated by the Hilliard smelting works.

Following is an accurate statement of the value of Wyoming forest products for the year 1877:

| | |
|---|---:|
| Lumber, sawed | $345,000 |
| Railroad ties, wood and fencing | 455,360 |
| Charcoal | 240,000 |
| Total | $1,040,360 |

Professional lumbermen, from the forests of Maine, are employed by the principal companies. These receive from $4 to $5 per day, while ordinary loggers and laborers get $30 to $40 per month and board. About 1,000 men are employed in this interest and in the production of charcoal during busy seasons, and two-thirds of the number find work the year round. Ordinary rough lumber sells at railroad stations at an average of $25 per thousand feet; finishing lumber, $40 per thousand. The railroads and local markets consume nearly the entire product. It is estimated that these forests in southern Wyoming have in the past ten years supplied 7,000,000 railroad ties, which have sold for $5,000,000, and 50,000,000 feet of lumber, worth $4,500,000, besides several million dollars' worth of wood, fencing, telegraph poles, etc.; and yet our best forests are practically untouched, and our market scarcely a tithe of what it will be in the near future when other resources are developed.

# CHAPTER VII.

## THE MANUFACTURING INTEREST.

IN Wyoming, as in other Rocky Mountain Territories and States, there exist hundreds upon hundreds of germs which at no very distant day will give life to the grandest of manufacturing enterprises, and make new cities quiver with proud activity. Nature paved the way along the western ranges for the sway of the forge, the shuttle and the loom as she never paved it in the older States and worlds. The resources of iron, coal, lumber and wood have always been among the first to enlist the attention of careful investors, and have yielded such men wealth and place, while they have clustered about them new interests, new dependencies and incalculable prosperity.

Iron ores which rival the metals of Michigan and Missouri, forest productions second to those of no State, and pasturage soon to produce its millions in wool, hides and meat, are among the incentives here offered; while for their profitable utilization are numberless well-distributed and unexcelled water powers, vast deposits of the finest coals, and already a market eager to consume a large home product. The very center and dome of the continent, Wyoming pays constant tribute to either the mills, foundries and machine shops of the far east, or else to the smelters of the west and south. Railroads are not always modest in their charges upon our productions, which only journey far toward the rising sun to again return in due time,—once more well levied for transportation,—manufactured into staple articles. It is a broad assertion, but a true one, that a few of the eastern States are today swallowing the major part of the results of our best western enterprise and energy, with the inevitable sweep of a grand industrial maelstrom.

From official statistics we learn that Massachusetts employs 54,000 people in the manufacture of boots and shoes, annually consumes $40,000,000 worth of raw material, which is largely from the west, pays as wages nearly $30,000,000, and ships prin-

cipally to western marts $90,000,000 worth of boots and shoes per
annum. During the past year Wyoming has sent nearly $300,000
worth of the raw material in this line, there or elsewhere worked
up. To have tanned it, manufactured and sold it here, without
paying the item of several thousand miles of transportation,
would have built up a thriving little village, would have materially stimulated productive enterprise, and would have kept six
or seven hundred thousand bright dollars in continued home
circulation. The manufacture of woolen goods in the same
State gives constant employment to 20,000 operatives, who
receive as wages and put into circulation annually over $7,000,-
000, and convert $24,000,000 worth of wool into $39,000,000
worth of cloths. Success is as sure to attend those who would
engage in this business, if energetic and persevering, as it has
those iron men of New England, who have made their barren
and rocky country flourish through the industry of her looms
and spindles. Nowhere do they produce a better article of wool
than we can produce in these Territories. Only give us the
machinery to transform it into fabrics for which we are sending
thousands of miles. Our prosperity would then be well based —
something that never fails — and add more wealth to the country
than the sluice-box or silver veins, and be more evenly prosperous.

There is plenty of surplus capital here that ought to be invested in spindles instead of brocade silks and furbelows — the
products of eastern looms and industry. No country in the
world can compete with us in the production of wool, and we
are enriching the east — piling wealth into the laps of those who
are willing to use their money at a fair and steady profit, and
giving work to thousands of men, women and children. We
have heard it said that labor is too high to make it profitable
business. Not so, for laborers here would work for as low a
figure as in the east, if these products were as cheap, and the reduction can only come through home manufactories. The eastern imports are what enhance the price of living with us. Why
is it that the scattering manufactures that are established about
us, on a small scale, are standing up under the pressure of high
wages for labor? Their products are sold as cheap as you can
buy imports of like quality, and they are giving employment to
a limited number and keeping the money in the country.

In Dr. Latham's eloquent and enthusiastic outburst upon

this subject a few years ago, after describing the vast pasturages directly tributary to Cheyenne on the north, occurred these rather pertinent words: "This 6,400,000 acres of land would give ample pasturage to as many sheep or to all the sheep in the great State of Ohio, which annually produce 24,000,000 pounds of wool, valued at $8,000,000. It would also produce annually 500,000 mutton sheep, worth in market $2,500,000. What would be the effect upon Cheyenne to be the entrepôt for the trade incident upon the growing and shipping (or manufacture) of 24,000,000 pounds of wool, such as is used in making the lustrous black broadcloths and French merinos, or the growing of an equal amount of the long, silken, floss-like combing wools of England, and the shipment of 500,000 mutton sheep to market?"

The forges and furnaces of Pennsylvania, located 1,000 miles from their largest iron supply, employ 40,000 men, producing $120,000,000 worth of staple iron goods annually, and ship a large percentage of those staples across the continent, past our magnificent mountains of iron and over our vast depths of coal measures. When our incomparable pyramids of the base metal and our blackened strata of never-ending lignites are once utilized to supply even home demand we will have accomplished more than the conquering of a city. The crushing and smelting of ores carrying the precious metals must also eventually prove a great interest here. As much additional income could thus be saved to our miners as the amount of tariff now paid in transporting refractory ores to distant markets or smelters. It is seldom the *small* quantity of *rich* ores, bearing shipment abroad, which render mining regions prosperous, but it is the *vast* deposits of *low-grade* ores, *worked economically at home*, which have given to most mining regions their permanent wealth.

The production of soda from the wonderful deposits of native sulphates and carbonates in our soda lakes is already attracting attention, and must soon prove a large addition to our manufacturing interests. As is elsewhere stated, these lakes are capable of supplying the whole of the 250,000,000 pounds of merchantable soda used annually in the United States, and can therefore keep in home circulation over $7,000,000 in gold which now annually goes abroad for the imported article.

To these interests may be added the utilization of our quarries of marble, yet to astonish the world by their extent and beauty of product; and of our deposits of iron oxides, from which a superior quality of paint sufficient to supply the entire West for an indefinite period can be economically manufactured.

The writer has bestowed no little time and labor in compiling the following comparative table showing the progress of Wyoming in the manufacturing line:

The official reports of 1870 were taken as a basis for comparison, but have been found very inaccurate in numerous instances. The hitherto almost total absence of statistics regarding the Territory's productions, compiled either by public or private enterprise, has rendered such work extremely difficult, and in a few minor cases — where principals in enterprises could not be personally visited by the writer — necessarily imperfect:

| INDUSTRIES. | No. of Establishments. | | Capital Invested. | | Product. | |
|---|---|---|---|---|---|---|
| | 1870. | 1877. | 1870. | 1877. | 1870. | 1877. |
| Boots and shoes ... | 4 | 22 | $6,200 | $18,500 | $41,640 | $78,400 |
| Blacksmithing .... | 4 | 31 | 108,500 | 185,000 | 55,628 | 235,500 |
| Brewing ........... | .. | 8 | ........ | 54,000 | ........ | 80,500 |
| Bread, crackers, etc. | .. | 7 | ........ | 21,500 | ........ | 70,000 |
| Confectionery ..... | .. | 3 | ........ | 4,500 | ........ | 19,300 |
| Charcoal........... | .. | 8 | ........ | 54,000 | ........ | 240,000 |
| Clothing, men's ... | 1 | 6 | 1,500 | 14,000 | 8,500 | 50,000 |
| Dentistry ......... | .. | 4 | ........ | 2,500 | ........ | 9,000 |
| Drugs & chemicals. | .. | 6 | ........ | 13,400 | ........ | 18,000 |
| Gunsmithing...... | .. | 5 | ........ | 3,000 | ........ | 10,000 |
| Jewelry .......... | 2 | 5 | 10,500 | 14,000 | 42,167 | 51,000 |
| Lumber, sawed.... | 8 | 10 | 110,500 | 241,000 | 268,000 | 345,000 |
| Lime.............. | .. | 3 | ........ | 1,800 | ........ | 4,940 |
| Masonry, brick and stone .......... | .. | 7 | ........ | 9,000 | ........ | 37,500 |
| Metallic paint..... | .. | 1 | ........ | 25,000 | ........ | 5,000 |
| Millinery ......... | .. | 12 | ........ | 18,500 | ........ | 44,800 |
| Machinery, railroad repairing, etc.... | 5 | 8 | 590,500 | 837,000 | 226,569 | 1,429,420 |
| Printing and publishing ......... | 1 | 6 | 1,800 | 32,000 | 6,000 | 74,800 |
| Photography ...... | .. | 9 | ........ | 7,000 | ........ | 24,900 |
| Quartz, milled .... | 4 | 13 | 46,000 | 78,500 | 76,000 | 215,000 |
| Railroad ties, poles, posts and wood.. | 2 | | 60,000 | ........ | 110,000 | 455,360 |
| Saddlery and harness............. | .. | 7 | ........ | 18,000 | ........ | 65,000 |
| Tin, copper and sheet-iron ware.. | 3 | 6 | 13,900 | 22,000 | 40,320 | 58,500 |
| Sales of tanned robes, hides and furs ............. | .. | 10 | ........ | ........ | ........ | 295,000 |
| Totals ...... | 34 | 197 | $1,149,400 | $1,674,200 | $874,824 | $3,918,120 |

The very large increase noticed in the items of machinery, railroad repairing, etc., is due, to a considerable extent, to the product of the rolling mills. These have been established at Laramie City since the first report was made. In the estimate of quartz milled the yield of several mills in the Black Hills, known to be located in Wyoming, is included. That the manufacturing interest has here quadrupled in these half-dozen unfavorable years — while the whole country has been groaning under a gloomy depression, and Wyoming enterprise has been confined to one-fourth of its rightful scope — and that we have seen but the "beginning of the dawn," are facts plain and bright as the noonday sun.

It is a golden truth that home production is the only solid foundation for perfect and permanent prosperity. When the unnatural stimulus — received by young western cities and commonwealths from their first flushed and enthusiastic comers — is gone, there is a universal casting about for genuine "underpinning." "What have we to show for all this stir and bustle, and what can we send abroad as an equivalent for the world's coveted dollars?" are the anxious inquiries. To enjoy such resources as are truthfully credited to Wyoming in these pages, and then to properly utilize those resources, must force homage and draw wealth. *Proper utilization*, then, is, in the end, the lever: for in this fast age the hare, with all his advantages of speed, strength, elasticity and beauty, wakes up to find that the homely and despised, but energetic tortoise has long since gained the goal.

# CHAPTER VIII.

## PHYSICAL GEOGRAPHY AND CLIMATOLOGY OF THE GREAT PLAINS AND ROCKY MOUNTAIN REGIONS.

By George W. Corey, M.D., Cheyenne, Wyoming.

IT is our purpose to present in this chapter a brief outline of the physical geography and climatology of the great plains and Rocky Mountain regions. A general knowledge of the physical geography of a country is indispensable in studying its climate, and it is impossible to consider intelligently the climatic conditions of any arbitrary political division, such as Wyoming, Colorado and Utah, without taking into account to some extent the whole of this vast elevated region of table lands and mountains.

The elevation and direction of these mountain ranges and their accompanying plateaus are the prominent physical features of the western portion of our continent. The bulk and elevation of these lofty mountain ranges and elevated plateaus, when compared with the bulk and diameter of the earth, appear very insignificant; yet, slight as it may seem, this element of altitude most powerfully affects the climate of these regions and the productions of organic life. If at the equator we ascend vertically until we reach an altitude of 18,000 or 20,000 feet, we find a region of perpetual frost. A difference then of a few thousand feet of elevation changes entirely the character of a country, other things being equal. These mountain ranges also influence more or less the direction and character of the winds and the distribution of rain.

*Mountain Formation.*—The Pacific mountain formation extends from the Sierra Nevada and Cascade ranges, which lie along the western border of the continent to the great plains that stretch away from the eastern base of the Rocky Mountains. This region comprises these two great marginal ranges, and the great plateau or basin that lies between them. The elevation of this plateau within the boundaries of the United States is from

4,000 to 6,000 feet. In old Mexico it reaches an elevation of 8,000 feet, while away to the north its elevation is only 800 feet. Unlike the plains east of the Rocky Mountains that have for the most part a smooth, undulating surface, the surface of this plateau through its whole extent is broken up by an infinite perplexity of mountain spurs and broken ranges, while no less than five distinct and pretty well defined mountain chains extend across it from one marginal range to the other. Its surface is one vast net-work of mountain chains and broken mountain masses, interspersed with rivers made up of innumerable torrents that pour down the flanks and deep gorges of the mountains, fertile valleys, parks, or intra-mountain basins, fresh and salt-water lakes, sandy and alkaline wastes. This mountainous region covers about two-sevenths of the superficial area of the continent. Along the thirty-ninth parallel its breadth is about 1,000 miles, and it extends from the Isthmus of Tehuantepec to the Arctic Ocean, about 4,000 miles.

*The Sierra Nevada and Cascade Mountains.*—The Sierra Nevada mountains through the whole length of the State of California are lofty and continuous, presenting an almost unbroken front, with an average elevation of 10,000 feet. This "great sea-wall" perfectly shuts off the mild, beautiful climate of the coast. But little moisture ever surmounts its lofty crest, and the regions along its eastern base are extremely barren and desolate. The Cascade range, which extends along the coast through Oregon and Washington Territories and the mountains farther north, are uniformly low and broken, and the contrast between the county east of them and the regions east of the lofty Sierra Nevada is most striking.

*The Rocky Mountains.*—This range is the main axis, or backbone of the continent. It is known as the Snowy Range, the Sierra Madre of the Spaniards, and in Mexico as the Cordilleras, but is essentially one vast chain of enormous bulk and great elevation. It is composed of apparently distinct ranges, approximately parallel and bound together by numerous cross ranges. From old Mexico northward to the north line of Colorado the crests of these mountains are uniformly high — 10,000 to 12,000 feet — and the direction of the range is nearly exactly north and south.

The most elevated region in North America is attained along

this range between the thirty-ninth and forty-first parallels of north latitude, within the boundaries of the State of Colorado, and known as the Parks. These are immense irregular basins, walled in on all sides by lofty mountain ranges, and are three in number — the North, Middle and South Parks.

The contrast of climate, soil and verdure between these mountain-locked plateaus, and the grand old desolate peaks and mountain crests that surround them, is without a parallel anywhere else in nature. The surfaces of these plateaus are diversified by innumerable streams fed by the melting snows of the mountains around them. The foot-hills and ridges that separate these water-courses are covered with a dense growth of pine, while the valley portion of the parks is clothed with luxuriant grasses and flowering plants of many species, and are extremely fertile. The elevation of these parks is from 9,000 to 10,000 feet and the area of each is about 2,500 square miles.

In the vicinity of these parks, and standing about them like grim old sentinels, are some of the loftiest peaks of the Rocky Mountain range. The summit of Mount Lincoln attains an elevation of 17,000 feet; Pike's Peak, 14,216 feet; Long's Peak, 14,056 feet; Gray's Peak, 14,251 feet. The average elevation of the range here is about 12,000 feet, and its base 6,000 feet. At the southern boundary of Wyoming the range trends rapidly to the north and passes across this Territory, Montana and the British possessions in a northwest course. It is here very much broken, and, through the whole extent of this Territory, apparently disconnected. Its summit and general direction is, however, well defined. If we ascend the North Platte river and the Sweetwater and go on through the South Pass, the ascent is so gradual and the regions on either side so vast, with scarcely a mountain crest in sight, we can hardly appreciate that we have attained an elevation of more than 7,000 feet and are crossing the backbone of the continent through this immense gateway of the mountains.

In the vicinity of the Yellowstone Lake, in the northwest corner of Wyoming, the range again attains an elevation of 10,000 feet, but rapidly falls off, and through Montana is uniformly low — 6,000 to 8,000 feet. Through the regions north of Montana the mountains continue to decrease in elevation, furnishing less obstruction to the warm winds that naturally flow across from the Pacific Ocean.

*The Great Plains.*—That vast treeless region that stretches away from the eastern base of the Rocky Mountains, known as the Great Plains, has an average width of about 450 miles, and extends from near the Gulf of Mexico to the Arctic Ocean. Its eastern boundary should be located about the 99th degree of west longitude. For purposes of accurate description this country should be divided into zones or regions of different elevations. The line which we have mentioned as the eastern boundary of the plains is very nearly the line of 2,000 feet elevation. Very little of the country west of that line will be found to have less than 2,000 feet elevation, while very little of the country east of it has as great an elevation as 2,000 feet. Coming west from the Missouri river anywhere south of the Platte we shall find, as we approach that line, that a very considerable swell or terrace occurs in the surface of the plain; that west of this a marked diminution in the annual rainfall occurs; that forest trees grow only in the valleys near the streams; that vegetation is scant, and that the grasses of the plain dry up and cure on the ground during the latter part of the summer and early fall, and that agriculture without irrigation will be found to be impracticable. Along this line, north of the Platte, extending to the great divide between the upper Missouri basin and the slope toward the Arctic Ocean, changes in elevation, climate, etc., occur similar to those we have mentioned as occurring south of the Platte.

Passing on westward in the regions south of the Platte, we shall find another very rapid increase in the elevation of the plain as we reach the vicinity of the 102d degree of west longitude. This swell or terrace is even more abrupt and marked than the other of which we have spoken, and its brow marks the line of 4,000 feet elevation. From the base of this terrace flow out the Colorado and Brazos rivers of Texas, the Red river of Louisiana, prominent confluents of the Canadian river and the Arkansas, also the Kansas and Republican. From the headwaters of the Republican the line of this terrace is deflected rapidly to the northwest, and the Niobrara river, the White river and the two forks of the Cheyenne river that encircle the Black Hills flow out of its base. It is lost in the foot-hills at the south end of the Big Horn mountains, and the line of 4,000 feet elevation continues close along the base of the mountains and among the foot-hills to the line of the British possessions and beyond. We have now reached the most elevated table-lands of the continent, and as we leave the line of 4,000 feet elevation and continue to travel westward in New Mexico, Colorado or southern Wyoming the ascent is gradual until the undulations of the plain swell up abruptly into the foot-hills of the great Snowy Range. These foot-hills are the outliers of the main range — they mask its crest and break and graduate its descent. Their surfaces are for the most part smooth and grass-grown to their summits, with here and there considerable forests of timber. At some points, however, they are rugged and abrupt, and crowned with rocky escarpments. The elevation of the base of these foot-hills is from 5,000 to 6,000 feet. This most elevated region of the Great Plains is well watered, and the valleys of the streams where irrigation is practicable are rich and fertile, and it is on these elevated table-lands that about one-half of the population of the Great Plains and the Rocky Mountain regions is at present to be found — in New Mexico, Colorado and Wyoming principally engaged in agricultural and pastoral pursuits. Almost the entire region of the Great Plains north of the Platte river falls within the lines of 2,000 to 4,000 feet elevation, and from the Platte to the British possessions are entirely within the Great Basin of the upper Missouri. It is in this region that the Black Hills, the Powder river and Big Horn gold fields are situated — it is here that a greater portion of the buffalo remaining are to be found in their original home, and it is here that the most numerous and warlike tribe of Indians that have ever existed on the continent have roamed about at will until recently. This region of the Great Plains presents a more mountainous, uneven surface than the region south of the Platte. Its rivers are more numerous, its river valleys and mountain flanks are better timbered, its soils of valley, plain and hill-side are more fertile, and vegetation is everywhere more abundant.

*Climatology.*—In discussing the climatology of any particular region of country, it is necessary to consider, to a greater or less extent, the climatology of the whole continent, especially that portion of it that is subject to similar climatic influences, and also that portion in the same latitude that is subject to different climatic influences. And it is often very necessary, and the source of a great deal of interesting information, to compare the climates of the continents, and also different portions of the continents in the same latitudes. It is our purpose to speak in a general way of the climate of the Great Plains and the Rocky Mountain regions, and, closing this chapter, to speak particularly of the region specially under consideration in this volume. Although a great deal has been said in late years in a desultory way about the climate of the Rocky Mountain regions, the subject is probably less understood than almost any other in reference to this country.* The climate of these highlands is entirely unlike that of the States east of the Missouri river, or that of the Pacific coast west of the Sierra Nevada mountains. Those regions are designated as having marine climates, being more fully under the influence of the great oceans than are the interior highlands which are designated as having continental climate. If these highlands, with their present latitude and altitude, were subject to the same climatic influences as the Atlantic coast of the continent, or the same as the Mississippi basin east of the Mississippi river, four-fifths of this important division of the country would be uninhabitable on account of the rigor of its climate. But the influence of the great elevation of these regions, and even the high latitudes of portions of them, is overcome by other influences, as we shall see, making them not only habitable, but giving them a climate extremely healthful and pleasant, more so than that of the Atlantic coast of the continent, at the sea level, in the same latitudes. It is a fact well understood that degrees of latitude, or the distance of any given region from the equator, does not absolutely control its temperature, nor the other physical conditions that go to make up its climate. The western coasts of the continent in the northern hemisphere are found to be warmer than the eastern. This fact is due to the influence of the atmospheric currents, and the thermal currents of the great oceans in distributing the heat of the tropics to

* The most distinguished author on climatology in the United States, wrote for a publication of 1874 as follows: "The mean temperatures for the winter are significant and valuable guides to the climate in its relations to vegetable and animal life. The absolute limit of the growth of grass is coincident with the isothermal line of 32°, which passes near Philadelphia, Baltimore, Washington, Cincinnati and St. Louis — thence westward to Denver, north of Santa Fé, and northwestward past Salt Lake to the forty-ninth parallel in northern Oregon. Very little winter pasturage exists in all the regions north of this line, except in winters unusually mild." Wyoming, Montana and Idaho, all entirely north of the line above designated, had, according to the census of 1870, 177,000 cattle and 10,000 sheep. Sheep are fed in these districts from five to fifteen of the stormy days of each winter, and no one any more thinks of feeding cattle, that graze on these plains the year round (except a few milch cows), than they think of gathering in herds of buffalo and feeding them.

7

these shores. The most remarkable example of the difference in the temperature between the eastern and western shores of the continents in the same latitude, is found between North America and Europe. The difference between eastern Asia and western North America is also very great. The isothermal line of 50° Fahr. leaves the eastern coast of Asia about the forty-second parallel — 2° north of Pekin, China. In crossing the Pacific Ocean it is deflected north about 8° and strikes the western coast of North America at the fiftieth parallel, 556 miles north of its point of departure from the eastern coast of Asia. Crossing North America, it is deflected southward to about the fortieth parallel — 10°, or 695 miles — passing near the city of New York. Extending across the Atlantic it shows its greatest deflection to the north, and reaches the city of London in latitude 51°, or 764 miles north of New York city. The line of 40° shows still greater departures. It leaves the eastern coast of Asia at the forty-fifth parallel and reaches Sitka, Alaska, in latitude 57°, or 834 miles north of the forty-fifth degree. And again it leaves the eastern coast of North America somewhere about Halifax, in Nova Scotia, latitude 45°, and is deflected rapidly to the north, passing the south coast of Ireland, and on the western coast of Norway extends north of the Arctic Circle. At this point it is 1,300 miles north of Halifax. England, situated 764 miles farther north, has a warmer and more equable climate than Long Island. Newfoundland, in the same latitude as the north of France, has a rigorous, cheerless climate. The interior of the island is barren and desolate. Where timber grows it is stunted fir, pine, birch and aspen, while large tracts of the country are covered with lichen and reindeer moss.

Wheat never matures. In the same latitude in France the vine and fig are cultivated successfully, and all the fruits and cereals of the middle temperate zones of the earth reach their greatest perfection. The whole of Europe may be said to be in high latitudes. Madrid, in Spain, is a little north of New York city, and with a very slight exception the whole of Italy is north of the latitude of Philadelphia. Still the climate of Europe is very mild, compared with that of other portions of the globe in the same latitudes. This tempering of the winds, and this mild climate of Europe, is due to the influence of the gulf stream coming in from the heated regions of the tropics, whose vast flow of thermal waters constantly leave its western shores.

The surface of Europe gradually rises from its western coast until we reach the bases of the mountain ranges of the interior. The soft, balmy winds, heated by the gulf stream and laden with moisture, pass over the whole surface, giving to the north of Ireland the myrtle, blooming as luxuriantly as in Portugal,* the vine, the ivy and the geranium to central Europe, and even invading the realms of the winter king far up the sides of the lofty mountain ranges of the interior. Influences exactly similar to this prevail upon the western coast of our continent in a less marked but very considerable degree. The great equatorial current of the North Pacific Ocean — the Kuro Sivo, or Black Water of Japan — is analogous to the gulf stream of the Atlantic. The warm waters and warm humid winds of this vast tropical stream constantly coming in upon the western coast of our continent, give it a mild equable climate. To what extent this warm breath of the tropics influences the mountain regions and the great plains in the interior of the continent, we shall attempt to show. The effect of this great tropical current of the Pacific Ocean upon our western coast is, however, modified by conditions not met with on the western coast of Europe. Most important of these, and more important than all others, are the mountain ranges along our western coast. The coast range, so called, is low and of no consequence. The Sierra Nevada range is by far the most lofty and rugged, having but few passes and those very high. It extends, as we have seen, through nearly the whole length of the State of California. Its western slope is covered to a height of 8,000 feet by a dense forest, which is succeeded by naked granite and perpetual snow. It shuts off most perfectly the mild climate of the coast from the interior. East of this mighty wall through the central portions of the State of Nevada, from the mud lakes of the north through the Humboldt desert and the great salt valley which extends to the south line of the State, and on south to Death Valley, in California, this whole region is extremely arid and barren. The small amount of moisture that surmounts the lofty crests of these mountains does so from January to May each year, during the rainy season of California, and during which time all the rains of this region fall — five to ten inches annually. At about the fortieth parallel of north latitude the influence of the Japanese current begins to be felt. This fact is

* Humboldt.

evinced by the rapid increase of the rainfall of the immediate coast, as we advance to the north from San Francisco. It is also evinced by the fact that all along the coast, as far north as Victoria, the annual temperature is only a trifle lower than that of San Francisco, as the following table shows:

| STATIONS. | North Latitude. | Annual Temperature. | Annual Rain-fall. |
|---|---|---|---|
| San Francisco | 37 48 | 54.9 | 23.50 |
| Fort Reading, Cal. | 40 30 | 62.1 | 29.11 |
| Fort Orford, Or. | 42 44 | 53.6 | 70.59 |
| Astoria, Or. | 46 11 | 52.2 | 86.35 |
| Victoria, Vancouver | 48 27 | 53.9 | 83.19 |

The rain-fall continues heavy and the climate comparatively mild along the coast to Sitka, Alaska, in latitude 57°, the annual temperature being 43° and the rain-fall 83 inches. About the forty-first parallel, near the north boundary of the State of California, the Sierra Nevada mountains and the Coast Range unite by means of a short transverse range in which is situated Mount Shasta. From this point north through Oregon, Washington Territory and the British possessions, the Cascade and other ranges are comparatively low and broken. The country east of these mountains compared with that east of the Sierra Nevada presents a wide contrast. There we find an almost rainless region — only five to ten inches falling annually, from January to May; here, an annual rain-fall of 12 to 16 inches distributed through nine months of the year. There, a region of arid deserts, with few and unimportant streams of water that evaporate in their courses, sink into sands or fall into shallow mud lakes and evaporate,— none of them ever reaching the ocean; here, a region of innumerable mountain torrents that form mighty rivers that have broken through great mountain walls seeking the ocean. There, a treeless region, almost destitute of vegetation; here, a region of forests with vegetation abundant. The difference between this region and that has been brought about by two causes — first, the Japanese current sending in its warm, humid winds upon the land, and secondly, by the mountain crests being less elevated and less continuous here than there. "The general system of atmospheric circulation is from west to east, all the upper volumes of the air steadily moving in that direction at all seasons; and this upper atmosphere constantly brings with it a vast volume of moisture evaporated from tropical seas. The trade winds of the equatorial regions, driven unremittingly over vast oceans of tropical seas at high temperatures, take up moisture far more rapidly than in any temperate latitudes."[*] These tropical winds accompany the Japanese current many thousands of miles, and as they approach the land their temperature is so rapidly lowered that vast quantities of rain are precipitated upon the immediate coast; the average amount at Astoria for a single year being equal to a sheet of water seven feet two and one-half inches deep. These warm winds passing over the great plateau, through its valleys, along its mountain flanks, across the comparatively low and broken rocky range in Montana and Wyoming and out upon the great plains, give these vast highlands a climate not only habitable but extremely salubrious and pleasant. These same conditions extend over that portion of the great plateau, mountains and plains that lie north of Montana and Washington Territories, modified, of course, by the higher latitudes of those regions.

*Rain-fall.*—These Pacific currents of air, after passing the Coast and the Cascade ranges, come upon the great plateau with their lower strata largely deprived of moisture. Passing over this region, and constantly coming in contact with mountain ranges and mountain peaks, they deposit during each year from 12 to 16 inches of water in the shape of snows and rains; and as they approach the more elevated regions of the Rocky Mountains they precipitate, during the latter part of spring and early summer, considerable quantities of rain, and during the winter and early spring vast deposits of snow-fall in the mountains. Also during March, April and May, considerable quantities of wet snows fall upon the plains, always melting away in a few hours. These deposits of snow on the mountains are a kind of reservoir of moisture for the great plains during summer. They are melted by the warm sun of June and July, and fill the mountain streams at a time water is most needed for irrigation on the plains. At the same time large quantities of these mountain snows are taken up by evaporation, and, gathering into rain-clouds over the mountains during the middle of the day, come down over the plains almost every afternoon in beautiful refreshing showers. All over the regions of the Great Plains proper

* Blodget.

the rain-fall is from 12 to 16 inches annually,— the smallest amount noted at any single point for one year being about 6 inches and the largest amount 30 inches. The average rain-fall here, being about 14 inches, is one third that of the regions east of the Mississippi, which is set down at from 40 to 45 inches.[*] There it is distributed about equally over the year: here it is distributed as follows: for the spring months, 7 inches; summer months, 4 inches; autumn, 2 inches; winter, 1 inch. The precipitation of moisture during the cold season of the year is entirely in the shape of light, dry, fleecy snows, never covering the ground for any length of time.

The following table is compiled from medical statistics of the United States army, the points compared being Forts Laramie and Bridger, Wyoming; Salt Lake City, Utah; Santa Fé, New Mexico, with Fort Independence, Boston Harbor. Mean number of fair, cloudy, rainy and snowy days, with annual rain-fall, compiled from a period of ten years' observations:

| STATIONS. | Fair. | Cloudy. | Rain. | Snow. | Rain-fall, Inches. |
|---|---|---|---|---|---|
| Fort Independence.......... | 191 | 157 | 89 | 22 | 39½ |
| Fort Laramie............. | 227 | 120 | 45 | 29 | 15¼ |
| Fort Bridger.............. | 253 | 161 | 40 | 29 | 13½ |
| Salt Lake ................ | 281 | 76 | 44 | 46 | 17 |
| Santa Fé................. | 226 | 103 | 46 | 27 | 17 |

These figures would not be materially changed were the comparison made between the above-named points and Chicago or Buffalo. It will also be remembered that comparing the density of the clouds of these highlands with that of the clouds of the sea-coast, the former will have a density about one-third that of the latter — a comparison of rain-fall and snow-fall of days will show about the same ratio. The most important facts deserving attention in reference to the precipitation of moisture over these regions is the abundant rains and wet snows of the months when moisture is most needed — the spring and early summer — and the extremely small amount of moisture precipitated in the form of dry snows during the cold seasons of fall and winter; and also the fact that there is no other region on the face of the earth that is subject to such small periodical rains, that is so little subject to drouth or entire absence of rain. On the great plateau

* Blodget.

the rain-fall is subject to much greater variations in reference to quantity. From the southern boundary of the United States northward to about the forty-first parallel, including the great basin of the Colorado river and most of the great Salt Lake basin, we have more nearly a rainless region than is anywhere else to be found in the United States. At points along the eastern base of the Sierra Nevada mountains the annual rain-fall is reported as low as five and even three inches, and some seasons no rain or snow falling at all for a whole year. To the east, along the western slope of the Wausach mountains, eight, ten and twelve inches fall annually, and at Salt Lake City, which lies between mountain ranges, seventeen inches. The western slope of the Rocky Mountains in this region receives from eight to twelve and eighteen inches of rain annually. The confluents of the great Colorado river, the Green, Grand and Rio Gila, drain more than 1,000 miles of this mountain slope. North of about the forty-first parallel the rain-fall increases considerably from causes that we have mentioned, and it is probable will be found to gradually increase as we extend our observations northward through British Columbia. That this is so is evident from the greater number of lakes and running streams, and also the larger volume of water in the streams, together with great increase of forests and other vegetation throughout this region, as compared with the regions south of the forty-first parallel.

*Temperature.*—The Great Plains and Rocky Mountain regions within the boundaries of the United States have an annual temperature ranging from 60° to 44°. Leaving the southern boundary when an annual temperature of 60° prevails, and passing northward along the 104th meridian until we reach the vicinity of Fort Union and Santa Fé, near the thirty-fifth parallel, we find in northern and western New Mexico an extensive region with an annual temperature ranging from 50° to 47°. There is no other region in the United States, in this latitude, where so low a temperature obtains, except a very small extent of country in western North Carolina and eastern Tennessee. This region in New Mexico has an elevation of over 6,000 feet. Points near the thirty-fifth parallel are Santa Fé, temperature 50°; Fort Union, 49°; Fort Defiance, 47°. Points in the same latitude east of the Mississippi are Knoxville, Tennessee, temperature 55°, and Chappell Hill, North Carolina, 59°. In the same latitude on the Pacific coast. Monterey has 55.° The isothermal line of 52°, which reaches considerably south of Santa Fé and passes to the northeast by Fort Lyon across five parallels of latitude, from the thirty-fifth to the fortieth, intersects the latter south of Fort Kearney, Nebraska. From this point it extends nearly due east along the fortieth parallel to the Atlantic seaboard. Again, the isothermal of 52° passes northwest from the thirty-fifth parallel in New Mexico to the vicinity of Salt Lake, thence westward to Austin, Nevada, and thence across the Cascade range about the forty-first parallel on to the Pacific coast. and extends along the coast as far north as the forty-eighth parallel in the vicinity of Victoria.* The regions of the Great Plains and Rocky Mountains north of this line seem to be under entirely different climatic influences from those south of it. The regions south of it are the most arid and barren to be found on the continent of North America, and west of the Rocky Mountains are fully under the influence of the South Pacific Ocean. The waters of the ocean from San Francisco as far south as the thirtieth parallel of north latitude are extremely cold, their annual temperature being 55°. The interior regions south of the thirty-fourth parallel have an annual temperature of 60°, and at many points in the deserts the extremes of summer reach 118° to 121°.

The winds coming in from the ocean find an atmosphere considerably warmer than they, and any moisture they may bring in the shape of clouds or fogs is at once dispelled, and the result is little or no rain-falls until the lofty mountain ranges of the interior are reached. This region west of the Rocky Mountains comprises southwestern New Mexico, Arizona, western and southern Utah, Nevada and eastern California.

The regions of the Great Plains south of the isothermal of 52° and east of the Rocky Mountains are probably quite fully under the influence of the Gulf of Mexico, and is a country of high temperature of floods and drouths. This region consists of the western portion of Kansas, the western portion of the Indian Territory, western Texas, and eastern and southern New Mexico. The regions under consideration that lie north of the isothermal line of 52° seem to be, as we have said, under almost entirely different climatic influences from those south of that line.

* See Temperature Chart, Vital Statistics. Census of 1870.

These regions within the boundaries of the United States comprise eastern Oregon and Washington Territory, Idaho, a small portion of northern Nevada, eastern Utah, northern New Mexico, Colorado, Wyoming, Montana, western Dakota and western Nebraska. Their annual temperature ranges from 52° to 44°. Some small unimportant mountain plateaus may fall as low as 40° or even 36°, while the valley of the Columbia river east of the Cascade Mountains as far up as Walla Walla, and the valley of the Snake river as far up as Boise City, have the same temperature as the coast west of the mountains, 52°. We have seen that the climate of the Pacific coast from the fortieth parallel northward to Sitka, the Japanese current being felt in full force, is extremely mild, and that the warm currents of air that accompany this vast thermal stream pass on to the highlands, meeting comparatively little obstruction from the Cascade Mountains and other ranges in British Columbia. All over this vast highland region north of the fortieth parallel, extending to the Arctic Ocean, these Pacific currents of air are more important than all other climatic influences. They bring warmth and moisture, and carry the line of forest trees and other vegetation along the valley of the Mackenzie river far up toward the seventieth parallel of north latitude.

"The mountain valleys of the Peace and Laird rivers, latitude 56° to 60°, are thus influenced by the Pacific winds, and wheat and other cereals are successfully cultivated." [*] These regions are five to seven hundred miles north of the north boundary of the United States. In the vicinity of Salt Lake these Pacific currents of air begin to be deflected southward. They are probably influenced by the Wahsatch and Uintah mountains, and are forced into the basin of the Colorado river and along the western base of the Rocky Mountains, as far south as the thirty-sixth parallel in northern New Mexico. They carry to these regions, as we have seen, a lower annual temperature than is to be found anywhere else in the United States in similar latitudes. It is thus that a considerable belt of country along the western base of the Rocky Mountains, from Washington Territory to northern New Mexico, is subject to exactly similar climatic influences, as the following table shows — Fort Colville, Washington Territory, being only

[*] Sir Roderick Murchison, in Ross Brown's "Mineral Resources," 1868. Appendix, page 14.

about thirty-five miles south of the line of British Columbia, and
Fort Defiance, New Mexico, being only a short distance north of
the thirty-fifth parallel:

| Stations. | Latitude. North. | Altitude. | Temperature. | Rain-fall. Inches. |
|---|---|---|---|---|
| Fort Colville, W. T. | 48  54' | 2,800 | 45.60 | 25.75 |
| Fort Lapwai, Idaho | 46  32' | 3,148 | 52.49 | 14.5 |
| Fort Hall, Idaho | 43  7' | 4,700 | 46.00 | 11.10 |
| Salt Lake, Utah | 40  46' | 5,030 | 50.61 | 17.19 |
| Fort Defiance, N. M | 35  44' | 6,500 | 46.76 | 16.64 |

Crossing the Rocky Mountain range to its eastern base, in the
vicinity of Santa Fé and Fort Union, we find climatic influences
similar to those we have noted along its western base. Here we
find a vast belt of country stretching away to the east from the
base of the mountains, extending from Santa Fé to Fort Benton,
Montana, and probably to the line of the British possessions, over
all of which the same prominent climatic features extend. At
Santa Fé this belt is probably 100 to 150 miles wide, and rapidly
increases in width as we advance northward into the great basins
of the Platte river and the upper Missouri, where it is 300 to 400
miles wide. It extends from south to north over twelve to thir-
teen parallels of latitude, 800 to 1,000 miles. The following
table of stations, with their latitude, altitude, annual temperature
and rain-fall, are points along the boundaries of this region. They
are widely separated and are representative positions for vast
areas of country.

| Stations. | Latitude, North. | Altitude. | Temperature. | Rain-fall. |
|---|---|---|---|---|
| Santa Fé, N. M. | 35  41' | 6,846 | 50.6 | 17. |
| Fort Union, N. M. | 35  54' | 6,670 | 49.14 | 19.24 |
| Fort Lyons, Col. | 38  5' | 4,000 | 49. | 11. |
| Denver, Col. | 39  44' | 5,000 | 50. | 16. |
| Fort McPherson, Neb. | 41  3' | 2,770 | 51.12 | 18.48 |
| Cheyenne, W. T. | 41  12' | 6,072 | 48. | 16.20 |
| Fort Laramie, W. T. | 42  12' | 4,517 | 50.1 | 15.16 |
| Fort Benton, Mon. | 47  50' | 2,663 | 48.2 | 12.50 |
| Fort Pierre, D. T. | 44  23' | 1,456 | 51.9 | 13.51 |

It will be noticed that while there is a difference of twelve
degrees of latitude between Fort Benton and Santa Fé and Fort
Union, there is but one or two degrees difference between their

temperatures. We have seen that a considerable portion of northern New Mexico along the thirty-fifth parallel is colder than points in the latitude east of the Mississippi. If, now, we compare points along and near the fortieth parallel, we find these highlands and points eastward along this line have the same temperatures. Salt Lake has a temperature of 50°, Denver 50°, Cheyenne 48°, Fort McPherson, Nebraska. 51°, Logansport, Indiana, 50°, Pittsburgh, Pa., 50°, and New York City 51°. Going north to the forty-seventh parallel and instituting comparisons along that line, Fort Benton has a temperature of 48°, Michipicoten, on one of the islands of Lake Superior, 38°, and Fort Kent, Maine, 37°. Fort Benton being 10° warmer than the former and 11° warmer than the latter, has the same temperature as Albany, New York, and Boston, Mass., these places being near the forty-second parallel, five degrees farther south. Fort Benton is two degrees warmer than Chicago, which lies nearly 500 miles farther south. By comparing the tables above submitted, and from what has been said, it will be seen that the climates of the great plateau and the Great Plains from about the northern boundary of the United States southward to the vicinity of the fortieth parallel are, in most respects, similar. The average temperature and rain-fall are identical, while the extremes of each are also the same. Elevated mountain basins or regions of limited extent that are subject to peculiar local influences are, of course, exceptions to this general statement. The Pacific currents of air moving from west to east, coming upon the Rocky Mountain range, which extends from northwest to southeast, striking it where its crests are low and its acclivities gradual, are influenced by this vast mountain chain and forced south of the fortieth parallel over five degrees of latitude, carrying along both the eastern and western base of the mountains the climate of eastern Oregon, Washington Territory and eastern Montana.

An important source of heat for these highlands is from the unobstructed rays of the sun. On account of the extreme dryness of the atmosphere there are few cloudy days. There is no sufficient growth of vegetation to protect the earth from the full force of the sun's rays, and from six to eight months of the year there is little or no moisture on the earth's surface, and consequently little or no evaporation, thus absorbing or making heat latent. As a consequence the daily range of temperature is very great. The earth's surface being rapidly heated by the sun's rays during the day, is as rapidly cooled by radiation during the night. Anywhere along the base of the mountains a hot sultry night is a thing unknown. The plains become heated, and the atmosphere over them very much rarefied, during the day; the air from the more elevated regions, cool and bracing, comes down in gentle breezes during the evening, until the equilibrium of the temperature between the two regions has been restored. The hotter and more sultry the day the more certain will the night be cool and pleasant. A difference of forty or fifty and even sixty degrees of temperature during twenty-four hours is frequently noted. The difference in temperature between winter and summer is less here than in regions east of the Missouri; and while the extremes of temperature for the year are about the same, spells of low temperature do not continue as long here as there. Owing to the extreme dryness of the atmosphere during the cold season of the year, men and animals do not suffer as much from a temperature of 20° below zero in this country as they do from a temperature of zero in a climate as moist as that of Chicago. The snow-line on the western slope of the Sierra Nevada Mountains, in the same latitude as the Park regions of Colorado, is 8,000 feet above the level of the sea.

On the Atlantic coast, in the same latitude, on the Allegheny Mountains, the line of perpetual snow would be (were these mountains sufficiently high) 7,000 feet above the sea. In the Park regions of Colorado the snow-line is 12,000 feet above the sea. On the summits of these lofty mountains, 10,000 and 11,000 feet above the sea, are to be found some beautiful open spots without a tree, and covered with grass and flowers surrounded on all sides by dense forests of pine. Just on the edges of these park-like areas considerable banks of snow may be seen during the whole summer, and, within a few feet of them, multitudes of flowers bloom, and even the wild strawberry seems to flourish.* In these open areas and in the more extensive parks, cattle graze for six months each year on lands from 9,000 to 11,000 feet above the sea. The high winds that are extremely prevalent all over these elevated regions are about the only unpleasant feature of the climate. The almost entire absence of moisture in them during

* Hayden. Report of 1867 to 1869, page 84.

the cold season of the year renders them much more tolerable than they would otherwise be; and while high gales of wind are common, hurricanes such as visit the Atlantic coast and the Mississippi basin almost annually never occur here. The winds at these altitudes are fitful, but usually of short duration, and when moving as rapidly as at the sea level their force is very much less, as the atmosphere here is much lighter.

*Resources.*—The physical conditions that go to make up the climate of a country have largely to do with deciding its value as a habitation for man. It is probable that pastoral agriculture will be the leading and most important industry of these mountain and plain regions when they shall have fallen fully under the control of civilized man. Mining and agriculture will also develop, we imagine, into proportions that no one now has the slightest conception of. Within the boundaries of the United States the Great Plains and the Rocky Mountain regions occupy an area of about 1,650,000 square miles, or more than a billion of acres, most of which is one vast pasture ground. Here the buffalo, antelope, elk, deer and mountain sheep — their numbers reaching far into the millions — have found their food winter and summer for untold centuries, grazing on these vast grassy tables as far south as the thirtieth parallel of north latitude, and as far north as Slave Lake, latitude 64°. The total number of horses, cattle and sheep in the United States, according to the census of 1870, was 65,242,752. On these vast pastures, within the boundaries of the United States, each of these animals could have an area of over fifteen acres on which to graze, and one hundred million of such animals could each have an area of ten acres. It is no exaggeration to say that, with the care and attention of flock-masters and herdsmen, as great a number of horses, cattle and sheep could be subsisted winter and summer on these vast areas as are now to be found in all the States east of the great plains. The value of these animals could not fall short of a billion of dollars. Winter grazing all over these regions is no longer a problem; that it is a great success is a fixed fact. The American people are, and have been, slow to comprehend the value and importance of these highlands as an integral part of the noble domain of the United States. It is within a decade that a distinguished and possibly a learned member of Congress from the great State of Ohio, said, in his place in the house, that the regions now comprised within the boundaries of Wyoming "were as broad and worthless as Sahara." Now this statement did not change one single fact in reference to Wyoming—it simply showed how little a man might know about some things and still be a member of Congress. All of the people of this country, and their ancestors from the earliest times, have inhabited countries of marine climates. They have never known anything of elevated regions with continental climates, and are constantly making comparisons between these arid regions and the country east of the Missouri and the Mississippi. Comparing these regions with those, they find no similarity, and consequently conclude that this country is a desert and worthless.

One reason this country has been looked upon with great disfavor, and its grand resources very much derided and belittled, is due to the fact that no civilized people in the world's history have ever inhabited a region whose latitude, altitude and climate is similar to this. There is indeed no country on the earth corresponding perfectly with this in these respects. Even the elevated plateaus and mountain regions in central Asia, lying in similar latitudes, are, in many respects, dissimilar. That continent and its elevated regions are much more extensive, the mountain ranges more lofty, and having an east and west direction, in some cases shut off a tropical climate on one side, producing a cold, temperate climate on the other; or with a temperate climate on one side, have almost a frigid region on the other. They are also dissimilar in this, that they are much farther removed from the influence of the great oceans, while the highlands of this continent lie along near the shore of the greatest of the oceans. They have a much less precipitation of moisture, their vegetation is more scant, and their deserts more extensive; all those regions being only cultivatable when irrigation is practicable, and there, like here, flocks and herds graze the year round on natural pastures. Glancing hastily over these vast areas of central Asia that lie between the thirtieth and the forty-ninth parallels of north latitude, nearly corresponding to the south and north boundaries of the United States, we find a region of elevated table-lands, plateaus and mountains, more than 1,000 miles wide from north to south, and extending 4,500 miles from the Caspian sea east to the great Kinghan mountains of eastern China. The climate and general characteristics of the various regions of this vast country, its resources, products, and the condition of the people inhabiting it, have been but little known until within the last quarter of a century. We find here in these desert highlands of Asia everywhere finely developed races of men, brave, independent and high spirited, and who, though not a tithe as numerous, have often overrun and conquered the most powerful nations of the lowlands. And when in time they have been conquered by the people of the lowlands, their subjugation has always cost vastly more than their vassalage was worth. They are generally as well educated as the people of the lowlands, schools of their kind are as numerous in proportion to population in Toorkistan, Afghanistan, Thibet, Cashmere, and even in Mongolia, where the country will admit of settled habitations, as in India or China. They are also as well versed in the arts and sciences as the other nations of Asia, many of their manufactures having for centuries attracted great attention in the markets of the world. Comparing the Asiatic races of these two regions, we readily perceive the influence the different climates have had upon them, and it is but fair to suppose that our own highlands, with their clear, elastic atmosphere and bracing, healthful climate, will produce here upon these plains and in these mountains a very superior race of people, noted for great physical endurance and mental power, despising alike all fetters of mind and body.

*Wyoming.*—Being centrally located in the mountain and plain regions of which we have spoken, and north of the isothermal line of 52 degrees, Wyoming will require little special attention on the subject of her climate further than what has been already said. The Great South Pass, situated near the western boundary of the Territory, about equally distant from its north and south boundaries, has a very decided influence on the climate of the interior of Wyoming. The valley of the Sweetwater and the extensive basin of the North Platte are very fully influenced by the warm winds from the Pacific coast, and have from the first advent of white men into the country had the reputation of being one of the most desirable locations for winter grazing in the Rocky Mountain regions. This whole country would long since have been filled with flocks and herds had it not been constantly exposed to predatory raids from the Sioux. The Laramie Plains, in southeastern Wyoming, are a part of the park system of Colorado. The Rocky Mountain range, as we have seen, is deflected rapidly to the west and northwest at the southern line of the Territory. A considerable mountain spur continues almost directly north, known as the Laramie mountains, and terminates in the Laramie Peak about twenty miles west of Fort Laramie. Between this mountain spur and the main range is situated the Laramie Plains, a beautiful valley with an elevation of from 6,000 to 7,500 feet, and an extremely salubrious, healthful climate. It is watered by the Laramie river, which takes its rise in the Rocky Mountains among perpetual snows. There are no other peculiarities in reference to the climate of Wyoming worthy of mention except it be the increased rain-fall in the Black Hills. This short mountain range lies in the extreme northeast corner of the Territory, and extends from north to south one hundred miles. It stands up very abruptly in the midst of the plain two to three thousand feet. Clouds approaching it have their temperature lowered, and a very considerable greater rain-fall occurs here than on the surrounding plain — twenty to twenty-five inches falling annually. The same condition obtains in the Big Horn mountains and the Wolf mountains, where very extensive forests of pine are found. As we shall speak in a subsequent chapter of Wyoming as a health resort, we shall defer further remarks on the special climatic conditions of Wyoming until then.

# CHAPTER IX.

## MANNERS AND SOCIETY, WITH A FEW REFLECTIONS.

OF manners and morals of western people generally, much is said that is far beyond the pale of truth. Nearly every eager itemizer, from the manager of a representative eastern paper down to the senseless and superficial scribbler for the eastern backwoods press, comes to the new west with mind literally charged with glaring absurdities, and with an unyielding determination to realize only those absurdities. Why this should be so is partially explained by the fact that eastern readers demand experiences from the western plains and mountains which smack of the crude, the rough and the semi-barbarous. To point out the reckless, rollicking traits of character, to tell of the marvelous and wild-cat speculations, and to describe the gilded dens of gaming and profligacy (which the writers only know of by hearsay), is magnificently popular. But to write of our model men, to enlarge upon their carefully conducted enterprises and to tell of our churches, schools and societies,— that would fall like a chilly drizzle after the glittering rainbow.

It is also quite the fashion to create thrilling episodes from whole cloth, in which the savage plays a prominent part, and is valiantly assisted by the writer. While this does the new Territory great injustice, and fills the emigrant with an unfounded dread, it still gratifies the popular demand; and what matters it if a burning at the stake scene *is* laid on a level plain where wood does not exist and buffalo chips are scarce? Or what matters it if more Indians than ever belonged to the tribes of America *are* concentrated along the Black Hills road? That is what readers must have, and it is so comfortable and satisfactory to sit in one of the cosy Cheyenne reading-rooms and indite articles in which "armed to the teeth," "dangerous lookout on top of the coach," "redskins seen on every bluff," "the gory graves in Killemquick canyon," etc., are only mild expressions.

Our settlements are full of odd characters, as are the eastern:

8

but it must be confessed that much of the devil-may-care
manner and dress attributed to real frontiersmen belong to
eccentric emigrants who have scarcely learned to distinguish our
crisp, invigorating atmosphere from the heavy, enervating fluid
they had just breathed beyond the Mississippi. The swagger and
swell of a recent heavily-armed and buckskinned arrival is as
commonly noted and of more disgusting originality than that of
the worst "hoodlum" of the plains. And here is where the
modern paragraphist shines. During the recent brief sojourn in
our midst of the " funny man " on a prominent New York newspaper, he stepped up to a representative business man of Cheyenne and asked:

"Can you point me out a real original westerner — regular
frontiersman, you know. that shows the 'out west' character
from head to foot?"

"Why, yes sir," replied the resident, "a good many of us
here have been west from ten to twenty years. There's Judge
C——, owns that block of brick buildings over there — made his
money in the stock business, and there comes Captain O——,
that well-dressed man, you see — he has fought Indians and built
posts all over these plains; and if you will come down to the
bank I'll introduce you to ——"

"Oh, pshaw! Those are not the kind of men I'm hunting.
Now here is a capital subject (pointing to a long-haired man clad
in a greasy suit of buckskin, and leaning listlessly against a
store-box). Now, come, I'll warrant that man is a dyed-in-the-
wool border genius, and he will answer my purpose gloriously."

"That fellow? Why, he came out here from Natchez about
two months ago and called himself 'Buckskin Jack.' He has
been loafing around ever since, eating free lunches, and is a first-
class deadbeat. Those are not the kind of men to build our
towns, raise our cattle and find the gold in the Big Horn
mountains."

" He suits me, anyhow," said the man of the glowing quill,
"and I propose to interview him."

The interview undoubtedly resulted in a thrilling narrative
of border experience, for Jack had been west just long enough to
distinguish a "tender-foot" and to learn how to manufacture
sensational yarns."

If the ambitious newcomer desires to appreciate thoroughly

and report honestly upon the native intelligence and enterprise, let him try his own metal against it. If he wishes to do credit to Wyoming's manners and customs, let him — instead of unearthing the outcasts and loafers, who often come from the dens of the east, a prey upon our prosperity — take as examples the large proportion in every community of earnest, thrifty western workers.

It is not the case, as is often assumed in the east, that distinctions in society — which are generally deemed essential to well-organized communities — are lacking here in the new west. As the merits and demerits of settlers are disclosed these distinctions inevitably appear here as elsewhere. In expecting to find boors and gentlemen upon a common social level the visitor will find himself happily or unhappily disappointed according to his own taste or disposition. Intelligence, industry, culture and integrity will be here found to draw the lines of social distinction as closely as anywhere. Churches and benevolent societies are as numerous in proportion to our population as elsewhere, while schools are as plentiful and as well conducted. Lectures, libraries, public and private parties, and select assemblies for instruction, amusement and social enjoyment are all found here as well as in the east. The press of Wyoming is perhaps more noticeable for its general excellence and thorough occupancy of the field than any other institutions. Numerous daily and weekly papers are published which would do credit to a population furnishing twice as many readers. Papers like these, beaming with frontier news, furnishing well-filled columns of spicy editorials, and special and associate press dispatches, tell in language unmistakable of the morality, the intelligence and the thrift of communities.

Wyoming stands out bravely in her support of universal suffrage. The better citizens, as a rule, are not only well satisfied with the measure which grants women the privilege to vote, but they are proud of it. The matter, so purely an experiment, has of course aroused liberal discussion, and from this many points of interest have been developed. Among these are the statements quite recently put forth by prominent officials and citizens of the Territory in answer to questions asked by a well-known local pastor. A few of these statements are appropos here.

"At the time of the passage of the law creating female suffrage, the project was opposed by a large majority of the people of Wyoming. The enactment was an experiment, and intended as such. At the next session of the legislature an attempt was made to repeal the law; but it failed, in consequence of the change of sentiments of the people upon the subject. . . . Since that time no serious attempt has been made to repeal the law. It is now no longer a political question. The attempt to repeal the law would now be a much more unpopular move than its original enactment. The most bitter enemies of the system have, by reason of its beneficial results in actual practice, become its warmest advocates. . . .

"Eight years' experience has shown that evil associations at the polls or in politics, on the part of ladies, is the result of choice, as in every other relation in life, and not of necessity. . . The women are not contaminated or degraded in any respect or degree by the exercise of their political rights, but, on the contrary; their appearance in politics has always the effect of quieting the most turbulent crowds. . . . Not a single case in which a respectable woman has been knowingly or wantonly insulted or treated with indignity while exercising the right of suffrage has been known. The practical result of the exercise of the right of suffrage by the women of Wyoming has been noticed in several instances to change the result in favor of the better candidate, and against the less competent and less worthy.

"We have had an opportunity to watch the practical effect of woman suffrage here from the first, and have seen none of the evil results prophesied for it by its opponents. We have never heard of a case of domestic trouble growing out of it; women have not been degraded or demoralized; on the contrary, they have, in a quiet, lady-like manner, exercised their elective franchise, as a rule, in favor of law, order and good government. Their influence has done much to refine the politics of our Territory, and to divest them of their objectionable features. All lovers of law and order, of whatever political faith, acknowledge the benefits of woman's refining influence in our local government."

The Territories have assumed a significance, yes, a grandeur, unthought of twenty years ago. The men who have so nobly cast their fortunes here, and have reared industrial monuments

which now astonish the wildest dreamers of the last decade are
not to be underestimated. They are representatives of the "best
enterprise, the best talent and the best energy from the old States
and nations," and have broken away from all hereditary ties to
face all dangers and endure all hardships in the cause of development. It has taken talent, energy and nerve to prove that the
Rockies are the treasure-vaults of the world, that our plains and
valleys can produce food and clothing for three Americas, and
that we possess here an empire complete in itself, of health,
wealth and beauty. One of the most learned and ready editorial
writers in the Union, after eloquently pointing to such representative western characters as Benton and Houston, does us the
credit to say: "We need not be surprised if the west and the
Pacific Slope furnish hereafter the strongest minds in public
affairs."

Brains will find ready recognition and employment in the
west, but they must strive, as did the first invoice, and not take
it for granted that such commodities are sufficiently scarce to
warrant unjust criticism, fault-finding and a "hunt-me-up" disposition. Willing hands are also wanted, and the writer has
never observed a case in which the man who earnestly sought
work — with a determination to do *something* — did not get it.

# CHAPTER X.

## WYOMING FOR HEALTH AND PLEASURE.

IT is not difficult to demonstrate that Wyoming possesses more natural and genuine attractions for the health and pleasure seeker than any region of similar extent in the known world. Her towering mountains and mountain-locked parks, her grand rivers and awe-inspiring cañons and her broad areas, so tempting to the research of all, are almost daily reaping richest homage from the most capable explorers and the best scholars of our land. The savant, the sportsman and the pleasure seeker alike find their ideal, and the invalid requiring an elevated region, and in search of health-giving waters or the purest of ether, can never be disappointed.

*Game and Fish.*—Wyoming is the huntsman's and angler's paradise. On her plains the buffalo and antelope find an agreeable all-the-year home; in her mountains the elk, deer, mountain sheep, bear and mountain lion abound; and in her thousand crystal streams and lakes the gamiest and most delicate of all fish, the mountain trout, are always ready for the bait. Sage hens, grouse and partridge are always found in numerous localities, while geese, ducks and other wild fowl are native to nearly all the lakes and water-courses. The settler has no trouble in providing himself with the best wild meats the year round, and indeed often makes a good living by hunting game for local markets. From the moment the tourist enters the Territory until he departs, his bill of fare teems with these riches of forest, plain and river. Fur-bearing animals of almost every description are also taken by the hundreds of trappers who inhabit the frontier, and the number of beavers and wolves especially, which are annually trapped for their skins, is enormous. A day's ride from almost any station will take the nimrod into hunting grounds of the best class.

*Natural Curiosities.*—Of the wonderful petrifactions and such other natural curiosities as garnet, topaz, jasper, agate, chalcedony and crystallizations, much has been written. Not only have these treasures been widely sought for their natural interest and beauty, but a very large business is being carried on in the way of manufacturing them into every variety of jewelry. Rare petrifactions of animals, trees and shells and monster fossils abound in many localities.

*Mineral Waters.*—Mineral springs of almost every nature are found in accessible localities. The great hot springs near Camp Brown, Sweetwater county, probably excel any of this class in the Rocky Mountain region, for their extent, and for the healing properties of their waters. The water is emitted from numerous orifices in the bottom of a pool or basin, which covers 6,000 square feet, and a large stream is constantly discharged into the ice-cold current of Little Wind river, near by. Carbonic acid and chloride of lime are given off abundantly, the temperature running from 100 to 120. Rheumatic affections and diseases of the skin are often eradicated by a short season of bathing, and the Shoshone Indians, whose agency is located here, have a delightful tradition making this out the mythical "fountain of youth." A fine bath-house is at hand for the accommodation of visitors.

GIANT GEYSER. YELLOWSTONE PARK.

A great many cold sulphur, iron and soda springs are found at Rawlins, Evanston, Hilliard and other points along the railroad, while in more remote locations there are hundreds of these fountains of health and beauty. Near Piedmont is a cluster of the most wonderful soda springs in the west. The sediment thrown out by the principal one has built up a beautiful conical-shaped body, fifteen feet in height. The water is delicious, and for health-giving properties cannot be surpassed by others of the kind in the Union. A short distance from Evanston is another interesting group of soda springs, occupying an area over six miles square. Fremont, many years ago, named some of these "Steamboat Springs," on account of their graceful but noisy steam vents.

*The Yellowstone Park.*—The Senate and House of Representatives of the United States did a very wise thing a few years ago when they passed the act which reserved and withdrew from settlement, occupancy and sale that portion of Wyoming's unique northwestern corner known as the Yellowstone Park. If readers may believe half that is written about it, it is the wonder-land not only of America but of the world. "This whole region," says Dr. Hayden, the United States geologist, "was, in comparatively modern geological times, the scene of the most wonderful volcanic activity of any portion of our country. The hot springs and geysers represent the last stages — the vents or escape pipes — of these remarkable volcanic manifestations of the internal forces. All these springs are adorned with decorations more beautiful than human art ever conceived, and which have required thousands of years for the cunning hand of nature to form." "It is probable," he remarks elsewhere, "that during the Pliocene period, the entire country, drained by the sources of the Yellowstone and the Colorado, was the scene of volcanic activity as great as that of any portion of the globe. It might be called one vast crater, made up of a thousand smaller volcanic vents and fissures, out of which the fluid interior of the earth, fragments of rock and volcanic dust, were poured in unlimited quantities. Hundreds of the nuclei or cones of these vents are now remaining, some of them rising to a height of 10,000 to 11,000 feet above the sea."

The Yellowstone Park embraces an area of fifty-five by sixty-five miles, and contains the most striking of all the mountains, gorges, falls, rivers and lakes in the whole Yellowstone region. The hot springs on Gardiner's river, for example, are along its

northern boundary; the Grand Cañon lies toward its northeastern corner, and toward its southeastern corner stretches Yellowstone lake. The springs in active operation on Gardiner's river
cover an area of about one square mile, and three or four square
miles thereabout are occupied by the remains of springs which
have ceased to flow. "Small streams flow down the sides of the
Snowy Mountain in channels lined with oxide of iron of the most
delicate tints of red; others show exquisite shades of yellow,
from a deep bright sulphur to a dainty cream-color; still others
are stained with shades of green;—all these colors as brilliant as
the brightest aniline dyes. The water after rising from the
spring basin flows down the sides of the declivity, step by step,
from one reservoir to another, at each one of them losing a portion of its heat, until it becomes as cool as spring water." The
natural basins into which these springs flow are from four to six
feet in diameter and from one to four feet in depth. The principal ones are located upon terraces midway up the sides of the
mountain. "The largest living spring is near the outer margin
of the main terrace. Its dimensions are twenty feet by forty,
and its water so perfectly transparent that one can look down
into the beautiful ultramarine depth to the very bottom of the
basin. Its sides are ornamented with coral-like forms of a great
variety of shades, from pure white to a bright cream yellow,
while the blue sky reflected in the transparent water gives an
azure tint to the whole which surpasses all art."

The banks of the Yellowstone river abound with ravines and
cañons, which are carved to the heart of the mountains through
the hardest rocks. The most remarkable of these is the cañon
of Tower Creek and Column Mountain. The latter, which extends along the eastern bank of the river for upward of two
miles, is said to resemble the Giant's Causeway. It is composed
of successive pillars of basalt overlying and underlying a thick
stratum of cement and gravel resembling pudding-stone. The
pillars are about thirty feet high, and are from three to five
feet in diameter. The cañon of Tower Creek is about ten
miles in length, and is so deep and gloomy that it is called "The
Devil's Den." About two hundred yards before it enters the
Yellowstone the stream pours over an abrupt descent of one hundred and fifty-six feet. The falls, which are about two hundred
and sixty feet above the level of the Yellowstone at the junction,

are surrounded with columns of volcanic breccia, that extend to the base and rise fifty feet above the top of the falls. "Some resemble towers, others the spires of churches, and others still shoot up as lithe and slender as the minarets of a mosque. Some of the loftiest of these formations, standing like sentinels upon the very brink of the fall, are accessible to an expert and adventurous climber." The view from these old rocky watch-towers is a grand one, but few are daring enough to climb to their rugged summits for the sake of it. "Below the fall the stream descends in numerous rapids, with frightful velocity, through a gloomy gorge, to its union with the Yellowstone. Its bed is filled with enormous boulders, against which the rushing waters break with great fury."

Where Tower Creek ends the Grand Cañon begins. Twenty miles in length, it is impassable throughout, and inaccessible at the water's edge, except at a few points. Its rugged edges are from two hundred to five hundred yards apart, and its depth is so profound that no sound ever reaches the ear from the bottom. "The stillness is horrible. Down, down, down, we see the river attenuated to a thread, tossing its miniature waves, and dashing, with puny strength, against the massive walls which imprison it. All access to its margin is denied, and the dark, gray rocks hold it in dismal shadow. Even the voice of its waters in their convulsive agony cannot be heard. Uncheered by plant or shrub, obstructed with massive boulders, and by jutting points, it rushes madly on its solitary course. The solemn grandeur of the scene surpasses description. The sense of danger with which it impresses you is harrowing in the extreme."

Concerning a view of the Grand Cañon and surroundings, Colonel Wm. Ludlow, of the engineer corps United States army, beautifully says: "The view of the Grand Cañon from the point where we stood is perhaps the finest piece of scenery in the world. I can conceive of no combination of pictorial splendors which could unite more potently the two requisites of majesty and beauty. Close at hand, the river, narrowed in its bed to a width of some seventy feet and with a depth of four or five feet, through the pure, deep green of which the hardly wavering outlines of the brown boulders beneath are distinctly visible, springs to the crest with an intensity of motion that makes its clear depths fairly seem to quiver. Just before making the plunge, the stream is again contracted, and the waters are thrown in from both sides toward the center, so that two bold rounded prominences or buttresses, as it were, are formed where green and white commingle. Lying prostrate and looking down into the depth, with the cold breath of the cañon fanning the face, one can see that these ribs continue downward, the whole mass of the fall gradually breaking into spray against the air, until lost in the vast cloud of vapor that hides its lowest third, and out of which comes up a mighty roar that shakes the hills and communicates a strange vibration to the nerves. From far below this cloud emerges a narrow, green ribbon, winding and twisting, in which the river is hardly recognizable. so dwarfed is it, and creeping with so oily and sluggish a current, as though its fall had stunned it. On either hand the walls of the cañon curve back from the plunging torrent, and rise weltering with moisture to the level of the fall, again ascending 500 or 600 feet to the pine-fringed margin of the cañon; pinnacles and towers projecting far into the space between, and seeming to overhang their bases.

"These details are comparatively easy to give, but how find words which shall suggest the marvelous picture as a whole! The sun had come out after a brief shower, and, shining nearly from the meridian straight into the cañon, flooded it with light, and illuminated it with a wealth and luxuriance of color almost supernatural. The walls appeared to glow with a cold, inward radiance of their own, and gave back tints of orange, pink, yellow, red, white and brown, of a vividness and massiveness hopeless to describe, and which would overtax the powers of the greatest artist to portray. The lower slopes, wet with spray, were decorated with the rich hue of vegetation, while through the midst the river, of a still more brilliant green, far below pursued its tortuous course, and the eye followed it down through this ocean of color until two or three miles away a curve in the cañon hid it from view and formed its own appropriate background."

The Grand Cañon is not all poetry, however, as those who have descended into it have discovered. It contains a great multitude of hot springs of sulphur, sulphate of copper, alum, etc.; and the river, when it is finally reached after four miles of wearisome clambering over masses of rocks and fallen trees, is warm, and impregnated with a villainous taste of alum and sulphur. Its margin is lined with various chemical springs, some depositing craters of calcareous rock, others muddy waters of different colors. The explorers have been unfortunate in selecting their point of descent, which has been at the northern end of the chasm, for at the southern end nothing but magnificence is apparent. There the Yellowstone plunges down in two grand cataracts, known as the Upper and Lower Falls. For some distance before it reaches the former the river breaks into rapids, and, narrowed between the rocks as it approaches the brink, leaps, in a sheet of snow-white foam, over a nearly perpendicular precipice about one hundred and forty feet high. The stream, which is about two hundred feet wide between the falls, narrows again as it approaches the Lower Fall to one hundred and fifty feet, where it plunges over a level shelf of rock three hundred and fifty feet high in a compact solid sheet. The Cañon here is one thousand feet in depth, its vertical sides rising darkly to shelving summits.

But the brightest jewel of our wonderful park,— the Yellowstone lake — must not pass unnoticed. It is about twenty miles long and fifteen miles broad, with a rough and irregular, but almost enchanting, shore line. Its superficial area is about three hundred square miles, its greatest depth three hundred feet, and its elevation above the sea seven thousand four hundred and twenty-seven feet. "Lying upon the very crown of the continent, Yellowstone lake receives no tributaries of any considerable size, its clear, cold water coming solely from the snows that fall on the lofty mountain ranges that hem it in on every side. In the early part of the day, when the air is still and the bright sunshine falls on its unruffled surface, its bright green color, shading to a delicate ultramarine, commands the admiration of every beholder. Later in the day, when the mountain winds come down from their icy heights, it puts on an aspect more in accordance with the fierce wilderness around it. Its shores are paved with volcanic rocks, sometimes in masses, sometimes broken and worn into pebbles of trachyte, obsidian, chalcedony, cornelians, agates, and bits of agatized wood; and again, ground to obsidian sand sprinkled with crystals of California diamonds."

Of the springs at the southwestern edge of the lake, Professor Hayden says: "Our second camp was pitched at the Hot Springs, on the southwest arm. This position commanded one of the finest views of the lake and its surroundings. While the air was still, scarcely a ripple could be seen on the surface, and the varied hues, from the most vivid green shading to ultra-marine, presented a picture that would have stirred the enthusiasm of the most fastidious artist. Sometimes, in the latter portion of the day, a strong wind would arise, arousing this calm surface into waves like the sea. Near our camp there is a thick deposit of silica, which has been worn by the waves into a bluff wall, twenty-five feet high above the water. It must have originally extended far out into the lake. The belt of springs at this place is about three miles long and half a mile wide. The deposit now can be seen far out in the deeper portions of the lake, and the bubbles that rise to the surface in various places indicate the presence, at the orifice, of a hot spring beneath. Some of the funnel-shaped craters extend out so far into the lake that the members of our party stood upon the silicious mound, extended the rod into the deeper waters, and caught the trout, and cooked them in the boiling spring, without removing them from the hook. These orifices, or chimneys, have no connection with the waters of the lake. The hot fumes coming up through fissures, extending down toward the interior of the earth, are confined within the walls of the orifice, which are mostly circular and beautifully lined with delicate porcelain."

Lieutenant Barlow contributes the following very interesting description of the great Geyser Basin, and of the points of interest near the Yellowstone Falls: "Entering the basin from the north, and following the banks of the Fire Hole river, whose direction there is about northeast, a series of rapids, quite near together, is encountered, when the river makes a sharp bend to the southeast, at which point is found a small steam-jet upon the right. A warm stream comes from the left, falling over a bank ten feet in height. A short distance beyond a second rapid is found, and then another, about 100 yards farther on, where the gate of the Geyser Basin is entered. Here, on either side of the river, are two lively geysers, called the Sentinels. The one on the left is in constant agitation, the waters revolving horizontally with great violence, and occasionally spouting upward to the height of twenty feet, the lateral direction being fifty feet. Enormous masses of steam are ejected. The crater of this is three feet by ten. The opposite Sentinel is not so constantly active, and is smaller. The rapids here are 200 yards in length, with a fall of thirty feet. Following the banks of the river, whose general course is from the southeast, though with many windings, 250 yards from the gate we reach three geysers acting in concert. When in full action the display from these is very fine. The waters spread out in the shape of a fan, in consequence of which they have been named the Fan Geysers. A plateau, opposite the latter, contains fifteen hot springs, of various characteristics; some are of a deep blue color, from sulphate of copper held in solution, and having fanciful caverns distinctly visible below the surface of the water. The openings at the surface are often beautifully edged with delicately wrought fringes of scalloped rock. One variety deposits a red or brown leathery substance, partially adhering to the sides and bottom of the cavern, and waving to and fro in the water like plants. The size of these springs varies from five to forty feet in diameter.

"One hundred yards farther up the side of the stream is found a double geyser, a stream from one of its orifices playing to the height of eighty or ninety feet, emitting large volumes of steam. From the formation of its crater it was named the Well Geyser. Above is a pine swamp of cold water, opposite which, and just above the plateau previously mentioned, are found some of the most interesting and beautiful geysers of the whole basin. First we came upon two smaller geysers near a large spring of blue water, while a few yards beyond are seen the walls and arches of the Grotto. This is an exceedingly intricate formation, eight feet in height and ninety in circumference. It is hollowed into fantastic arches, with pillars and walls of almost indescribable variety. This geyser plays to the height of sixty feet several times during twenty-four hours. The water, as it issues from its numerous apertures, has a very striking and picturesque effect. Near the Grotto is a large crater, elevated four feet above the surface of the hill, having a rough-shaped opening two by two and a half feet. Two hundred yards farther up are two very fine large geysers, between which and the Grotto are two boiling springs. Proceeding one hundred and fifty yards farther, and passing two hot springs, a remarkable group of geysers is discovered. One of these has a huge crater five feet in diameter, shaped something like the base of a horn—one side broken down—the highest point being fifteen feet above the mound on which it stands. This proved to be a tremendous geyser, which has been called the Giant. It throws a column of water the size of the opening to the measured altitude of one hundred and thirty feet, and continues the display for an hour and a half. The amount of water discharged was immense, almost equal in quantity to that in the river, the volume of which, during the eruption, was doubled. But one eruption of this geyser was observed. Another large crater close by has several orifices, and, with ten small jets surrounding it, formed probably one connected system. The hill built up by this group covers an acre of ground, and is thirty feet in height.

"Toward the western verge of a prairie of several miles in extent, above the Yellowstone Falls, a hill of white rocks was discovered, which, upon investigation, proved to be another of the 'Soda Mountains,' as they are called by the hunters. Approaching nearer, I found jets of smoke and steam issuing from the face of the hill, while its other side was hollowed out into a sort of amphitheatre, whose sides were steaming with sulphur fumes, the ground hot and parched with internal fires. Acre after acre of this hot volcanic surface lay before me, having numerous cracks and small apertures at intervals of a few feet, whence were expelled, sometimes in steady, continuous streams, sometimes in puffs like those from an engine, jets of vapor more or less impregnated with mineral substances. I ascended the hill, leaving my horse below, fearful that he might break through the thin rock-crust, which in many places gave way beneath the tread, revealing caverns of pure crystallized sulphur, from which hot fumes were sure to issue. The crystals were very fine, but too frail to transport without the greatest care. A large boiling spring, emitting strong fumes of sulphur and sulphuretted hydrogen, not at all agreeable, was also found. The water from the spring, overrunning its basin, trickled down the hill-side, leaving a highly-colored trace in the chalky rock. Upon the opposite side was found a number of larger springs. One, from its size and the power displayed in throwing water the height of several feet above the surface, was worthy of notice. Near this was a spring having regular pulsations like a steam engine, giving off large quantities of steam, which would issue forth with the roar of a hurricane. This was in reality a steam volcano, deep vibrations in the subterranean caverns, extending far away beneath the hills, could be distinctly heard."

The only blemishes in all this exquisite workmanship are chargeable to man. Colonel Ludlow tells us that the mouldings and carvings about the craters and pools have been chipped and defaced by visitors, or scrawled over with the vacuous names of self-important sightseers. We heartily concur in his opinion that such practices should be stopped at once, together with the whole system of plunder and vandalism which is wasting the reservation. "Hunters have for years devoted themselves to the slaughter of the game, until within the limits of the park it is hardly to be found. I was credibly informed by people on the spot, and personally cognizant of the facts, that during the winter of 1874 and 1875, at which season the heavy snows render the elk an easy prey, no less than from 1,500 to 2,000 of these, the largest and finest game animals in the country, were thus destroyed within a radius of fifteen miles of the Mammoth Springs. From this large number, representing an immense supply of the best food, the skins only were taken, netting to the hunter some $2.50 or $3 apiece; the frozen carcasses being left in the snow to feed the wolves or to decay in the spring. A continuance of this wholesale and wasteful butchery can have but one effect, viz., the extermination of the animal, and that, too, from the very region where he has a right to expect protection, and where his frequent inoffensive presence would give the greatest pleasure to the greatest number."

P. W. Norris, Esq., superintendent of the park, has issued a series of rules for the regulation of visitors. All hunting, fishing or trapping, except for purposes of recreation or to supply food for visitors or actual residents, is strictly prohibited; no fires must be left burning; no lumber must be cut without a written permit from the superintendent; visitors are prohibited from breaking the silicious or calcareous borders or deposits surrounding or in the vicinity of the springs or geysers for any purpose, or the removal, carrying away or sale of specimens found within the park. Persons will not be permitted to reside permanently within the limits of the park without permission from the secretary of the interior. The superintendent also complains that for the past two years great injury has been done by the careless use of fire, wanton slaughter of rare and valuable animals and vandalism of matchless wonders, and he appeals in the interest of science to all to abstain, and to use all influence in urging others to desist, from future vandalism of all kinds in the lofty, romantic " wonderland."

Now that our Indian problem seems so near a final settlement, and that highways are being rapidly constructed to this great national pleasure ground, we may hope to soon see the world's attention more strongly riveted upon this object than the Yosemite has ever known. Adding this to Wyoming's other charms of magnificent scenery, healing waters, invigorating atmosphere and choice hunting grounds, she possesses more attractions for the tourist and health seeker than any other State or Territory. To the hundreds of enthusiastic opinions offered by visitors as to the future of this section, Colonel Ludlow adds his own, that " the day will come, and it cannot be far distant, when this most interesting region, crowded with marvels and adorned with the most superb scenery, will be rendered accessible to all; and then, thronged with visitors from all over the world, it will be what nature and Congress, for once working together in unison, have declared it should be — a National Park."

There are at present two feasible ways of entering the park, the first from the Montana settlements on the north, and the second from the Wyoming settlements on the south. Travel is now confined principally to the northern routes, although they are much more inconvenient and expensive, as the following tables of distances, with accompanying explanation, will show. Routes are laid down from different stations on the Union Pacific railroad, according to official reports, and we will commence with those of Montana:

|  | Miles. |
|---|---|
| Ogden, Utah, to Franklin, Idaho, (rail) | 80 |
| Franklin to Virginia City (stage) | 317 |
| Madison River (private conveyance) | 14 |
| Driftwood, or Big Bend of Madison, (private conveyance) | 28 |
| Henry's Lake (private conveyance) | 18 |
| Tyghes Pass      " | 3 |
| Gibbon's Fork      " | 23 |
| Upper Geyser Basin   " | 15 |
| Yellowstone Lake    " | 14 |
| Total | 512 |

The Bozeman route is similar to the above so far as distance is concerned. From either Virginia City or Bozeman there are

9

fair wagon roads, with numerous desirable camping places and generally fine trouting. Ranches extend within sixty miles of the lake, while animals, camping "outfits" and guides are always available at reasonable rates. Following is the Bozeman route:

| | Miles. |
|---|---|
| Ogden, Utah, to Franklin, Idaho, (rail) | 80 |
| Bozeman, Montana, (stage) | 405 |
| Boteler's Ranch, Yellowstone river, (private conveyance) | 39 |
| Second Cañon of Yellowstone " | 13 |
| Devil's Slide, at Cinnabar Mountain, " | 8 |
| Mouth of East Fork of Yellowstone " | 24 |
| Crossing at Cascade Creek " | 24 |
| Yellowstone Lake | 12 |
| Total | 605 |

The nearest and most feasible Wyoming route at present is that leaving the Union Pacific at Green River City. Daily stages of the Sweetwater line run into the Wind River region to Camp Brown, a distance of 155 miles, and from there a passable wagon road leads to Yellowstone lake, 150 miles farther. From Green River City the distances are—

| | Miles. |
|---|---|
| Alkali Station (stage) | 21 |
| McCoy's Ranch " | 27 |
| Dry Sandy " | 22 |
| Pacific Springs " | 13 |
| Atlantic City " | 14 |
| Miner's Delight " | 9 |
| Eagle Ranch " | 18 |
| Camp Brown " | 21 |
| Head of Wind River (private conveyance) | 110 |
| Yellowstone Lake " | 50 |
| Total | 305 |

At Camp Brown the tourist will find ample facilities for providing himself for the trip. Leaving that post, a splendid wagon road ascends Wind River valley for a distance of 110 miles to Two Ocean Pass, where the new gold-diggings known as the Rhodes Mining District are found. The balance of the distance—fifty miles—is usually made with pack animals; but the grade is easy, and could be readily followed with wagons. The entire route is noted for the grandeur of its scenery, its ever present and beautiful trout streams, and its superb, continuous hunting grounds. Stages leave Green River City every morning, reaching Camp Brown in thirty-six hours. Fare, first-class, $27.

Capt. William A. Jones, of the United States engineers, who was in 1873 sent to find a shorter route to the Yellowstone Park and Montana settlements, was very emphatic in his recommendations of one of these southern outlets. His report also was quite pointed and valuable upon the advantages to be derived by the government from building either a rail or wagon road into Montana. He says:

"At present there are two routes to Montana, over which the interchange of products between that Territory and the east is carried on, and government supplies shipped to the military posts and the Indians in that country. These are: 1st, the Missouri River route, by which supplies are carried by steamboat as far as Fort Benton, Montana, and from thence distributed through the Territory by wagons; and, 2d, the Union Pacific Railroad route, over which supplies are carried by rail as far as Corinne, Utah, and from thence northward, by wagons, to Idaho and Montana. In the government's freighting contracts of 1873 the rates from Fort Benton to points in the Territory, and from Corinne to the same points, are exactly the same. Of course, so far as *rates* are concerned, the land-route cannot compete with the water-route; but the river-route is only open during a few months of the year, and during the remainder of the time the land-route is not brought into competition with it. Furthermore, during the season that the river is open, its navigability is far from being certain and reliable at all times; so that shipments over it are detained a very long and wholly uncertain length of time *in transitu*. As the business of the country is now conducted, men can ill afford to have their money lying idle for months or weeks, or even days, locked up in goods *in transitu*. Every day saved on goods, of *whatever character*, is the equivalent of money gained. It is this element of *time and its money equivalent* that underlies the astounding success of railroads as competitors with water-lines of traffic — success through which the steamboat is disappearing from our rivers; success that is proving to us that there is no such thing as slow freight; that men want some kinds of freight shipped *faster* than others, but that there is none they want shipped in a slow and unreliable manner.

"These considerations are so potent that, were a railroad

constructed to Montana from some point on the Union Pacific railroad, it would in all probability be followed by virtual disappearance of steamboat traffic from the Missouri river; and it is by no means improbable that the great saving in distance effected by the new Yellowstone route will, even without any more railroad, enable the land-route to compete successfully with that *via* the Missouri. In all events, the proposed route is fraught with benefit to the people of Montana, through the bringing of the rival lines into a closer competition.

"The present land-route leaves the Central Pacific railroad at Corinne, Utah, and runs in a northerly direction through Idaho to Montana, crossing the Bannock mountains on the divide between the Snake and Missouri rivers. The distance from Corinne to Fort Ellis, Montana, is four hundred and three miles. The proposed [wagon] road should leave the Union Pacific railroad in the vicinity of Point of Rocks, Wyoming, and run about north into the Wind River valley; thence following up that valley to its head, and through Togwotee Pass, northerly, to Yellowstone lake, and through the Yellowstone National Park to Fort Ellis. This route would pass directly by all of the principal phenomena of the park, except the geysers, which could easily be reached by a short side-road. By it, the distance from Point of Rocks to Yellowstone lake is two hundred and eighty-nine miles, and to Fort Ellis four hundred and thirty-seven miles."

Captain Jones surveyed a line from Point of Rocks station, on the Union Pacific, and indulges in a few comparisons which, even at this late day, are worthy of close attention. The freight and passenger rates have changed a trifle, but these answer our purpose just as well:

COMPARATIVE TABLE OF DISTANCES.

Omaha, Neb., to Corinne. Utah...................................1,055 miles.
Omaha, Neb., to Point of Rocks. Wyoming.................. 805 "
Distance saved by rail....................................... 250 "

OMAHA, NEB., TO YELLOWSTONE LAKE.

Omaha to Corinne...............................1,055 miles.
Corinne to Fort Ellis. Montana .................. 403 "
Fort Ellis to Yellowstone Lake................... 118 "
Omaha to Yellowstone Lake (present route)....... ——     1,576 miles.
Omaha to Point of Rocks.................. 805 "
Point of Rocks to Yellowstone Lake.............. 289 "
Omaha to Yellowstone Lake (proposed route)...... ——     1,094 "
Proposed route shortens distance to Yellowstone Lake ........ 482 "

OMAHA, NEB., TO FORT ELLIS AND BOZEMAN, MONTANA.

Omaha to Corinne............................1,055 miles.
Corinne to Fort Ellis............................ 403  "

Omaha to Fort Ellis (present route)..............     1,458 miles.
Omaha to Point of Rocks...................... 805  "
Point of Rocks to Fort Ellis ..................... 437  "

Omaha to Fort Ellis (proposed route) ............     1,242  "

Proposed route shortens distance to Fort Ellis............... 216  "

"It is fair to presume that the freight and passenger rates will be about the same over the proposed as they are over the present route, as the distances are nearly the same. A reasonable comparison between these rates can therefore be made from the following table, showing those paid by the government to the Union Pacific railroad:

### TABLE OF RATES.

#### TRANSPORTATION OF PERSONS—(AMOUNT FOR EACH PERSON.)

Omaha to Corinne..................................................$79 25
Omaha to Point of Rocks ......................................... 57 25

Amount per man saved by the proposed route.....................$22 00

### TRANSPORTATION OF FREIGHT.—THIRD CLASS.

#### (FOUR CENTS PER TON PER MILE.)

Omaha to Corinne (1,055 miles), per ton...........................$42 20
Omaha to Point of Rocks (805 miles), per ton ...................... 32 20

Amount per ton saved by the proposed route .......................$10 00

### SHIPMENTS OF FREIGHT TO MONTANA.

#### SHIPMENTS TO MONTANA VIA UNION PACIFIC RAILROAD.

| Years. | Pounds. |
|---|---|
| 1869 ............................................................. | 1,125,960 |
| 1870 ............................................................. | 6,896,723 |
| 1871 ............................................................. | 7,501,280 |
| 1872 ............................................................. | 6,129,644 |
| 1873............................................................. (about) | 6,000,000 |

"The proposed route will not be blocked by snow so much as the present one, as the snow belt lies in a heavily-timbered country, in which the snow will not drift much. This will include a distance of fully 150 miles north from Wind River valley. It will open up a body of 2,000,000 acres of timber land, well watered and with a rich soil. There is considerable frost even during the summer, but in spite of it the vegetation is always quite luxuriant.

"There is good reason for believing that the Yellowstone National Park will in time become the most popular summer resort in the country, perhaps the world. This of itself is a sufficient reason for opening the way to it at once.

"To sum up: the proposed route will save 250 miles of distance by railroad, 482 miles in reaching Yellowstone lake, and 216 miles in reaching the principal cities of Montana; it is a direct route to the Yellowstone National Park, which at present is practically inaccessible; it opens up a very large tract of low-lying timber land, a feature of rare occurrence in the great Rocky Mountain plateau; it will open up to settlement the Wind River valley, the Teton Basin, and the valley of the Upper Yellowstone; and, finally, will throw open the Yellowstone National Park to the wonder-seekers of the world."

*Wyoming's Healthfulness.*— Concerning Wyoming as a resort for invalids, Dr. George W. Corey, of Cheyenne, contributes the following: "More than forty years ago a kind of vague but quite general impression prevailed among the people inhabiting what was then the frontier of the United States that the Plains, as they were then designated, were peculiarly valuable as a health resort for those suffering from pulmonary consumption, and for those young persons who were weakly and cachectic. As early as 1850, Dr. G. K. Wood wrote as follows from Fort Laramie: 'The climate of these broad and elevated table-lands, which skirt the base of the Rocky Mountains on the east, is specially beneficial to persons suffering from pulmonary diseases, or with a scrofulous diathesis. This has been known to the French inhabitants of the upper Mississippi and Missouri for many years, and it has been their custom since the settlement of that portion of the country to send the young members of their families who showed any tendency to diseases of the lungs to pass their youth among the trappers of the plains and mountains. The beneficial results of this course no doubt depends in a great measure upon the mode of life led by these persons — their regular habits, constant exercise in the open air, and the absence of enervating influences incident to life in cities. But that more is due to the climate itself is shown by the fact that among the troops stationed

THE GREAT FALLS OF THE YELLOWSTONE, 350 FEET HIGH.

in this region (whose habits are much the same everywhere) this class of disease is of very rare occurrence.'

"A vast amount has been written during the last ten years in reference to the marvelous beauty of the Rocky Mountain scenery and the wonderful curative properties of the climate of these regions, especially in cases of disease of the respiratory organs, such as consumption, asthma, bronchitis, etc. etc., and it would seem that the subject had been pretty well exhausted. Most of this writing has, however, been done by industrious adventurers of particular localities, who have not always observed the strictest regard for exact truth, but have magnified features of scenery and climate that were pleasant and favorable, and sought to cover up or pass unnoticed those that are unpleasant and unfavorable. This method of proceeding is certain to react unfavorably, and statements of the best established facts in reference to the benefits arising to certain classes of invalids from a residence in these highlands are even now beginning to be looked upon with many grains of allowance by people of the east. This country is beginning to be looked upon as a quack nostrum, and statements favorable to it as a health resort considered as advertising dodges. It is our purpose to show in this article that these elevated plains and mountain regions are the most healthful districts in the United States, and that Wyoming is as healthful as the most favored of them; that in these elevated regions, where the inhabitants enjoy the greatest degree of immunity from lung diseases, the climate has an actual curative influence upon most diseases of that class; that this climate cures some diseases, while others are made worse; that consumption, in its early stages, may be cured by a residence here, while in a more advanced stage of the disease the sufferer sinks more rapidly here in these highlands than he would down near the sea-shore; that while this clear, bracing, tonic mountain air is a great, good medicine, it is no quack nostrum that cures everything. We shall also attempt to show that Wyoming, today, possesses more advantages as a health resort for people of all classes than any other region in these highlands, being more accessible from both east and west, and having larger areas unoccupied where people may make homes and follow lucrative pursuits while they improve their health.

"In presenting the claims of any region or country as being

peculiarly salubrious and valuable as a resort for invalids or those seeking the improvement of their health, it would seem quite proper in the outset to inquire into the general health, comparatively, of those that may be considered as nearly as possible its permanent residents. For this purpose we have selected several important regions of the United States, and, taking the medical statistics of the United States army,* have compiled a tabular statement of the ratio of sickness and mortality among the troops in these various regions, so that they may be compared with the ratio of sickness and mortality among the troops in Wyoming.

"It will be noted that the troops of the United States army are subject to exactly the same conditions and surroundings, and have the same habits everywhere more nearly than any other class of people. They are frequently moved from one region to another; their food, clothing, medical attendance and places of abode are nearly identically the same wherever they go, and, consequently, comparing the ratio of sickness and mortality among them in these different regions will enable us to obtain a more correct estimate of the actual healthfulness of each region than could possibly be obtained in any other way.

TABLE

Showing comparative sickness and mortality, from disease, among United States troops in different localities; averaged for five years, from 1869 to 1874. Compiled from the official reports of the War Department.

| Localities by States and Territories. | Average number of troops per y'r stationed in each locality. | Average number treated in hospital per year for disease. | Average number died per year from disease. | Ratio to 1.000 of mean strength. | |
|---|---|---|---|---|---|
| | | | | Treated each year for disease. | Died ea. y'r from disease. |
| Atlantic Coast, from New York to Maine......... | 841.21 | 1,486.90 | 15. | 1,768.01 | 17.83 |
| Arizona ................ | 1,168.32 | 2,481.15 | 14.15 | 2,124.14 | 12.11 |
| New Mexico............. | 954.79 | 1,176.02 | 7.42 | 1,231.70 | 7.77 |
| California and Nevada.... | 1,393.24 | 2,212.60 | 9.60 | 1,587.65 | 6.88 |
| Pennsylv'nia, Indiana and Michigan ............ | 438.25 | 561.75 | 2.65 | 1,282.53 | 6.05 |
| Montana................ | 622.74 | 720.90 | 3.50 | 1,157.62 | 5.62 |
| Dakota ................ | 2,004.37 | 2,453.35 | 9.55 | 1,224.06 | 4.76 |
| Wyoming.............. | 1,919.10 | 2,406.24 | 9.05 | 1,253.77 | 4.71 |
| Oregon, Washington and Idaho.............. | 730.56 | 1,074.60 | 3.40 | 1,471.23 | 4.66 |

* Circular No. 4, War Department, Surgeon-General's Office, Washington, December 5, 1870, and Circular No. 8, May 1, 1875. We regret not being able to make this table more full and complete, for want of time, but hope to do so in the future.

"It will be observed that deaths from all other causes except disease have been excluded from the above statement, and that while Dakota, Wyoming, Washington and Idaho Territories, and the State of Oregon, show the smallest ratio of mortality, Montana shows the smallest ratio of sickness.  It should also be remembered that the troops in Dakota, Montana and Wyoming were, during the years included in the above table, almost constantly harassed and kept on active field duty, assisting a lot of robbers and lunatics to civilize the wild Sioux on the 'peace plan.'  This plan consisted in the robbers robbing the Sioux of their annuities, while the lunatics taught them to sing psalms. This constant duty brought with it exposure and fatigue, and consequent increase of sickness and mortality.  In spite of this, these last named regions show as small a sick-rate, and within a trifling fraction as small a death-rate, as any of the most healthy regions of the United States.

"*Some of the Acute Diseases of Wyoming.*—The acute diseases of these mountain regions are the same in many respects that prevail in similar latitudes in the Mississippi basin, modified of course by the very great difference that exists in the climate of the two regions.  The most striking peculiarities of this climate are the extreme dryness of the atmosphere and the great daily range of temperature.  The season of greatest relative humidity is from October to April, and again from April to October is the season of least relative humidity; the atmosphere of July being the driest of the whole year.  The greatest daily ranges of temperature occur during the season of the driest atmosphere. These climatic conditions seem to have a controlling influence upon disease,—catarrhal affections prevailing most during seasons of greatest humidity of the atmosphere, while diseases of the bowels, such as diarrhœa and dysentery, prevail while the air is dryest and the greatest daily ranges of temperature occur. Catarrh, or, as it is popularly called, cold, is the most common disease here, as it is everywhere in this latitude.  When special regions of the air passages are attacked, the disease is designated accordingly: cold in the head or coryza, quinsy or tonsilitis, laryngitis or bronchitis.  Quinsy is very prevalent, and embraces much the larger proportion of all the cases of sore throat.  While catarrhal affections of the upper portions of the air passages are extremely common, inflammatory diseases of the lungs, such as bronchitis, pneumonia or lung fever, and pleurisy, are extremely rare. Intermittent fever, or ague, never occurs here except in persons who have lately arrived in the country from malarious districts either east or west. There is, however, a species of remittent fever called 'mountain fever,' which is indigenous, and is a very severe disease. It prevails most in autumn and early winter following dry summers, but may occur at any season of the year. Some physicians report a great many cases of this disease, which are simply bilious attacks, and have no resemblance to 'mountain fever' whatever. Biliousness, or 'bilious attacks,' are extremely common, and prevail most during the spring and summer months, and are speedily cured by remedies that promote the action of the liver. Typhoid fever occurs but rarely. Rheumatism and neuralgia are not very common, and seem to prevail epidemically; more cases of rheumatism have occurred in this place (Cheyenne) during the last year than occurred in eight years before. Childbed fever occurs rarely, and mothers recover from confinement rapidly and successfully, while children born here are extremely fine, well developed and healthy. Scarlet fever and diphtheria have never prevailed epidemically in Wyoming except in one instance,—a quite malignant form of scarlet fever prevailed in Laramie City in 1873.

"The disease that is most fatal among children in Wyoming is a species of brain affection. Many children are born here with very high-strung, irritable nervous organizations — seem quite healthy at first — grow unusually well, and are extremely precocious. They are often quite fleshy, but are noticed to have a bloodless, pearly-white skin, with large, finely-formed, but unnatural-shaped heads. Such children seldom live through their second year. Some of this class of children, however, recover from the most severe attacks of sickness, showing that remarkable tenacity of life sometimes possessed by children, and continue to grow and thrive in spite of the disease and the predictions of the doctors. Diarrhœa, dysentery and cholera infantum, while they occur here among children, have never proven to be such severe scourges as they frequently do in the regions east of the Missouri.

"*Wyoming as a Resort for Invalids.*—We come now to speak of Wyoming as a resort for invalids; and first, for those suffering from diseases of the respiratory organs. If we were called upon to select a climate well calculated to benefit invalids suffering from any particular malady, it would seem the most natural thing in the world for us to select a region where that particular malady, or the class of diseases to which it belonged, were least prevalent, and where climatic conditions prevailed best calculated to prevent its occurrence. The climate of North America is rough and harsh compared with that of Europe, notably so on account of its sudden changes, and great fluctuations of temperature in short spaces of time. The opinion has long prevailed that severe and sudden changes of temperature played a most important part in the production of diseases of the lungs, especially bronchial catarrh and other milder diseases of the air passages. Such, however, is found not to be the case, unless these sudden changes are accompanied by great relative humidity of the atmosphere; and as we have before stated, the ratio of relative humidity here in these highlands is very low, while the absolute humidity is even less. The correctness of the latter opinion is constantly verified in this country, where we see persons who have weak lungs spending most of their waking hours in the open air without regard to winds or weather, and suffering no inconvenience, but, on the contrary, being constantly improved in health. The great daily oscillations of temperature are more than counterbalanced by the dryness of the atmosphere and other climatic conditions that exist here. Just what it is that makes up these other conditions it may be difficult to say. It may be an excessive amount of electricity. It may be ozone, or an increased amount of oxygen or diminished pressure of the atmosphere. It may be found in the perfect freedom of the atmosphere from noxious vapors of the lower altitudes, or the clear, pure, unobstructed light of the sun. It may be found in that antiseptic property which is known to exist in the air of these regions, that heals wounds rapidly, and prevents the flesh of slain animals, when exposed in the open air, from rapid decay. It may be any one or, as we suspect, all these combined that produce tonic air.

"The fact that the extremely rough, harsh, changeable climate of New England produced greater ratios of consumption than almost any other, long since led to the conclusion that a climate as nearly the opposite of that — mild and equable — would be the one most likely to benefit consumptives. Such climates, however, are found not to possess tonic properties, such as we have just spoken of; but, on the contrary, are enervating, and the benefits anticipated from them have not been realized. We are of the opinion that the influence of this mountain air upon the lungs, directly or locally, is not as important as the profound change it produces upon the whole system during the process of acclimation, giving new life and new energy to constitutions that appeared to be shattered and broken down. It acts as a slow and gentle stimulant and tonic to the nervous system — the center of life — and through it upon all the functions of the body. We are not to be understood as saying that this climate produces this effect in every case. This is the rule, to which, however, there are some exceptions.

"*Chronic Nasal Catarrh.*—This is an extremely common disease in these dry regions. Persons afflicted with it coming here from the east are about as often made worse as better. The evaporation from the surfaces of the mucous membranes of the nose, caused by the currents of dry air passing in over them at every respiration, keeps them on a constant strain to secrete moisture sufficient to lubricate their surfaces, and an extremely unpleasant feeling of dryness in the nose is experienced by newcomers for some time on this account. This form of catarrh is a very manageable disease except when it attacks persons of feeble constitution.

" Chronic laryngitis and bronchitis are speedily cured by a residence here unless they exist as complications of pulmonary consumption.

"*Asthma.*—It may be said of these regions that they are the paradise of asthmatics. An uncomplicated case of asthma was never seen here that was not either cured or very much benefited by a residence in these regions. Hundreds of the very worst cases have come to Wyoming, both from the Atlantic and Pacific coasts, and the longer they reside here the freer they become from the disease. Persons of advanced age are as uniformly benefited as those that are younger. Asthmatics who have organic disease of the heart may often stay on the Great Plains, in the elevations of from 2,000 to 4,000 feet, such as the regions around the Black Hills, with great relief from their asthma and slight inconvenience from their heart trouble.

" *Emphysema.*—As a rule this disease seems to be benefited by long-continued residence in high regions. One case that we have seen occasionally for seven years past remained perfectly free from the disease while living for two years at an altitude of 8,000 feet, but on taking up his abode at 6,000 feet elevation has had an attack about every six months, lasting from ten days to two weeks.

"*Consumption.*—This terrible scourge of the human race unquestionably originates in imperfect or faulty nutrition. This defect may be either hereditary or acquired. A tendency to consumption may exist during a long life and not be developed, because of the correct habits of the person having this constitutional defect. And again consumption may be developed in a person having no constitutional taint—it being brought on by poor diet, long-continued transgression of hygienic laws, or residence in an unhealthy, depressing climate or poorly-ventilated dwellings. In view of these facts the prevention of consumption becomes an important consideration. For all persons who are predisposed to consumption these regions offer a more certain lease of life than any other on this continent. Persons whose habits of life do not allow or compel them to fully expand their lungs in a pure atmosphere—pale, thin, bloodless clerks, or those of sedentary habits, with hacking coughs; nervous and dyspeptic persons, children with narrow, stooping shoulders, flat breasts and impaired digestion;—all these should seek the mountains, if possible. The light air of these elevated regions necessitates full breathing. Every nook and corner of the lungs is forced into activity. The chest becomes full and round, the stooping shoulders straighten up, the breathing capacity becomes greater, the blood flows more rapidly and freely through the lungs and is more perfectly purified or aerated. These people will find no occasion to devote a certain amount of time every morning or evening to dumb-bell exercises and spasmodic efforts to inflate their lungs. They will find that this exercise goes on all through the twenty-four hours of the day and night; that it is involuntary and not fatiguing; that it is constant and natural, and infinitely more beneficial than over-exertion for a short time each day at dumb-bell and gymnastic labors. All such persons as we have mentioned above will find their appetites and digestion improved, their weight increased, and their physical and mental energy greater than they have ever known them before.

" *Developed Consumption.*—After consumption has been developed the question arises whether highlands or lowlands are preferable to relieve the sufferer and prolong his existence, or in rare instances cure him. The extent to which the disease has advanced; the amount of the lung-substance that has been destroyed or rendered useless, and the degree of general emaciation that has taken place, must be the guide in deciding whether the sufferer should go to the highlands or lowlands, or remain at home and die among his friends. The responsibility of the physician is very great in these cases where the patient is seen in the early stages of the disease, and an opinion should be made up at once as to what should be done. As a rule, hemorrhage from the lungs is the first occurrence that fully settles the question in the minds of the patient and his friends as to the true nature of his disease. It is looked upon as a symptom of seated consumption. We have seen a great many persons who, frightened by this occurrence in their cases, have left homes in the east and come here at once, and at least nine out of ten of them have been benefited. We should, then, as a rule, advise all persons, as soon as hemorrhage from the lungs has occurred, to come to the mountains as soon as convenient, say within a month. There are, of course, some exceptions to this rule, such as extremely acute cases, where inflammation and rapid softening and breaking down of the lungs is followed in a short time by death. After softening of tubercular deposits in the lungs, except in cases where these deposits are of extremely limited extent, the sufferer should not be brought to these elevated regions, as he will only hasten the fatal termination by so doing. Quite a number of these unfortunate people who have been on their way to California over the Union Pacific railroad, have died in their seats while passing over these elevated regions. Chronic inflammation of the lungs and chronic pleurisy never exist here, except as complications of consumption.

"*Other Chronic Diseases.*—As a rule, persons suffering from organic disease of the heart, like those in the advanced stages of consumption, should avoid these highlands and remain nearer the sea-level. Chronic diseases peculiar to females are usually made worse by a residence here, unless they exist as a complication of pulmonary disease.

"Those suffering from general debility or nervous dyspepsia are almost certain to be cured by a residence here for a sufficient length of time to become acclimated."

# PART SECOND.

# COUNTIES, CITIES, MILITARY POSTS, ETC.

### WITH MISCELLANEOUS INFORMATION FOR THE

### CITIZEN OR PROSPECTIVE SETTLER.

# COUNTIES AND CITIES.

## CHAPTER I.

### COUNTIES, CITIES, MILITARY POSTS, ETC.

IN this chapter it is the purpose of the writer to briefly describe the counties, cities, towns, etc., giving merely the important features of location, size, population, wealth, and similar points. As the most important industries tributary to the principal cities, or belonging to the different counties, have already been treated of in appropriate articles, exhaustive descriptions are rendered superfluous here. In the estimates of area following, no allowance is made for the new counties of Crook and Pease, which were created by the last legislature, and which yet lack organizations. Taking up the counties first we naturally commence at the eastern boundary of the Territory.

### COUNTIES.

*Laramie.*—Occupying the extreme eastern portion of the Territory, Laramie county presents an area of 16,800 square miles, consisting largely of high rolling plains. It is watered principally by the Laramie, North Platte and Cheyenne rivers, and its settlements are confined wholly to the valleys of the two first named and their tributaries. The county contains a larger proportionate area of summer and winter grazing land than any of the other counties, while its valleys susceptible of cultivation are quite numerous and extensive. The valleys of Horse Creek, Chugwater river, Pole Creek, the Laramie river, and numerous other streams, contain good lands, easily irrigated, and will produce fine crops, with a good market always at hand. Timber is found in abundance within a convenient distance. Nearly 75,-000 head of cattle and 50,000 head of sheep are now feeding upon less than one-third of its pasturage, and are confined to the region lying south of the Platte. The sales from these herds the present year will reach $500,000. Assessed valuation of all property for 1877, $3,000,000; estimated population, 9,540. Rich deposits of gold, iron and copper are found in accessible localities, and coal abounds in the extreme northern portions.

*Albany.*— Next on the west lies Albany county, containing 10,400 square miles of unexcelled grazing, forest, agricultural and mineral lands. The Big and Little Laramie, North Platte and Medicine Bow rivers are the principal streams, while the great natural feature of interest — the Laramie plains — furnishes an immense area of available farm and pasture lands. This wonderful basin or park contains nearly 3,000,000 acres, and has an average altitude of 7,150 feet. Over 50,000 head of stock are grazing in this region, and many of the finest ranch sites in the west are still to be had for the simple taking. The lumber, marble, iron and soda interests have already awakened much attention, and are destined to soon make Albany the banner county for the value of productions. Taxable wealth, $2,500,000; estimated population, 8,500; productions of all kinds for 1877, $1,850,000.

*Carbon.*— Carbon county occupies 22,080 square miles of the central portion of the Territory. Population, 2,500; assessed valuation, 1877, $1,900,000. The importance and diversity of its resources is a matter worthy of more than usual note. The valleys of the North Platte, Sweetwater, Medicine Bow and Snake rivers have a total length, within the county, of over 300 miles. Along these can be found large areas of good lands, plenty of water for irrigating purposes, and plenty of timber within easy distance. There are numerous small streams all through the county, principally tributaries of the streams already mentioned, whose valleys contain thousands of acres of good lands, well adapted to the purposes of agriculture and stock-raising. All these valleys will produce fine crops of small grain, potatoes, beets, onions, cabbage and all other kinds of hardy vegetables. Pine timber is always abundant near the sources of the streams. Thousands of railroad ties are made every year from this timber and are floated down the Medicine Bow river to the line of the railroad. The mining interest is also destined to be very extensive. In the northern, central and extreme southern portions, rich deposits of gold and silver are being developed. Coal and iron abound, the former underlying at least one-fourth of the surface. The Carbon coal mines are yielding from eighty to ninety thousand tons of coal per annum. This county is also the source of the western paint supply, and detailed mention of this interest is made elsewhere.

*Sweetwater.*—This county has the princely area of 29,532 square miles and occupies a large proportion of the western half of the Territory. Green, Sweetwater, Wind, Sandy and Popoagie are the principal rivers, and with their numerous mountain tributaries render this entire region unusually well watered. Thus far Sweetwater is the banner agricultural county, nearly every variety of small grains and vegetables being regularly produced along Wind and Popoagie by thrifty and well-satisfied ranchmen. Wheat, oats and barley are the principal crops at present, and a home market is found for all that can be raised. The government purchases all the grain offered for sale, and pays good prices, giving eastern prices with cost of transportation added. Potatoes yield well and are of superior quality; they sell very readily in the mining towns at good prices. Cabbage, turnips, beets, carrots, parsnips, onions, etc., are raised easily and successfully; cucumbers, melons, tomatoes and egg-plant mature well and are of an excellent flavor. The rich Sweetwater and Wind river gold and silver mines are located in this county, and, indeed, a large proportion of the Big Horn range, with its vast undeveloped wealth. The Rock Springs coal measures, so famous all over the trans-Missouri region, are also in this county. Pine timber is abundant everywhere. Sweetwater county contains more desirable unoccupied farming lands than any other in the Territory, has vast summer and winter pasturage for stock and presents strong inducements to the prospector or the capitalist seeking investment in mines. Total valuation of property, $1,918,449. Population, 3,500.

*Uintah.*—This county occupies the extreme western portion of the Territory and contains 17,064 square miles. Its resources in coal lands, forests, pastures and arable soil are as extensive, in proportion to its area, as are those of any region in the west. Uintah county supplies the Central Pacific railway, Utah, Nevada, Idaho and portions of California with coal. It sustains the Utah and Wyoming smelters with charcoal and coke, and it furnishes vast quantities of lumber, ties and wood for local and railroad consumption. The Yellowstone, Bear and Snake rivers and Henry's and Ham's forks of Green river are the principal streams. These and their tributaries water finely situated and fertile valleys, only waiting for the labor of man to make them equally as productive as the best sections of the States. There are several large valleys which offer extraordinary inducements to settlers, and large colonies will experience but little difficulty in obtaining desirable locations; they will find it to their interest to examine some of these valleys before deciding upon a location. The many growing towns afford a home market for everything produced; the supply at present is totally inadequate, and large quantities of vegetables, eggs, butter, etc., are imported from Utah and the east. The soil will produce nearly every variety of the hardy cereals and vegetables. Flax grows spontaneously and luxuriantly in many parts of the county. No better location for stock-raising and dairying can be found than here, and many are already laying the foundations for competence by earnest efforts in this direction. That mountain-locked gem of all America, Yellowstone Park, lies in the northern portion of Uintah county. A good route can easily be constructed thither through the county, and will undoubtedly soon be a popular highway.

### CITIES, VILLAGES, POST-OFFICES, ETC.

*Cheyenne.*—The writer recently asked one of the first settlers of Cheyenne whether he knew who erected the first house in the city, and received as an answer: "Well, one fine day, early in July, 1867, four or five hundred of us pitched our tents here, where there wasn't a sign of civilization, and about half of us woke up at daylight the next morning to find that the other half were living in board shanties!" That is the history of the founding of western cities, in a very small nut-shell, with the exception that while many other cities are short-lived, Cheyenne was founded as permanently as her western walls of granite. The city is situated in the southeastern corner of Wyoming, 516 miles west of Omaha, and is the seat of Territorial government as well as of Laramie county. Her population closely approximates 4,500, and her taxable wealth for the present year is estimated at nearly $3,000,000.

No city of like population in the west can boast as rapid and permanent a growth during the past two years as Cheyenne. During this period the population has been doubled, over 200 residences and twenty massive business blocks have been completed at a cost of $700,000, and at this writing plans are drawn or work progressing on improvements worth over $100,000 more. Among public improvements may be noted a public school building costing $13,000; a court-house costing $40,000; city hall, $12,000; Odd-Fellows hall, $15,000; five fine churches, belonging to the prominent denominations, and a large outlay upon the grading of streets, construction of sidewalks, etc. An excellent system of water-works, well under way, will soon supply the city with water for both fire and domestic purposes, while arrangements have just been completed for illumination by gas. Several immense reservoirs or lakes, supplied by Crow Creek, occupy elevated positions near the city, and are drawn upon for water for irrigating purposes. Thus, the site once so barren and desolate is not only teeming with wonderful life, but will soon, through the beautifying influences of tasty residences and rich foliage, be a really handsome city.

In order to show the present importance of Cheyenne in a commercial way we will quote figures of business in a few leading lines. During 1876 there were received at the Union Pacific and Denver Pacific freight depots here over 80,000,000 pounds of freight. During the same time nearly $250,000 were received by these roads at the Cheyenne offices for passenger tickets and extra baggage.

For the six months ending June 30, 1877, the Cheyenne and Black Hills Stage Company — the finest organization of its kind in the whole west, and of which every citizen is justly proud — carried 3,128 first and second class passengers, for which the fares amounted to $48,766.22. The same company, during this period, has carried 5,680 express packages, on which were charges to the amount of $19,471.47. This company has nearly $200,000 invested in its elegant coaches, fine stock, etc. On its Black Hills lines eighty men are regularly carried on the pay-roll, and their wages foot up the snug sum of $7,000 per month. It requires 600 head of stock to run this "broad-gauge" line, which is only second to a narrow-gauge railway; and all other appointments are on the same liberal plan.

Cheyenne's two solid and well-conducted banks — the First

National and Stebbins, Post & Co.—have, during the past year, sold exchange to the amount of $4,225,000; have bought $1,200,-000 worth of Black Hills gold dust, and have had an average of $300,000 regularly on deposit. These institutions are officered and conducted by Cheyenne men, and have no superior for systematic and legitimate management.

The business of the telegraphic companies is another fair indication of the general prosperity. The Western Union, Atlantic & Pacific and Cheyenne and Black Hills companies have offices here. The total number of messages received by these during the past year is 267,971; cash receipts, $35,000; money transfers, $22,000. The Cheyenne and Black Hills line is emphatically a home institution, and the far northern settlements owe to Superintendent W. H. Hibbard a debt of gratitude which cannot soon be repaid. The wires were first stretched to Deadwood, December 1, 1876, since which date over 700,000 words have passed over them to or from Cheyenne.

The three leading hotels of Cheyenne have registered 10,800 arrivals during the past year, and a dozen smaller institutions have probably done as much more.

Real estate transfers for the past year have numbered about five hundred, with the handsome consideration of $175,000. Business lots have increased in value from fifty to seventy-five per cent., and residence lots from twenty to twenty-five per cent. Large areas of outside property are still held by the Union Pacific company at very reasonable figures. First-class business lots 24 × 132 feet sell readily at from $2,000 to $3,000; first-class residence lots 66 × 132, $500 to $800. Good outside property sells for less than half these prices, and that portion held by the railway company still sells in best plats at the uniform rate of $100 per lot. Rents are usually high, and the supply of desirable business or residence structures is never equal to the demand. Strictly first-class brick business houses rent for from $100 to $125 per month for a single floor, while cottages of five and six rooms are eagerly sought at $30 to $35. Insurance premium on first-class brick houses, $1.25. Risks on frame business houses are not taken. Over $600,000 in policies are now out on Cheyenne property.

What Omaha has been to Nebraska, Dakota and Iowa, or Denver to Colorado and New Mexico, Cheyenne is and will be to Wyoming, Montana and so much of Dakota as is covered by the

Black Hills region. No outlet for all the vast northwest can present half the natural advantages and no northwestern city can approach Cheyenne for real downright enterprise, sagacious business management or spirit of permanency. Already possessing two important railway lines, the "Magic City" is constructing a third, and by the avowed determination of Union Pacific authorities will soon have her fourth — that to connect her with the rich Big Horn and Black Hills regions, and to lay at her feet the offerings of all the fertile valleys and metal-seamed mountains of Montana. Already her heavy wholesale houses are securing much of the northern and western trade which originally went to the cities of the east, and with their constantly enlarging facilities and liberal spirit this important feature of prosperity has the brightest possible outlook. The stock interests have thus far had more to do with the erection of her elegant blocks and residences, and her prosperity generally, than any other single item, and this, simply inaugurated, promises the grandest possibilities. Of Cheyenne's relations to the Big Horn and Black Hills regions more is said in chapters devoted to those sections. However, in closing this hasty and imperfect sketch, the writer desires to state that, all things being considered, there are no points aspiring to reap the benefits of the travel and trade of those regions which can be compared with Cheyenne.

Cheyenne is justly proud of her newspapers, and we doubt if all other interests combined have promoted development to a greater extent than these. There are three large dailies, the *Sun*, *Leader* and *Gazette*, the two first-named issuing fine weekly editions, all publishing the associated press and special telegrams, and columns of spicy editorial and local matter. The *Leader*, published in the morning, is the pioneer, having been established during the earliest settlement, and grown in importance and influence with the general prosperity. The *Sun*, E. A. Slack, editor and proprietor, and J. P. C. Poulton, associate editor, is one of the brightest, newsiest and most original journals in the whole northwest, and for solid worth or genuine merit is praised in every hamlet of Wyoming. It is also issued as a morning daily. Published in the afternoon, the *Gazette* occupies a field exclusively its own, and occupies it in a very satisfactory manner, as shown by its excellent patronage.

*Laramie.*— Laramie City is beautifully situated on the east bank of the Laramie river, on the line of the Union Pacific railroad, 572 miles west of Omaha. It is not only "Queen of the Laramie Plains," but of all Wyoming, for beauty of location, finely laid out streets and tree-embowered homes. The first building was erected in 1868, and without the serious collapse usually suffered by western towns, it has steadily advanced to the importance of a thriving, well built city of 3,500 souls, and is today more noticeable for its grand local resources, its large number of elegant churches, public improvements and residences, and its excellent society, than any other city between Omaha and Salt Lake.

Besides being the supply point for the entire Laramie plains, the great lumbering districts of southern and central Wyoming and of the grand mining region encircling her — all of which are elsewhere described — Laramie city contains the only rolling mills on the line of the Union Pacific railway. These were built by the Union Pacific company in 1875, at a cost of $250,000, and have a capacity of 20,000 tons of railroad iron per annum. An average of 200 men are constantly employed, and these, with a large force of machinists at work in the company's extensive car-shops, put many dollars into home circulation.

The long rows of shade trees, well-kept lawns, and pretty flower gardens, are stimulated by the crystal waters of spring brooks which flow through all the streets, and by the utilization of an excellent system of water-works. The latter consist of iron pipes laid from a spring several miles back from the city, and which have so great a fall that an immense pressure is obtained from hydrants on all the streets.

Business at the Laramie freight depot and at the post-office will give readers an idea of its extent in other lines. For the year ending June 30, 1877, freight was received to the amount of 17,-000,000 pounds, and collections on this amounted to $117,629.18. The post-office, conducted by Dr. J. H. Hayford, is a marvel of system and a fitting pattern for other institutions of the public service. During the fiscal year ending June 30, 1877, $7,514.78 worth of stamps were sold; money orders issued to the amount of $56,237.84; surplus money order funds remitted, $40,400; fees on orders, $469.50; number of registered letters sent and received, 3,301.

Laramie City is ably represented in the newspaper line by

the daily and weekly *Sentinel*, Hayford & Gates, proprietors. It is one of the oldest institutions of the kind in Wyoming, is a thoroughly representative western paper and is appreciated as it should be by a large circle of readers.

Few cities have assurances of a brighter future. The wealth of mines and forests, pastures and farm lands, and the grand auxiliaries furnished by unexcelled deposits of marble and soda, will, at Laramie, in the not distant future, command an attention and insure a prosperity not yet dreamed of even by her own far-seeing and enthusiastic citizens. Laramie is also the county-seat of Albany county.

From Laramie there is a tri-weekly mail route to the Hahn's Peak gold mines, in northern Colorado, 112 miles; to White River agency, Colorado, 228 miles; weekly to Fort Laramie, 85 miles; and weekly to the Centennial mines and Last Chance district, 30 and 40 miles respectively.

*Rawlins.*— Rawlins is the county-seat of Carbon county, named after the late General John A. Rawlins, chief of General Grant's staff, and afterward Secretary of War. It is situated on the line of the Union Pacific railroad, 710 miles west of the Missouri river, and 322 miles east of Ogden, at an altitude of 6,540 feet above the level of the sea, in the center of a rich mineral and grazing country, and has a population of about 1,000 people. It is the terminus of the Laramie freight division of the Union Pacific railroad, embracing a large depot, first-class railroad and mail facilities, round-house, and machine shops, at which about one hundred men are constantly employed. The town is well supplied with good water from large springs in the immediate vicinity, and distributed through iron pipes. It contains three good hotels, three general stores well stocked and doing an extensive business, two telegraph offices, court-house, public school-house, new stone jail, two churches, a first-class drug store, jewelry establishment, two blacksmith and wagon shops, livery and sale stable, and a large hall fitted up with stage and scenery for public entertainments. Masonic, Odd-Fellows, Good Templars and other societies flourish. Here are also the two extensive mills in which is manufactured the celebrated Rawlins Metallic paint, obtained by pulverizing a red hematite of iron ore found in large quantities about three miles north of Rawlins, on the route to the Big Horn. This paint is used exclusively by the Union Pacific and other railroad companies.

The county for miles about Rawlins, and especially along the North Platte river, is well stocked with cattle, and the valleys are being rapidly settled.

The merit which Rawlins, from its position on the Union Pacific railroad, possesses as a place of departure and outfitting for the Big Horn country will at once be seen by referring to the map. There are two excellent routes, descriptions of which are given in the chapters devoted to the Big Horn region. The large expedition to the Big Horn mountains sent out by the government in 1874, under the command of Captain Mills and conducted by Mr. Tom Sun, late government guide, going by one and returning by the other, passed over both routes, and the commander expressed himself as well pleased with both of them.

The excellent facilities for shipping stock from Rawlins are beginning to attract their deserved attention, and thousands of head of cattle from Montana and from the great ranges in the vicinity of the railroad are being shipped eastward to market this season. One firm, whose ranch is located south of Rawlins, on Snake river, has recently effected a sale of beef cattle, to be delivered here, the consideration of which was $52,000.

*Green River City.*—Three hundred and twenty-nine miles west of Cheyenne, on the Union Pacific railroad, and occupying a central position in the Territory, is Green River City. It is located on the east bank of Green river, here a clear, swift stream averaging seventy-five yards in width. Green River City is the county seat of Sweetwater county, contains 600 inhabitants, elegant court-house and other public buildings, and is well supplied with extensive business houses, representing every line. It is the southern terminus of the Sweetwater daily stage line, and has well-founded aspirations for the travel and business of parties en route to the Big Horn and Wind River gold regions. The capable postmaster of Green River, Judge S. I. Fields, is one of the oldest settlers, and is regarded as the "Father of the Town," in that he has extensive land interests and directs his best energies toward building it up. He has experimented quite extensively in the cultivation of the soil in the suburbs of the town, and has established the fact that all of the hardy grains and vegetables flourish when irrigated. Green River City is the western end of one of the Union Pacific divisions, has one of the company's large repair

GREEN'S RIVER CITY, WYOMING.

shops and round-house, and other extensive railroad buildings.
The *Daily Press* is published here every afternoon by Judge C.
W. Holden, and is a sprightly twenty-column paper, having for
its field the largest and perhaps richest county in the Territory.
See engraving of Green River on another page.

*Evanston.*—Evanston is the county seat of Uintah county,
and is located in Bear River valley, in the extreme western part
of the Territory. It contains 1,200 inhabitants, is built largely
of brick and stone and boasts as fine churches, schools and public buildings as any of the Wyoming cities. The lumber, coal
and charcoal interests, together with stock-growing, are the solid
foundations of Evanston's prosperity. It is the designated shipping point for a large proportion of the Montana cattle which
find a southern market every season. To the north for a distance
of 100 miles, extending into Utah and Idaho, is a fine agricultural and grazing country, which is settled by about 4,000 people.
Unexcelled trout fishing in Bear river and tributaries, large sulphur springs in the vicinity and most picturesque surroundings,
combine to render Evanston a point much sought by tourists
and health seekers. The bluffs surrounding abound with nearly
every species of game, from the rabbit to the elk, and lend additional charms for the sportsman. A ditch eight miles long
brings the clear mountain water from Bear river down to the
city and through its streets. Yellowstone Park is 290 miles due
north of Evanston, and a good route leads thither via Bear valley and Caribou. A desirable route for western miners to the
Big Horn is also located from here. Evanston post-office business for the fiscal year just ended is as follows: money orders
issued, $28,239; remitted on orders, $22,695; orders paid, $4,722;
fees and commissions, $191. The Evanston weekly *Age*, pub-
lished here by Wm. E. Wheeler, is one of the essential and mer-
itorious institutions. It faithfully represents the resources and
capabilities of western Wyoming and is a most valuable member
of the Territory's bright constellation of journals.

*Other Towns.*—Among other towns worthy of mention are
the following: Rock Springs, 320 miles west of Cheyenne, the
great coal mining town of central Wyoming. Population 450.
Besides producing immense quantities of coal, Rock Springs the
present season will ship 10,000 head of cattle. Hilliard, fourteen
miles east of Evanston, is one of the most prominent lumbering

centers, and manufactures many thousand bushels of charcoal annually. South Pass, Atlantic City, and Miners' Delight, are important mining camps in Sweetwater county, and are destined to swell the bullion yield of Wyoming to a very large extent, as low-grade ores and the poorer gulches can be worked profitably by more practicable appliances.

## MISCELLANEOUS INFORMATION.

*Post-Offices.*—Following is a complete list of the post-offices in Wyoming, with the counties in which they are located, and the names of postmasters. Names of money-order offices are marked with an *; county seats in small capitals:

| OFFICE. | COUNTY. | POSTMASTER. |
| --- | --- | --- |
| Almy | Uintah | N. Beeman. |
| Aspen | Sweetwater | J. N. Adams. |
| Atlantic City | Sweetwater | Robt. McAuley. |
| Bear Springs | Laramie | Isaac Bard. |
| Bordeaux | Laramie | Thos. Hunton. |
| Camp Brown | Sweetwater | J. K. Moore. |
| Camp Stambaugh* | Sweetwater | J. N. Baldwin. |
| CHEYENNE* | Laramie | H. Glafcke. |
| Chugwater | Laramie | John Phillips. |
| Chimney Rock | Laramie | J. McFarland. |
| Carbon | Uintah | W. C. Bangs. |
| Carter | Uintah | Richard Carter. |
| Centennial | Carbon | Thos. Markle. |
| Dixon | Carbon | Susan Hugus. |
| Davis Ranch | Laramie | Henry Davis. |
| Eagle Ranch | Sweetwater | B. F. Ward. |
| EVANSTON* | Uintah | E. S. Whittier. |
| Farrel | Albany | Edward Farrel. |
| Ferris | Carbon | H. W. Smith. |
| Fort Bridger* | Uintah | W. A. Carter. |
| Fort Fetterman | Albany | W. H. Murphy. |
| Fort Fred Steele | Carbon | J. W. Hugus. |
| Fort Halleck | Carbon | Robert Foote. |
| Fort Laramie* | Laramie | J. W. Ford. |
| Granger | Uintah | F. B. Carley. |
| GREEN RIVER CITY* | Sweetwater | S. I. Field. |
| Hat Creek | Laramie | J. Bowman. |
| Hilliard | Uintah | W. K. Sloan. |
| Lander | Sweetwater | P. P. Dickinson. |
| LARAMIE CITY* | Albany | J. H. Hayford. |
| Last Chance | Albany | J. Beagle. |
| Little Horse Creek | Laramie | Wm. McMinn. |
| Little Moon | Laramie | N. Janis. |
| Medicine Bow | Carbon | A. Trabing. |
| Miners' Delight | Sweetwater | James Kime. |
| North Fork | Sweetwater | H. R. Prather. |
| Percy | Carbon | A. J. Bowle. |
| Piedmont | Uintah | A. B. Cameron. |

| OFFICE. | COUNTY. | POSTMASTER |
|---|---|---|
| Pine Bluffs.............. | Laramie ........... | J. R. Gordon. |
| Pole Creek ............. | Laramie ........... | Fred Schwartz. |
| Rawlins* .............. | Carbon ........... | James France. |
| Red Buttes............. | Albany............ | Thos. A. McCool. |
| Rock Creek............. | Albany............ | Herbert Thayer. |
| Rock Springs* .......... | Sweetwater ........ | O. C. Smith. |
| Sherman............... | Albany............ | W. N. Gale. |
| South Pass City......... | Sweetwater ........ | James Smith. |
| Tie Siding.....:....... | Albany............ | J. W. Booth. |
| Walbach............... | Laramie ........... | D. Lannen. |
| Wyoming.............. | Albany............ | J. Allen. |

*Schools, Churches, Societies and Libraries.*—The following educational, religious and literary statistics will be found reliable, and generally interesting:

WYOMING PUBLIC SCHOOLS.

| COUNTIES. | Superintendents. | No. School Buildings. | Schools. | No. Pupils. | Am't paid Teachers. |
|---|---|---|---|---|---|
| Albany...... | W. E. Hamilton.. | 3 | 3 | 277 | $3,375 |
| Carbon...... | Daniel Clay...... | 4 | 4 | 260 | 1,826 |
| Laramie..... | J. Y. Cowhick.... | 1 | 6 | 432 | 7,010 |
| Sweetwater.. | Chas. Washington | 3 | 6 | 190 | 2,461 |
| Uintah...... | Wm. E. Wheeler. | 5 | 8 | 384 | 3,497 |
| Totals.... | ............... | 16 | 27 | 1,543 | $18,169 |

Total value of public school property, $60,500. All counties have surplus school funds, and several are arranging to erect new buildings and make other needed improvements.

All religious denominations are represented by good churches and membership. The total value of all church property closely approximates $100,000.

There are in Wyoming five lodges of the Masonic order, nine lodges of Odd Fellows, two lodges of Knights of Pythias, and six temperance societies. Trades unions are also well represented.

Seven good public and circulating libraries in the Territory (without including about an equal number at the military posts) contain an aggregate of 8,000 volumes.

*County Officers.*—Following is a list of all county officers in Wyoming, corrected up to July 15, 1877:

*Albany.*—Commissioners, Henry Wagner, John S. McCool, N. A. Heath; Sheriff, Daniel Nottage; Clerk, J. W. Meldrum;

11

Probate Judge, J. W. Donnellan; Prosecuting Attorney, M. C. Brown; Superintendent of Schools, W. E. Hamilton; Coroner, J. W. Dysart.

*Carbon.*—Commissioners, James France, William Brauer, Wm. H. Kobson; Sheriff, Isaac M. Lowry; Attorney, Homer Merrell; Clerk, Joseph B. Adams; Probate Judge and Treasurer, W. L. Ash; Assessor, Hower L. Bair; Superintendent of Schools, Daniel R. Clay; Coroner, Ed. S. Snow.

*Laramie.*—Commissioners, A. P. Swan, E. Nagle, J. Sparks; Sheriff, T. J. Carr; Probate Judge and Treasurer, C. F. Miller; Attorney, W. H. Miller; Assessor, W. C. Provines; Coroner, G. C. Goldacker.

*Sweetwater.*—Commissioners, W. P. Noble, James Calhoun, Wm. F. O'Nealey; Sheriff, John W. Dykins; Probate Judge and Treasurer, A. E. Bradbury; Clerk, A. McIntosh; Assessor, K. McLennan; Superintendent of Schools, J. H. Nason; Coroner, D. Rathbune.

*Uintah.*—Commissioners, C. A. Phipps, Noel Beeman, F. H. Harrison; Sheriff, George W. Pepper; Probate Judge and Treasurer, Frank M. Foote; Attorney, H. Garbanati; Clerk, Alf. G. Lee; Surveyor, Alf. G. Lee.

*Banks and Bankers.*—The following banks are in operation in Wyoming:

| City. | Name of Bank. | Paid-in Capital. | Cashier. |
|---|---|---|---|
| Cheyenne | First National | $75,000 | J. E. Wild. |
| " | Stebbins, Post & Co. | | J. V. Jillich. |
| Evanston | Mutual Exchange | | O. North. |
| Laramie City | Wyoming National | 50,000 | C. B. Root. |
| " | Wagner & Dunbar | | |

## MILITARY POSTS.

Wyoming is afforded the best system of military protection of any of the Territories. The different forts and posts are located at the most practicable points for the certain protection of the frontier from maranders, either white or red. This system enables the Territory to extend more certain assurances of safety to the prospective settler, or to parties bound for the northern gold fields, than can be offered by any other commonwealth

* Evanston should be credited with a second institution, data in regard to it being withheld by the manager.

adjacent.   Nearly all successful sallies during the progress of the Sioux war have been made from these posts.

*Fort D. A. Russell.*—Fort Russell is located two miles west of Cheyenne, in the southeastern corner of the Territory.   It is designed to accommodate twelve companies — six each of cavalry and infantry, and is used as a general rendezvous for troops passing to and from more isolated posts.   Immense quantities of supplies for northern posts are constantly stored at Camp Carlin, near by, and are distributed from there as they may be needed.

*Fort Sanders* lies on the Union Pacific railroad, on the Laramie plains, three miles south of Laramie City.   It was established in 1866, and with subsequent additions accommodates six companies.   During the incursions of Indians from the north, in the earlier history of the Territory, Fort Sanders was probably of more real utility than any of the others in Wyoming along the railroad.   Rows of trees encircling the parade ground and in front of the officers' quarters, with a clear stream flowing immediately by, add very much to the beauty of the place.   The fort and company gardens furnish fresh vegetables for the use of officers and troops.

*Fort Fred Steele.*—Fort Steele is beautifully situated in the southern central part of the Territory, at the crossing of the Union Pacific railway over the North Platte.   It was built in 1868 and is a six-company fort.   It is in the center of one of the finest agricultural and pastoral regions in the west, and the country for a hundred miles to the south has long been noted as the choicest hunting and trapping grounds.   These attractions have always served to render the fort a general rendezvous for hundreds of ranchmen, hunters and trappers.

*Fort Bridger.*—Fort Bridger is in Uintah county, in the valley drained by Black Fork of Green river, and is the most westerly of Wyoming posts.   It was established in 1858 as a means of protection and refuge for emigrants on the old California road. The soil in the valleys adjacent is fertile, and yields abundantly all the hardy grains and vegetables.   Streams in the vicinity are well stocked with trout, and fine hunting is afforded in spurs of the Uintah mountains thirty to forty miles south.   The staunch old fort has much unwritten and thrilling history of hardships and dangers incident to early pioneering.

*Camp Stambaugh* is situated in Sweetwater county, 100 miles north of the Union Pacific railway. It is one of the smaller forts, being designed for only two companies. It was established as a permanent fort in 1870, for the protection of the then large mining camps, South Pass, Atlantic City and Hamilton City, all within a few miles of the fort. The Sweetwater stage line carries daily mails from Green River City to this fort. Telegraph to the Union Pacific.

*Camp Brown.*—Camp Brown is also located in Sweetwater county, in the fertile valley of the South Fork of Little Wind river. It is 160 miles north of the Union Pacific railroad, and is connected with Camp Stambaugh by a good wagon road, over which stages of the Sweetwater line run daily. The post was established in compliance with the terms of a treaty with the Shoshone and Bannock Indians (who of late years have been faithful allies of the whites) for their protection against Sioux, Arapahoe, Cheyenne and other hostile bands. The agency of the friendly Indians above noted is located a mile and a half from the fort. This section of country has been the hunting ground and winter quarters for some few white trappers since 1849, and scattered over this and contiguous valleys are burnt ranches and rude graves, attesting the success with which hostile Indians have raided them. The valley in which the fort is located is about forty miles long and three miles wide. The soil is a dark, sandy loam, yielding large returns for the labor bestowed upon it.

*Fort Laramie* is located on the Laramie river, ninety-two miles north of Cheyenne, and is the oldest as well as the most important fort in Wyoming. There are barracks for seven companies, and among the relics of the earliest days are concrete block houses and rows of earthworks surrounding the site. The old overland road to Oregon passes up the North Platte here, and one of the routes to Montana and the Big Horn region, as well as the unexcelled Cheyenne and Black Hills stage road, lies across this reserve. Fort Laramie has daily mail service to Cheyenne and the Black Hills cities, semi-weekly to Fort Fetterman, eighty miles distant, and weekly to Laramie City, on the Union Pacific. It is also connected with Cheyenne by telegraphic wires, and in the same way with Fort Fetterman and other northern and northeastern points. It has for many years been the rallying point for trappers, prospectors and emigrants, and during the recent troubles with the Sioux has played a very important and necessary part. Some of the best stock ranges in Wyoming are located along the tributaries of the Laramie and Platte rivers, within fifty miles of the fort.

*Fort Fetterman.*—Eighty miles northwest of the fort just described is Fort Fetterman. It is located on the south bank of the North Platte, and for ten years has been the extreme northwestern fort in this section of Wyoming. It has been the starting and supply point for General Crook's different expeditions, and is looked to for protection by the scattering ranchmen located within fifty miles south and southeast. The Cheyenne route to the Big Horn region crosses the Platte here, and two good wagon roads run south to the Union Pacific railroad — to Medicine Bow station, eighty-five miles, and to Rock Creek, seventy miles.

*Cantonment Reno.*—Ninety miles northwest of Fort Fetterman, on Powder river, and near the base of the Big Horn mountains, is the temporary supply post, Cantonment Reno. It was established in the fall of 1876, near the site of old Fort Reno, as a base of supplies for the expeditions operating against the Sioux. The old Pumpkin Butte Trail, from the Black Hills, crosses the Powder near here, as does also the Cheyenne road, and the hundreds of miners who have recently flocked into the Big Horn region have made the cantonment their outfitting and organizing point. The southeastern base of the Big Horn range is about forty miles distant. Four companies of infantry at present (July 15) constitute the garrison, and are comfortably quartered in log huts built by themselves.

## MISCELLANEOUS INFORMATION.

*Altitudes.*—The following are the altitudes of prominent points in Wyoming as determined by capable engineers. In the case of the Black Hills peaks, observations of different engineers have not resulted alike, and the ones believed to be most reliable are quoted:

|  | Feet. |
|---|---|
| Laramie Bottom at mouth of Chugwater | 4,500 |
| Chugwater | 5,460 |
| Platte Valley at Fort Fetterman | 4,970 |
| Yellowstone Park (average) | 7,403 |
| Evanston | 6,770 |
| Millis | 6,790 |
| Gilbert's Peak | 13,250 |

|  | Feet. |
|---|---|
| Hilliard | 7,310 |
| Aspen | 7,885 |
| Piedmont | 7,540 |
| Bridger | 6,780 |
| Carter | 6,550 |
| Church Butte | 6,817 |
| Granger | 6,270 |
| Bryan | 6,340 |
| Green River City | 6,140 |
| Rock Springs | 6,280 |
| Rawlins | 6,732 |
| Fort Fred Steele | 6,840 |
| Carbon | 6,750 |
| Medicine Bow | 6,550 |
| Cooper's Lake | 7,044 |
| Laramie Peak | 10,000 |
| Snow's Peak (Wind River range) | 13,570 |
| Laramie City | 7,123 |
| Red Buttes | 7,336 |
| Sherman, highest point on U. P. R. R. | 8,242 |
| Cheyenne | 6,041 |
| Powder River at old Fort Reno | 4,340 |
| Clear Fork, of Powder | 4,560 |
| Old Fort Phil Kearney | 4,770 |
| Tongue River (average) | 3,500 |
| Cloud Peak (not official) | 13,000 |
| Lake Carpenter, Big Horn mountains | 11,000 |
| Inyan Kara Peak, Black Hills | 6,500 |
| Harney's Peak, Black Hills | 7,700 |
| Bare Butte, Black Hills | 4,800 |
| Belle Fourch, near Black Hills | 3,734 |
| Floral Valley, in Black Hills | 6,196 |
| Castle Creek Valley | 6,136 |

*Expense of Living.*—We will take Cheyenne as a fair example in different statements following. Board at first-class hotels, transient, $3 to $4 per day; board at first-class hotels, per week, $12 to $15; at ordinary boarding houses, $6 to $9 per week. Ordinary expenses of housekeeping are about twenty-five per cent. higher than at points east of the Mississippi.

*Wages.*—Wages in Wyoming settlements average about as follows: Salesmen, $75 to $125 per month; carpenters, $3 per day; bricklayers, $4; plasterers, $3; ranch hands and herders, $30 per month and board; teamsters, $28 per month and board.

*Building Material.*—Brick, $9.50 per thousand; common

native lumber, $25 per thousand; best dressed lumber, $45; lime, 40 cents per bushel; plastering cement, $5 per barrel. Hardware as low as in the east, with freight added.

*Railway and Telegraph Rates.*—First-class fare, Cheyenne to Chicago, $47; to Omaha, $31; to Denver, $7; to St. Louis, $47; to New York city, $70; stage fare to Deadwood, $50. Telegraphic rates, ten words, Cheyenne to Chicago, $1; to Deadwood, $2.50; Custer City, $2.

*To Outfitters.*—Those who desire to purchase their own teams for the transportation of miners and miners' supplies, can procure an outfit to much better advantage in Cheyenne than elsewhere. Groceries, provisions, clothing, mining tools, and all other necessary articles can be procured at this point. The following may be considered average prices for animals and wagons:

| | | |
|---|---|---|
| Team of two horses.... | $100 to | $250 |
| Team of two mules | 200 " | 300 |
| Oxen, per yoke | 80 " | 100 |
| Saddle horse | 40 " | 75 |
| Saddle mule | 40 " | 60 |
| Pack horse | 40 " | 60 |
| Pack mule | 40 " | 50 |
| Two-horse wagon | 100 " | 125 |
| Four-horse wagon | 125 " | 150 |

Following is the average price of provisions:

| | | | |
|---|---|---|---|
| Flour | per sack. $3 00 to | $4 50 |
| Bacon | per lb., | 15 " | 16 |
| Syrup | per gal., | 75 " | 1 25 |
| Coffee, Rio | per lb., | 26 " | 30 |
| Sugar | " | 12½ " | 15 |
| Tea | " | 60 " | 1 50 |
| Baking powders | " | 45 " | 50 |
| Beans | " | 6 " | 7 |
| Grain—corn | per cwt., | 1 90 " | 2 00 |
| "    oats | " | 2 50 " | 2 60 |

# CHAPTER II.

THE following synopsis of laws now in force in Wyoming, re-
lating to exemptions, limitations, interest, etc., and the
different mining and homestead laws applicable to the wants of
settlers, should be generally scrutinized:

*Exemptions.* — Every householder, being at the head of a
family, is entitled to a homestead not exceeding in value fifteen
hundred dollars, exempt from execution or attachment for any
debt, contract or civil obligation, while such homestead is actually occupied as such by the owner thereof, or his or her family.
The homestead may consist of a house and lot, or lots, in any
town or city, or a farm of not more than one hundred and sixty
acres. The owner of a homestead may mortgage the same, but
such mortgage shall not be binding against the wife of a married
man who may be occupying the premises with him, unless she
shall freely and voluntarily acknowledge and sign the same, and
the officer taking such acknowledgment shall fully apprise her of
her rights, and of the effect of signing such mortgage.

Besides the homestead above mentioned, the wearing apparel
of every person is exempt from judicial or ministerial process;
also the following property, when owned by any person being the
head of a family and residing with the same, to wit: The family
bible, pictures and school books, a lot in any cemetery or burial
ground, furniture, bedding, provisions, and such other articles as
the debtor may select, not to exceed in all the value of five hundred dollars, to be ascertained by the appraisement of three disinterested householders; *Provided*, that no personal property of
any person about to remove or abscond from the Territory shall
be exempt. The tools, team and implements, or stock in trade
of a mechanic, miner, or other person, and used and kept for the
purpose of carrying on his trade or business, is exempt to a value
not exceeding three hundred dollars; also the library, instru-
ments or implements of any professional man, not to exceed in

value three hundred dollars. The person claiming exemption must in all cases be a *bona-fide* resident of the Territory.

*Limitation of Actions.*—Civil actions can be brought only within the following periods, after the cause of action shall have accrued:

1. An action for the recovery of bonds, tenements and hereditaments, within twenty-one years.

2. An action of forcible entry and detainer, within two years.

3. An action upon a specialty, or any agreement, or contract, or promise in writing, within fifteen years.

4. An action upon a contract not in writing, within six years.

5. An action for trespass upon real property, or for taking, detaining or injuring personal property, including actions for the specific recovery of personal property, within four years.

6. An action for libel, slander, assault and battery, malicious prosecution, or false imprisonment, within one year.

7. An action upon the official bond or undertaking of an executor, administrator, guardian, sheriff, or other officer, or upon the bond or undertaking given in attachment, injunctions, arrest, or any cause whatever, required by statutes, within ten years.

8. An action for any cause not before enumerated, within ten years. If any person entitled to bring any of the foregoing actions — except an action for the recovery of real property, and except a penalty or forfeiture — be, at the time the cause of action accrues, within the age of twenty-one years, a married woman, insane or imprisoned, the action may be brought within the times above limited, after such disability shall have been removed. If, when the cause of action accrues against a person, he be out of the Territory, or shall have absconded, or concealed himself, the period limited for the commencement of the action shall not begin to run until he comes into the Territory, or while he is absconded or concealed. If, after the cause of action accrues, he depart or conceal himself, the time of such absence or concealment shall not be computed as any part of the period within which the action must be brought. Where the cause of action has arisen in another State or Territory, between non-residents of this Territory, and, by the laws of the State or Territory where the cause of action arose, an action cannot be maintained thereon by reason of lapse of time, no action can be maintained thereon in this Territory. In any case founded on contract, part payment

of principal or interest, or an acknowledgment of existing debt, liability or claim in writing signed by the party to be charged, takes the case out of the statute, and an action may be brought within the times limited, after such part payment or acknowledgment.

*Interest.*—Any rate of interest may be agreed upon in writing, but in the absence of express contract, all monies, claims or judgments draw interest at the rate of twelve per cent. per annum; unsettled accounts draw interests after thirty days from date of the last item. There is no usury law.

*United States Mining Laws—Qualifications of Mining Claimants.*—All citizens of the United States, or persons who have in due form declared their intention to become citizens, are qualified to locate for themselves mining claims on the public lands of the United States, and two or more persons or associations of persons thus qualified may make a joint entry of land under the mineral laws, and individuals who are not citizens and any persons whomsoever may afterward become joint or sole owners.

*Proof of Citizenship* in the case of an individual may consist of his own affidavit thereof; and in the case of an association of persons unincorporated, of the affidavit of their authorized agent, made on his own knowledge or upon information and belief: and in case of a corporation organized under the laws of the United States, or of any State or Territory of the United States, by filing a certified copy of their charter, or certificate of incorporation. These affidavits may be taken before the register or receiver of the land district, or any other officer authorized to administer oaths within the district.

*Placer Claims.*—No location of a placer claim can be made to exceed one hundred and sixty acres, whatever be the number of locators associated together, or whatever the local regulations of the district may allow; no location made by an individual can exceed twenty acres, and no location made by an association of individuals can exceed one hundred and sixty acres, which location of one hundred and sixty acres cannot be made by a less number than eight *bona-fide* locators; but whether as *much* as twenty acres can be located by an individual, or one hundred and sixty acres by an association, depends entirely upon the mining regulations in force in the respective districts at the date of the location; it being held that such mining regulations are in no way enlarged by said acts of Congress, but remain intact and in full force with regard to the size of locations, in so far as they do not permit locations in excess of the limits fixed by Congress.

The miners of each district may make rules and regulations not in conflict with the laws of the United States, or of the State or Territory in which such districts are respectively situated, governing the location, manner of recording and amount of work necessary to hold possession of a claim; but the location must be so distinctly marked on the ground that its boundaries may be readily traced. This is a very important matter, and locators cannot exercise too much care in defining their locations at the outset, inasmuch as the law requires that all records of mining locations made subsequent to its passage shall contain the name or names of the locators, the date of the location, and such a *description of the claim or claims* located, by reference to some natural object or permanent monument, as will identify the claim.

To make the identification clear the claimant should state the names of adjoining claims, or if none adjoin, the relative positions of the nearest claims; should drive a post or erect a monument of stones at each corner of his surface-ground, and at some point thereon should fix a post, stake or board, upon which should be designated the name or names of the locators and the extent of the claim in each direction from this point.

Within a reasonable time, say twenty days after the location shall have been marked on the ground, notice thereof, accurately describing the claim in manner aforesaid, should be filed for record with the proper recorder of the district, who will thereupon issue the usual certificate of location.

In order to retain the possessory right to any placer claim, it must be actually worked to a reasonable extent, and within a reasonable time, according to the local regulations, and if even after having been so worked it should be left beyond the time prescribed in the local regulations, it may be treated as abandoned, and be thereupon taken by another person.

*Patents for Placer Claims.*—The law provides, in respect of placer claims, that "where said person or association, they and their grantors, shall have held and worked their said claims for a period equal to the time prescribed by the statute of limitations for mining claims for the State or Territory where the same may be situated, evidence of such possession and working of the claims for such period shall be sufficient to establish a right to a patent thereto under this act in the absence of any adverse claim."

When an applicant desires to make his proof of possessory right in accordance with this provision of law, the register will not require him to produce evidence of location, copies of conveyances, or abstracts of title, as in other cases, but will require him to furnish a duly certified copy of the statute of limitations of mining claims for the State or Territory, together with his sworn statement giving a clear and succinct narration of the facts as to the origin of his title, and likewise as to the continuation of his possession of the mining ground covered by his application; the area thereof, the nature and extent of the mining that has been done thereon; whether there has been any opposition to his possession or litigation with regard to his claim, and if so, when the same ceased; whether such cessation was caused by compromise or by judicial decree, and any additional facts within the claimant's knowledge having a direct bearing upon his possession and *bona-fides* which he may desire to submit in support of his claim.

There should likewise be filed a certificate, under seal of the court having jurisdiction of mining cases within the judicial district embracing the claim, that no suit or action of any character whatever involving the right of possession to any portion of the claim applied for is pending, and that there has been no litigation before said court affecting the title to said claim or any part thereof for a period equal to the time fixed by the statute of limitations for mining claims in the State or Territory aforesaid, other than that which has finally been decided in favor of the claimant.

The claimant should support his narrative of facts relative to his possession, occupancy and improvements by corroborative testimony of any disinterested person or persons of credibility who may be cognizant of the facts in the case and are capable of testifying understandingly in the premises.

It will be to the advantage of claimants to make their proofs as full and complete as practicable.

The government price of the placer mines is two dollars and fifty cents per acre.

*Veins or Lodes.*—Any person who is a citizen of the United States, or who has declared his intention to become a citizen, may locate, record and hold a mining claim of *fifteen hundred linear feet* along the course of any mineral vein or lode subject to location; or an association of persons, so qualified, may make joint location of such claim of *fifteen hundred feet*, but in no event can a location of a vein or lode, except fifteen hundred feet along the course thereof, whatever may be the number of persons composing the association.

The lateral extent of locations of veins or lodes may in no case *exceed three hundred feet on each side of the middle of the vein at the surface*, and no such surface rights shall be limited by any mining regulations to less than twenty-five feet on each side of the middle of the vein at the surface, the end lines of such claims to be in all cases parallel to each other.

The act provides that no lode-claim can be recorded until after the discovery of a vein or lode within the limits of the ground claimed; the object of which provision is evidently to prevent the encumbering of the district mining records with useless locations before sufficient work has been done thereon to determine whether a vein or lode has really been discovered or not.

The claimant should therefore, prior to recording his claim, unless the vein can be traced upon the surface, sink a shaft, or run a tunnel or drift, to a sufficient depth therein to discover and develop a mineral-bearing vein, lode or crevice; should determine, if possible, the general course of such vein in either direction from the point of discovery, by which direction he will be governed in marking the boundaries of his claim on the surface, and should give the course and distance as nearly as practicable from the discovery-shaft on the claim to some permanent, well-known points or objects, such, for instance, as stone monuments, blazed trees, the confluence of streams, point of intersection of well-known gulches, ravines or roads, prominent butes, hills, etc., which may be in the immediate vicinity, and which will serve to perpetuate and fix the *locus* of the claim and render it susceptible of identification from the description thereof given in the record of locations in the district.

To make the identification clear, the claimant should state the names of adjoining claims, or if none adjoin, the relative position of the nearest claims; he should drive a post or erect a monument of stones at each corner of his surface-ground, and at the point of discovery or discovery-shaft should fix a post, stake or board, upon which should be designated the name of the lode, the name of the locator, and the number of feet claimed each way on the lode from the discovery point.

Within a reasonable time after the location shall have been marked on the ground, notice thereof, accurately describing it as above mentioned, should be filed for record with the proper recorder of the district, who will thereupon issue the usual certificate of location.

In order to hold the possessory right to a claim of fifteen hundred feet of a vein or lode, not less than one hundred dollars'' worth of labor shall be performed or improvements made thereon in each year, in default of which the claim will be subject to re-location by any other person or persons having the necessary qualifications, unless the original locator, his heirs, assigns or legal representatives shall have renewed work thereon after such failure and before such re-location.

These details in the matter of location, labor and expenditure should receive careful attention, because neglect of them may cause expensive litigation or totally invalidate an otherwise most valuable claim.

*Mill Sites.*—Where non-mineral land not contiguous to the vein or lode is used or occupied by the proprietor of such vein or lode for mining or milling purposes, such non-adjacent surface-ground may be embraced and included in an application for a patent for such vein or lode, and the same may be patented therewith, subject to the same preliminary requirements as to survey and notice as are applicable to veins or lodes: *Provided,* that no location of such non-adjacent land shall exceed five acres, and payment for the same must be made at the same rate as fixed for the superfices of the lode. The owner of a quartz-mill or reduction works, not owning a mine in connection therewith, may also receive a patent for his mill site.

To avail themselves of this provision of law, parties holding the possessory right to a vein or lode, and to a piece of land not contiguous thereto, for mining or milling purposes, not exceeding the quantity allowed for such purpose by the local rules, regulations or customs, the proprietors of such vein or lode may file

in the proper land office their application for a patent, under
oath, which application, together with the plat and field-notes,
may include, embrace and describe, in addition to the vein or
lode, such non-contiguous mill site, and after due proceedings as
to notice, etc., a patent will be issued conveying the same as one
claim.

In making the survey in a case of this kind, the lode-claim
should be described in the plat and field-notes as " Lot No. 37,
A," and the mill site as " Lot No. 37, B," or whatever may be its
appropriate numerical designation ; the course and distance from
a corner of the mill site to a corner of the lode-claim to be inva-
riably given in such plat and field-notes, and a copy of the plat
and notice of application for patent must be conspicuously
posted upon the mill site, as well as upon the vein or lode, for
the statutory period of sixty days. In making the entry no separate receipt or certificate need be issued for the mill site, but the
whole area of both lode and mill site will be embraced in one
entry, the price being five dollars for each acre and fractional
part of an acre embraced by such lode and mill-site claim.

In case the owner of a quartz-mill or reduction works is not
the owner or claimant of a vein or lode, the law permits him to
make application therefor in the same manner prescribed therein
for mining claims, and after due notice and proceedings, in the
absence of a valid adverse filing, to enter and receive a patent for
his mill site, at five dollars per acre.

In every case there must be satisfactory proof that the land
claimed as a mill site is not mineral in character, which proof
may, where the matter is unquestioned, consist of the sworn
statement of the claimant, supported by that of one or more disinterested persons capable from acquaintance with the land to
testify understandingly.

The law expressly limits mill-site locations made from and
after its passage to *five acres*, but whether so *much* as that can
be located depends upon the local customs, rules or regulations.

The registers and receivers will preserve an unbroken consec-
utive series of numbers for all mineral entries.

*Tunnel Rights.*—Where a tunnel is run for the development
of a vein or lode, or for the discovery of mines, the owners of
such tunnel shall have the right of possession of all veins or
lodes within three thousand feet from the face of such tunnel on

the line thereof, not previously known to exist, discovered in such tunnel, to the same extent as if discovered from the surface; and locations on the line of such tunnel of veins or lodes not appearing on the surface, made by other parties after the commencement of the tunnel, and while the same is being prosecuted with reasonable diligence, shall be invalid, but failure to prosecute the work on the tunnel for six months shall be considered as an abandonment of the right to all undiscovered veins or lodes on the line of said tunnel.

The effect of this section is simply to give the proprietors of a mining tunnel run in good faith the possessory right to fifteen hundred feet of any blind lodes cut, discovered or intersected by such tunnel, which were not previously known to exist, within three thousand feet from the face or point of commencement of such tunnel, and to prohibit other parties, after the commencement of the tunnel, from prospecting for and making locations of lodes on the *line thereof* and within said distance of three thousand feet, unless such lodes appear upon the surface or were previously known to exist.

The term "face," as used in said section, is construed and held to mean the first working face formed in the tunnel, and to signify the point at which the tunnel actually enters cover, it being from this point that the three thousand feet are to be counted, upon which prospecting is prohibited as aforesaid.

To avail themselves of the benefits of this provision of law, the proprietors of a mining tunnel will be required, at the time they enter cover, to give proper notice of their tunnel location, by erecting a substantial post, board, or monument, at the face or point of commencement thereof, upon which should be posted a good and sufficient notice, giving the names of the parties or company claiming the tunnel right; the actual or proposed course or direction of the tunnel; the height and width thereof, and the course and distance from such face or point of commencement to some permanent well-known objects in the vicinity by which to fix and determine the *locus* in manner heretofore set forth applicable to locations of veins or lodes; and at the time of posting such notice they shall, in order that miners or prospectors may be enabled to determine whether or not they are within the lines of the tunnel, establish the boundary lines thereof by stakes or monuments placed along such lines at proper intervals, to the terminus of the three thousand feet from the face or point of commencement of the tunnel, and the lines so marked will define and govern as to the specific boundaries within which prospecting for lodes not previously known to exist is prohibited while work on the tunnel is being prosecuted with reasonable diligence.

At the time of posting notice and marking out the lines of the tunnel as aforesaid, a full and correct copy of such notice of location defining the tunnel claim must be filed for record with the mining recorder of the district, to which notice must be attached the sworn statement or declaration of the owners, claimants or projectors of such tunnel, setting forth the facts in the case; stating the amount expended by themselves and their predecessors in interest in prosecuting work thereon, the extent of the work performed, and that it is *bona-fide* their intention to prosecute work on the tunnel so located and described with reasonable diligence for the development of a vein or lode, or for the discovery of mines, or both, as the case may be.

This notice of location must be duly recorded, and, with the said sworn statement attached, kept on the recorder's files for future reference.

By a compliance with the foregoing, much needless difficulty will be avoided, and the way for the adjustment of legal rights acquired in virtue of the act will be made much more easy and certain.

This portion of the law is very important and fruitful in adverse claims, and the United States land office is supposed to take particular care that no improper advantage of it is taken by parties making or professing to make tunnel locations, ostensibly for the purposes named in the statute, but really for the purpose of monopolizing the lands lying in front of their tunnels to the detriment of the mining interests and to the exclusion of *bona-fide* prospectors or miners, and it will hold such tunnel claimants to a strict compliance with the terms of the act; and as *reasonable diligence* on their part in prosecuting the work is one of the essential conditions of their implied contract, negligence or want of due diligence will be construed as working a forfeiture of their right to all undiscovered veins on the line of such tunnel.

*Government Titles to Vein or Lode Claims.*—The claimant is required, in the first place, to have a correct survey of his claim made under authority of the surveyor general of the State or

12

Territory in which the claim lies; such survey to show with accuracy the exterior surface boundaries of the claim, which boundaries are required to be distinctly marked by monuments on the ground.

The claimant is then required to post a copy of the plat of such survey in a conspicuous place upon the claim, together with notice of his intention to apply for a patent therefor, which notice will give the date of posting, the name of the claimant, the name of the claim, mine or lode; the mining district and county; whether the location is of record, and if so, where the record may be found; the number of feet claimed along the vein and the presumed direction thereof; the number of feet claimed on the lode in each direction from the point of discovery, or other well defined place on the claim; the name or names of adjoining claimants on the same or other lodes; or if none adjoin, the names of the nearest claims, etc.

After posting the said plat and notice upon the premises, the claimant will file with the proper register and receiver a copy of such plat, and the field-notes of survey of the claim, accompanied by the affidavit of at least two credible witnesses that such plat and notice are posted conspicuously upon the claim, giving the date and place of such posting; a copy of the *notice* so posted to be attached to, and form a part of, said affidavit.

Attached to the field-notes so filed must be the sworn statement of the claimant that he has the possessory right to the premises therein described, in virtue of a compliance by himself (and by his grantors, if he claims by purchase,) with the mining rules, regulations and customs of the mining district, State or Territory in which the claim lies, and with the mining laws of Congress; such sworn statement to narrate briefly, but as clearly as possible, the facts constituting such compliance, the origin of his possession, and the basis of his claim to a patent.

This affidavit should be supported by appropriate evidence from the mining recorder's office as to his possessory right, as follows, namely: Where he claims to be a locator, a full, true and correct copy of such location should be furnished, as the same appears upon the mining records; such copy to be attested by the seal of the recorder, or if he has no seal, then he should make oath to the same being correct, as shown by his records; where the applicant claims as a locator in company with others,

who have since conveyed their interests in the lode to him, a
copy of the original record of location should be filed, together
with an abstract of title from the proper recorder, under seal or
oath as aforesaid, tracing the colocator's possessory rights in the
claim to such applicant for patent; where the applicant claims
only as a purchaser for valuable consideration, a copy of the location record must be filed, under seal or upon oath as aforesaid,
with an abstract of title certified as above by the proper recorder,
tracing the right of possession by a continuous chain of conveyances from the original locators to the applicant.

In the event of the mining records in any case having been
destroyed by fire or otherwise lost, affidavit of the fact should
be made, and secondary evidence of possessory title will be received, which may consist of the affidavit of the claimant, supported by those of any other parties cognizant of the facts
relative to his location, occupancy, possession, improvements,
etc.; and in such case of lost records, any deeds, certificates of
location or purchase, or other evidence which may be in the claimant's possession, and tend to establish his claim, should be filed.

Upon the receipt of these papers the register will, at the
expense of the claimant, publish a notice of such application for
the period of sixty days, in a newspaper published nearest to the
claim, and will post a copy of such notice in his office for the
same period. The notices so published and posted must be as
full and complete as possible, and embrace all the *data* given in
the notice posted upon the claim. Too much care cannot be
exercised in the preparation of these notices, inasmuch as upon
their accuracy and completeness will depend, in a great measure,
the regularity and validity of the whole proceeding.

The claimant, either at the time of filing these papers with
the register, or at any time during the sixty days' publication, is
required to file a certificate of the surveyor general that not less
than five hundred dollars' worth of labor has been expended or
improvements made upon the claim by the applicant or his
grantors; that the plat filed by the claimant is correct; that the
field notes of the survey, as filed, furnish such an accurate
description of the claim as will, if incorporated into a patent,
serve to fully identify the premises, and that such reference is
made therein to natural objects or permanent monuments as will
perpetuate and fix the *locus* thereof.

It will be the more convenient way to have this certificate indorsed by the surveyor general, both upon the plat and field-notes of survey filed by the claimant as aforesaid.

After the sixty days' period of newspaper publication has expired, the claimant will file his affidavit, showing that the plat and notice aforesaid remained conspicuously posted upon the claim sought to be patented during said sixty days' publication.

Upon the filing of this affidavit the register will, if no adverse claim was filed in his office during the period of publication, permit the claimant to pay for the land according to the area given in the plat and field-notes of survey aforesaid, at the rate of five dollars for each acre and five dollars for each fractional part of an acre, the receiver issuing the usual duplicate receipt therefor; after which the whole matter will be forwarded to the commissioner of the general land office and a patent issued thereon if found regular.

In sending up the papers in the case the register must not omit certifying to the fact that the notice was posted in his office for the full period of sixty days, such certificate to state distinctly when such posting was done and how long continued.

*Adverse Claims.*—An adverse mining claim must be filed with the register of the same land office with whom the application for patent was filed, or in his absence with the receiver, and within the sixty days' period of newspaper publication of notice.

The adverse notice must be duly sworn to before an officer authorized to administer oaths within the land district, or before the register or receiver; it must fully set forth the nature and extent of the interference or conflict; whether the adverse party claims as a purchaser for valuable consideration or as a locator; if the former, the original conveyance, or a duly certified copy thereof, should be furnished, or if the transaction was a mere verbal one he will narrate the circumstances attending the purchase, the date thereof, and the amount paid, which facts should be supported by the affidavit of one or more witnesses, if any were present at the time, and if he claims as a locator he must file a duly certified copy of the location from the office of the proper recorder.

In order that the "*boundaries*" and "*extent*" of the claim may be shown, it will be incumbent upon the adverse claimant to file a plat showing his claim and its relative situation or position with the one against which he claims, so that the extent of the conflict may be the better understood. This plat must be made from an actual survey by a United States deputy surveyor, who will officially certify thereon to its correctness; and in addition there must be attached to such plat of survey a certificate or sworn statement by the surveyor as to the approximate value of the labor performed or improvements made upon the claim of the adverse party, and the plat must indicate the position of any shafts, tunnels, or other improvements, if any such exist upon the claim of the party opposing the application.

Upon the foregoing being filed within the sixty days as aforesaid, the register, or in his absence the receiver, will give notice in writing to *both parties* to the contest that such adverse claim has been filed, informing them that the party who filed the adverse claim will be required, within thirty days from the date of such filing, to commence proceedings in a court of competent jurisdiction, to determine the question of right of possession, and to prosecute the same with reasonable diligence to final judgment, and that should such adverse claimant fail to do so, his adverse claim will be considered waived, and the application for patent be allowed to proceed upon its merits.

When an adverse claim is filed as aforesaid, the register or receiver will indorse upon the same the precise date of filing, and preserve a record of the date of notifications issued thereon; and thereafter all proceedings on the application for patent will be suspended, with the exception of the completion of the publication and posting of notices and plat, and the filing of the necessary proof thereof, until the controversy shall have been adjudicated in court, or the adverse claim waived or withdrawn.

In the foregoing abstract of the mining laws of the United States it will be observed that reference is frequently made to *the mining statutes of the particular State or Territory* in which the claim is situated, and also to the local regulations of the Mining District. Many of the miners of the Black Hills are within the Territory of Dakota, the legislature of which has passed a law in relation thereto. This limits the width of a lode claim to 150 feet (instead of 300) on each side of the lode, but gives power to the *county* to increase or diminish the width by *vote at a general election.* Also that the discoverer must record his claim within three months after discovery with the recorder or register of deeds of the county, before which the claim must be located; and besides the discovery, shaft or equivalent adit, open cut, cross cut, or tunnel to be completed in sixty days from discovery, and the sign or notice posted there, the boundaries must be marked by *eight substantial posts*, hewed or blazed on the side facing the claim, and sunk in the ground, or if this is impracticable, held in place by stones — one at each corner, one at each end of the lode, and one at the centre of each side-line.

Re-locations are substantially like new ones. Not only must at least one hundred dollars' worth of work and improvements be done in a year, but, within six months after the time allowed, an affidavit of the fact must be made and recorded with the register or recorder of deeds.

There is no doubt that all locations which do not conform to this law will be void, whether they are in accordance with local regulations or not. For these latter the locator should consult the mining recorder and other people of the district.

Settlers wishing to obtain non-mineral land for agricultural purposes should study the following

## ABSTRACTS OF THE UNITED STATES HOMESTEADS AND PRE-EMPTION LAWS.

*Pre-emption.*—Every head of a family, or widow, or single man or woman, over twenty-one years of age, being a citizen, or having filed a declaration of intention to become a citizen, can pre-empt 160 acres of any American government lands, with the exception of some limited special reservations. The first act necessary is settlement, or the commencement of some work or improvement upon the land, and the pre-emption right dates from the first improvement or occupation of the land. Upon surveyed land a pre-emptor must, within three months of settlement, go or send to the land office in that district, pay $2, make a "filing" or written declaration of intention to pre-empt, and within thirty months from filing the land must be paid for. If within ten miles of a land grant railroad, the price is $2.50 per acre; outside of that distance, $1.25 per acre. No one can pay for land under the pre-emption law until the claimant and family (if he has one) has actually resided upon the land for six months, and he must not be the owner of 320 acres of land

within the United States (exclusive of pre-emption claim). No
person can make a settlement or improvements on land for
another, which will hold for pre-emption. No one can hire
another to live upon the land for six months in such a way to
answer the requirements of the law that the pre-emptor shall
have resided on the tract. One land warrant or Agricultural
College scrip in same manner can be laid on a quarter section
(160 acres) in pre-empting; but, if the land is $2.50 per acre,
the extra $1.25 per acre must be paid in cash. Soldiers have no
rights in pre-emption beyond any other person. Heirs may complete the pre-emption in their own names.

*Citizens' Homesteads.*—Any person qualified as for pre-emption
can acquire by occupation, and the payment of commission and
fees ($18 to $26), 160 acres of land held at $1.25 per acre, or 80
acres of land within ten miles of railroad, and held at $2.50 per
acre. Every homestead settler, except soldiers, must in person
go to the land office to make the filing, unless he is actually living
on the land, and then it is allowable to make the filing before the
clerk of the county within which the land is situated. The right
to land under homestead law dates back from filing (not from
settlement as under pre-emption), and the claimant is allowed six
months, within which time he must take possession of the land
by occupation and improvement. Not sooner than five, nor later
than seven years after entry, the settler must go to the land office
and prove by two witnesses that he has resided upon and cultivated the land for five years immediately succeeding the time of
filing, and thereupon he or she is entitled to a patent. Absence
from a homestead for more than six months at any one time
during the five years works a forfeiture of all right to the land,
if proven to the satisfaction of the United States Register.
Neither pre-emption nor homestead claims are liable for debts or
taxes incurred previous to completion of title.

In case of death before title is perfected, either by pre-emption
or homesteading, the right of the deceased descends to the widow
or heirs, or, in case of infant children only, it may be sold for
their benefit, even though the five years be not expired.

Each and every homestead settler, at any time after the end
of the third year of his or her residence, who, in addition to the
settlement and improvements required by the homestead laws,
shall have had under cultivation for two years one acre of timber

(the trees thereon being not more than twelve feet apart each way, and in a good thrifty condition) for each and every sixteen acres of said homestead, shall, upon due proof of such fact by two credible witnesses, receive his or her patent for said homestead.

One may take a homestead and a timber claim, or a pre-emption and a timber claim at the same time; but a homestead and a pre-emption claim cannot run together, because both require actual residence.

A soldier's actual or enlisted service in the army will be counted as equal to a like period of residence on the land.

The fact that a person has had the benefit of the Pre-emption Act does not in any case interfere with his right to homestead. The fact that a person has had the benefit of the Homestead Act does not prevent him from pre-empting, but no one can leave his or her own land in the same State or Territory to take the benefit of the Pre-emption Act. No person can pre-empt more than once. No person can homestead more than once. No person can make a second entry to a homestead unless the first was illegal.

*Commuting a Homestead.*—Homestead settlers may pay for their land in cash or warrants at the government price [$1.25], upon making proof of actual residence and cultivation for a period of not less than six months from the date of entry to the time of payment, but this does not interfere with the right to pre-empt.

*Desert Lands.*—Under an act of Congress, approved March 3, 1877, any person of lawful age who is a citizen of the United States, or who has declared his intention to become a citizen, may file his oath with the register and the receiver of the land office in the district in which any desert land is located, that he intends to reclaim not to exceed six hundred and forty acres of said land, in a compact form, by conducting water upon it within three years of the date of said oath, and by describing accurately the boundaries of said land, if surveyed, and if not surveyed, as near as possible without a survey; and paying to the receiver the sum of twenty-five cents per acre for all the land claimed.

Any time within three years after the filing of said oath a patent can be obtained by making proof to the register and receiver that he has reclaimed said land, and paying to the receiver the sum of one dollar per acre. But no person shall enter more than one tract of land.

By desert lands is meant all lands, not timber or mineral, which will not produce some agricultural crop without irrigation, which fact shall be established by proof of two or more credible witnesses under oath. Said oaths to be made before some person competent to take oaths, and filed in the land office of the district in which the land is situated.

This act only applies to desert lands in Wyoming, Utah, Montana, Idaho, Nevada, Arizona, Washington, Oregon, California, New Mexico and Dakota.

*Legal Weights and Measures in Wyoming.*—The law of Wyoming prescribes the following as the standard weights:

|  | Lbs. |
|---|---|
| Wheat | 60 |
| Rye | 56 |
| Corn | 56 |
| Corn in ear | 70 |
| Barley | 48 |
| Oats | 32 |
| Potatoes | 60 |
| Beans | 60 |
| Clover seeds | 60 |
| Timothy seed | 46 |
| Hemp seed | 44 |
| Buckwheat | 52 |
| Blue-grass seed | 14 |
| Corn meal | 50 |
| Onions | 57 |
| Salt | 80 |
| Lime | 80 |
| Mineral coal | 80 |

A perch of stone in mason work shall be considered sixteen and one-half (16½) cubic feet, and for brick-work measure, when laid up in wall, shall be counted twenty-two brick per cubic foot for foot wall, and fifteen brick for what is known as eight-inch wall; a common brick to be 8¼ inches long, 4¼ inches wide and 2½ inches thick. All grain and nearly all vegetables sold by the pound.

# PART THIRD.

# THE BIG HORN, BLACK HILLS AND YELLOWSTONE REGIONS.

### MINERALS, SOIL, GRASSES, SCENERY, CLIMATE, ETC.

# THE BIG HORN REGION.

## CHAPTER I.

### LOCATION AND PROMINENT NATURAL FEATURES.

IT has been quite natural for the average reader, when referring to the Big Horn Region, to cover with his imagination all of that vast country lying between the Yellowstone on the north and the Sweetwater on the south, and between the Black Hills on the east and the degree of longitude defining the line of Wyoming and Idaho on the west. While it should be remembered that within these generous bounds are three or four distinct and naturally separate mountain ranges, almost as large as the Big Horn, and with their own well defined system of drainage, yet there is no reason why one of the grandest of western rivers and this great central backbone should not give the region adjacent a distinguishing title. In these pages the Big Horn Region will be treated of as one covering the broad country above outlined, while its spurs or tributary regions, which are attracting less attention at present, will be briefly outlined as we progress.

The Big Horn mountains lie almost wholly in northwestern Wyoming, between the thirtieth and thirty-second degrees of longitude west from Washington, and the forty-third and forty-fifth parallels of north latitude. The mountain region proper is therefore 125 miles in extent north and south and about the same east and west, and contains 15,000 square miles. Rising near the head of the main fork of Powder river the range trends off to the northwest 200 miles, and then, turning almost directly west, soon loses itself in the different ranges bordering the Yellowstone National Park. At the southeastern terminus the range singularly doubles back upon itself to the west, and is said to have thus taken the significant name, "Big Horn." By a few of the old-time mountaineers we learn that the big horn of the mountain sheep, there so plentiful, is the source of the title, while others claim that the entire range, from its horn or cornucopia shape, has, from the earliest advent of the fur company employes, been thus distinguished. The average altitude of valleys at the immediate base of the range is 4,500 feet above sea level, and the higher peaks are from nine to twelve thousand feet.

A scene never to be forgotten is that which the visitor from the south, or the Cheyenne route, enjoys when this great watershed is first seen from the Powder river divide. Nearly the whole of the resplendent range, stretching off along the northwestern horizon 150 miles is grasped by the eager vision. "A cloud-land mirage!" we first exclaim, its lofty peaks appearing white, fleecy and ethereal enough to belong to cloud-land, and yet too surpassingly grand to be spared by even a beautiful earth. In most harmonious contrast to the great banks of glittering snowbanks of burnished silver, they looked to us, are the long, purple-tinged pedestals upon which they rest. These are the unusually rugged foot-hills, and they receive their rich coloring from dense forests of pine and spruce, which cover them from base to summit. From near the center rise Cloud and Hayes peaks, the proudest landmarks of all the northern country, while at frequent intervals on either side other snow-capped sentinels are clearly outlined against the sky. Even from this distant view the grand cañons of the Tongue river tributaries are defined — sombre and threatening gashes, and sometimes almost cavernous in their rocky mould.

It was the writer's good fortune to traverse this grand wilderness almost from end to end, and to several times cross the range in the vicinity of Cloud Peak. From the summit, at an altitude of some 12,000 feet, a view which can hardly be equaled in the mountain ranges of America was obtained. Eastward it swept from the Powder River region to that of the Yellowstone, and a radius of 250 miles was but a comprehensive panorama for the naked eye. The Tongue, Powder, Rosebud and other rivers could be traced almost from the feet of the enraptured visitor, out northward among their lesser mountains and flanking plains, until lost in the picturesque brakes of the Yellowstone, 150 miles away. Westward for over 100 miles stretched the valley of the

Big Horn, the crystal sheen of that river itself often emerging from graceful groves of richest green. Still beyond in that direction were the Wind River mountains, with their thousand rugged cañons and unbroken covering of snow. Yet beyond — over 200 miles distant — was the Shoshone range, bordering the National Park, its giant peaks rising up like spectres in the dim background saying "thus far and no farther shalt thy vision penetrate." Then the grand mass of granite upon which we stood, so long the fascinating *terra incognita* of the northwest, and today the richest field of promise in all our broad land, afforded a study never to be forgotten. Mountains upon mountains rolled up toward our common footstool like the exaggerated waves of an ocean — with "white caps" of snow for "white caps" of foam — these when analyzed becoming live forests of refreshing green or fire-licked forests of sombre brown and gray, sheltering hundreds of mountain torrents, leaping waterfalls, pine-embowered parks and rock-girt lakes. It was simply a survey of America's best hunting-grounds, her deepest and grandest solitudes, and her land richest in native tradition, adventure and "extravagant possibilities." Much abler pens filled columns with glowing descriptions of those "dizzy altitudes, blackened cliffs and awful gorges," and yet the half has not been told.

The formation is principally limestone, with granite and slate occasionally cropping out. There is also some conglomerate showing in the Big Horn cañon, and sandstone on the south fork of Powder river.

From foot-hill to summit the mountains north of Cloud peak are covered with a dense growth of pine; south of this bare ridges and peaks predominate. There are several high points, the most prominent being Hayes and Cloud peaks, whose bald heads rise one thousand feet above their fellows. On the south side of these mountains and on the main divide are a number of pretty little lakes, the largest about two miles in circumference. These are clear as crystal, often very deep, and some of them fringed with perfect masses of water lilies.

The creeks, owing to their rapid descent, have nearly all cut deep cañons in the solid limestone, making it almost impossible to travel lengthwise in the mountains when not near the summit. But they compensate the traveler for their roughness by their beautiful and grand scenery. Waterfalls and cascades, rocks

worn into fantastic shapes, and the ever-luxuriant foliage, where
it can obtain foothold, complete a picture never tiring to the eye.

During the recent jaunt of Generals Sheridan and Crook in
the Big Horn region, a determined effort was made by members
of the party to further explore the dizzy heights. Their success
is gossiped of as follows by the Chicago *Tribune:* "The party
left the Union Pacific railroad at Bryan, and proceeded north in
stages to Camp Brown, in the Wind River valley, Wyoming Territory, thence to a camp at the base of the Big Horn mountains.
At this point a scientific party composed of Lieutenants Bourke,
Schuyler and Carpenter was made up to ascend this heretofore
unexplored mountain. That is to say, no one has ever reached
the actual summit of Cloud Peak. After reaching an elevation
of about 13,000 feet they were unable to proceed farther, owing
to the inaccessible rocks encountered. They, however, reached
a higher point than any former party. Several like attempts
have been made during the occupancy of the Big Horn country
by United States troops in 1867-8, but none have been successful. Amongst other interesting occurrences of this exploration
was the discovery and naming of Hayes Peak, a point jutting
out from Cloud Peak, and the highest mountain of this range.
A large collection of the fauna was made, including some very
interesting discoveries of new species. These have been properly
preserved, and will be forwarded to the Smithsonian Institute.
While on this subject it may be as well to say that General Welsh,
of Chicago, who accompanied the expedition in the cause of scientific investigation, shot two of those rare animals known as
the prock and camelco,—so some of those who were there say.
Any persons interested in zoology should call on the general for
a detailed description. Of course all kinds of game were killed,
including black-tailed deer, mountain sheep, mountain bison,
and two bears. Of the latter, General Sheridan killed one and
General Crook the other. The generals were in luck. The bison
is a species much smaller than the buffalo, as fleet almost as a
deer, and as sure-footed as a big-horn sheep."

# CHAPTER II.

EVER since the explorers of our own race have commenced their efforts to penetrate and hold the Big Horn region, it has been the scene of strife and the jealously guarded rendezvous of different savage nations. The Crows and Shoshones, long the faithful allies of the whites, have for years disputed vainly with their powerful and deadly enemies, the Sioux, for its possession, and have sacrificed their best blood and treasured property in the never-ending war. These tribes and others call the Big Horn and Tongue River regions the most beautiful of America, the most favored for game and fish, and the natural home of the buffalo, elk and deer. The Crows say, beautifully, "The Great Spirit only looks at other countries in summer, but here he lives all the year." Another tribe have a tradition which tells them that this country is nearest the "happy hunting ground," and that the warrior who falls here is particularly favored, because he makes only one short step from the old scenes to the enchanting new.

Some of these savages tell us that many years ago, when their people had no horses, and, in fact, when tribes known by other names freely roved the land, that strange people came from the south and east, commenced to found homes in the solitudes, and worked among the rocks in the mountains. The country was made to yield rich treasures of not only furs, but something which was found in the ground, and native jealousy only brooked the loss for a few years, when it destroyed all of the strangers in their new homes. A little further down the ages the savages found these glittering treasures themselves, but they cared less for them than for their bales of furs. Then, still later, when missionaries and trappers appeared upon the scene, and the rightful owners of the wilds were taught the value of gold, trespassers were more closely watched than ever, the stronger tribes

13

announced their determination to hold this, their last and best hunting-ground, forever, no matter what the cost might be. Finally, with the establishment of fur-trading posts, came the oft-repeated proof of golden riches found somewhere in the region — proof furnished by the Indians themselves, who frequently showed pouches of gold and glittering ornaments of the same metal.

At the time when hordes of frenzied California gold seekers were crossing the continent, not a few penetrated portions of the Big Horn region, and subsequently laid claims to rich discoveries there. Again, during and after the Montana and Pikes Peak stampedes — which have resulted in the development of two of the grandest metal-yielding centers in the world — numerous small and a few large parties of miners entered this region, and found enormous prospects, but supernumerary savages as well. The writer has frequently interviewed members of some of these parties, and has always been met with the same general statement that gold was discovered in quantity, but that it would require thousands of men to hold the country against the Sioux — the latter a truth which the experiences of 1876 only too thoroughly demonstrated. These pioneers have faithfully bided their time; have followed our different military expeditions through the region, in the hope of again viewing their treasure vaults, and at this date they are delving early and late in the shadowy gulches of the Big Horn to attain the same end; and with the changes in the Indian policy inaugurated by President Grant early in 1876, and the advent of General Crook into this department, the present state of affairs promises a permanency never before thought of. Today hundreds of men are scattered from end to end of the region which one year ago was regarded as practically impenetrable by any force short of two or three regiments of well disciplined troops. Camps, trading posts and mail routes are established, and the daily six-horse coach is a thing of the not very distant future.

*Gold in the Big Horn Mountains.*—As to the existence of gold in the Big Horn mountains, the writer can only say that "colors" have been found in nearly all the streams between Powder river and the Yellowstone. Our personal knowledge in the matter is confined principally to tributaries of the Powder, and to a stream flowing westward from Cloud Peak. In these we know fair prospects were made from surface gravel. But in accepting the many testimonials in succeeding pages, which come from reliable sources, there is no room left for doubt; and it is now only a question of special locality, the general distribution of fine gold throughout the gulches clearly indicating that at some point in this great range the wonderful deposits referred to by Father De Smet will be found. Immense deposits of decomposed gold-bearing quartz are found at many points, from base to summit, of the higher mountains. The veins are clearly defined, and ledges of from five to twenty feet in width protrude from the vast walls of granite so plainly that they can be traced for miles. Among the early discoveries were several large masses of this rock, which were most beautifully seamed and specked with flakes of native gold. Within the past few weeks several small shipments of Big Horn gold have been made from Cheyenne and Laramie city, the specimens being very coarse (weighing from fifty cents to ten dollars each), and the gold of very fine quality. The latest arrivals at Cheyenne have most flattering news from the mountain tributaries of Tongue river. There are nearly 3,000 prospectors scattered along the different streams, and considerable coarse gold has been found. Owing to the melting of very deep snows, however, water had up to July 15 been too plentiful, and bed-rock could not be reached in the best localities on account of the floods. It is unfortunate that no more satisfactory intelligence is available at this writing, but the work of another month will undoubtedly prove the claims of those whose testimony follows:

In the month of July, 1859, Captain W. F. Reynolds, of the corps of topographical engineers, under orders from the War Department, penetrated from Fort Pierre, on the Missouri, to the Black Hills. He explored the northern and northeastern portion of them, and then wended his way to the Powder river, Yellowstone and Big Horn countries. In his report, on page 14, under head of "Mineral Products," he says: "Very decided evidences of the existence of gold were discovered by us in the valley of the Madison and in the Big Horn mountains, and we found some indications of its presence also in the Black Hills, between the forks of the Cheyenne. The very nature of the case, however, forbade that an extensive or thorough search for the precious metals should be made by an expedition such as I conducted through the country. The party was composed in the main of irresponsible adventurers, who recognized no moral obligation resting upon them. They were all furnished with arms and ammunition, while we were abundantly supplied with picks, and carried with us a partial stock of provisions. Thus the whole outfit differed in no essential respect from that which would be required if the object of the expedition had only been prospecting for gold. The powder would serve for blasting, and the picks and shovels were amply sufficient for the primitive mining of the gold pioneer, while the arms would be equally useful for defense and in purveying for the commissariat. It is thus evident that if gold had been discovered in any considerable quantity, the party would at once have disregarded all the authority and entreaties of the officers in charge and have been converted into a band of gold miners, leaving the former the disagreeable option of joining them in their abandonment of duty or of returning across the plains alone, through innumerable perils. It was for these reasons that the search for gold was at all times discouraged, yet still it was often difficult to restrain the disposition to 'prospect,' and there were moments when it was feared that some of the party would defy all restraint."

As early as 1869 Lieutenant Maynadeer wrote of that country, in his report of his explorations, the following: "The valley of the Yellowstone offers the greatest advantages of any part of the country explored. It is fertile enough to yield generously to the farmer, and the capacity of the hills for grazing is unlimited. It is the paradise of the Indian, and in every direction it is marked by the track of vast hordes of buffalo, antelope and elk, which subsisted upon it. This will apply to the Yellowstone from the mouth of the Big Horn river to the mountains. Nearly all the country inside the curve of the Big Horn mountains is also of this description. There is every reason to believe that the mineral wealth of the mountainous portion is very great. I purposely discouraged any desire among those under my command to search for gold, but in several instances small quantities of the sands of some of the streams were washed and found to yield gold. Moreover, the geological features of these mountains are precisely similar to those of California and the neighborhood of Pike's Peak (Colorado), which abound in gold. But it is hardly probable that the gold could be obtained profitably, except by large outlays of capital and concerted operations of organized companies."

Mr. Thomas Sun, late government guide and scout, from long continued travel, has a very general knowledge of the Big Horn country and its approaches, and all information given by him is vouched for as implicitly reliable. Mr. Sun makes Rawlins, Wyoming, his home when not in the mountains, and can be referred to for any farther particulars. In giving the writer a short sketch of his adventurous career in the mountains of the northwest, he said:

"I am a native of the Province of Quebec, and left my home when only eleven years old to come to the States. Three years afterward I joined some hunters and trappers on the Missouri river who had spent many years in the employ of the Northwestern American Fur Company. With them I lived several years, and have during that time and ever since trapped, hunted and prospected in the northwest, as well as acted in the capacity of guide to government expeditions and private hunting parties. During the past eight years I have hunted and prospected principally in the Big Horn mountains and Sweetwater country, and have traveled many hundreds of miles all over them, and I think for the miner, the farmer and the stock-raiser this country is, without doubt, the finest and best to be found anywhere. Gold, no doubt, from discoveries already made, exists in great abundance in the Big Horn mountains, and the valleys have the best ranch lands in the west.

"Sweetwater valley alone is about 75 to 80 miles long and from 35 to 40 miles wide, with an altitude of about 6,000 feet above the level of the sea. It is surrounded by mountains covered with fine large timber, and watered by a number of rivers and creeks along which are splendid hay lands. Very large bunch grass grows on the plains, affording stock plenty of good feed summer and winter. I am quite sure that no finer stock country is to be found in the world. Upward of 2,000 cattle are now on these plains, belonging to Montana stock-men, who have told me they intend driving a very large number in there this summer."

In speaking of gold in the Big Horn country, Mr. Sun said: "When I was on the Missouri river some twenty-three years ago, I saw the late Father De Smet at Yankton, in Dakota, and heard him giving an account of some portions of his life amongst the

Indians. He told my partners and myself that he had no doubt but that the Big Horn country was the richest gold field in the whole world, and he prophesied that when the Indian troubles were over his words would come true. He had seen several of the whites, who lived and hunted with the Indian tribes, panning dirt which showed gold in large quantities, and he had himself made many very rich discoveries, but could do nothing in the way of developing them, as the Indians would not permit white men to mine in the country. He had also seen large nuggets in the hands of the Indians on very many occasions.'"

Mr. Sun added: "My partners and myself have discovered good paying diggings and some rich quartz leads, and I know of several parties who have made some rich strikes at different points in the Big Horn mountains, but none of them could be worked, as it was too great a risk for small parties on account of the Indians.

"In 1862 a party consisting of five French Canadians, I. Patneen, J. Dubois, and three others whose names I have now forgotten, outfitted at the Sweetwater crossing of the old stage road (where the route from Rawlins to the Big Horn crosses this road), to go into the mountains and work some placer ground they had previously found, and which they said was very rich. It was during the rush to Idaho and Montana in that year. They endeavored all in their power to persuade some of the many parties traveling along this route, bound for those Territories, to join their party to the Big Horn to strengthen it, as they feared trouble with the Indians. But although they offered to show them very rich ground, they were unsuccessful, and had to go alone, and, as they were never heard of again, it is thought they must have been killed. Being quite certain that the representations made by these men were honest and true, and the prospects, from what they said, most favorable, as they were willing to risk their lives in an Indian country to work their discovery, my partners and myself, while out hunting, made a trip to the place where they said they had found the gold, and there saw traces where white men had camped and had prepared to mine. I have no doubt it was the same party, no other miners having ventured into the mountains at that time.

"The following was told me by old man 'Dakota,' who, if living, is the oldest mountaineer in the northwest, and I have heard the same statement from Bruere, Paul Packet and Lami-reaux, all old mountaineers, and also from many others: 'That before California was known as a mining country, an old free trapper named La Pondre, who always hunted and trapped alone, making long journeys into the Big Horn mountains — that being his favorite hunting ground — had in his possession several large nuggets sufficient to fill his bullet pouch, and which they all saw with him. But in those days the value of gold in its crude state was not known amongst the trappers, they having come into this country young boys, like myself. Old man La Pondre stayed round Fort Pierre, and exhibited his nuggets freely to his friends, amongst whom were the men I have named. He told them he was going to St. Louis, and if what he had in his hand was what he expected it was, namely, gold, he had done with trapping for furs, as he could find enough of the stuff to buy up the American Fur Company whenever he liked. He left St. Pierre to go to St. Louis, telling the men to be on hand and stay round, as he was coming back in the spring, and would take them with him to the place where the gold was. He said it was lying free in the bed of a creek, on bed rock, where there was any amount of it.

"Travel to St. Louis in those days was slow. The trappers used to make boats of buffalo hides and fill them with their bales of furs, paddling down stream to St. Louis, and returning in barges hauled or cordelled by ropes from shore. When old man La Pondre arrived at St. Louis he showed what he called his yellow bullets and found they were gold nuggets of great value. The American Fur Company at once offered him great induce-ments to show them where he had found them and wanted to buy him out, but he refused to tell them or sell at any price, as he said the company did not always act on the square with the people in their employ, and he was going to have the first show for himself and his friends.

"It was the custom for the trappers and hunters in those days to work for two or three years and then make a trip to St. Louis to draw their money and have a good time. Old man La Pondre, after finding that he had made such a wonderful discov-ery of gold, feeling rich on the strength of it, and knowing where he could make a good haul in the Big Horn if he got broke in St. Louis, took in too much bad whisky forced on him by some of the Fur Company's men, who wanted to get hold of his secret, and he died from this and cholera. Thus he died without disclosing anything about the place where the gold was to be found in the Big Horn, and was buried at St. Louis.

"I have myself seen gold in the possession of Indians at Boray's ranch and at several other places, which they traded at the posts for goods. But this is no reason for me to suppose that they took it from the ground themselves, and I should rather suspect that they had taken it from miners whom they had found in the mountains and killed."

Asking Mr. Sun to give his opinion of the new country as a hunting-ground, he enthusiastically replied: "For game no place in the world can beat the Big Horn country; there are any amount of antelope, black and white tailed deer, Rocky-mountain sheep, elk and moose, buffalo and bison, cinnamon, black and grizzly bear, and Rocky-mountain lion, wild cats, silver-gray, black and red foxes, etc. Mountain grouse, sage hens, geese, ducks and chickens are found in great abundance. Swarms of trout and other fish in the streams."

Interviewed by a reporter a month before his death, General Custer had the following to say about early gold-hunting in the Big Horn region, and the characteristics of the country:

"The mining party from Bozeman that I spoke of, set out for that region. A few persons had contrived in the past, when the Indians were not troublesome, to enter a portion of it, and they returned with wonderful stories of the riches hidden there; and fine specimens of gold were shown as proof. General Sheridan, in his letter to General Sherman, corroborates this view, and he thinks that the wealth of the Big Horn country will be found to surpass that of the Black Hills. Beyond report nothing positive is known about it.

"In passing westward from the Black Hills we find a low, rolling landscape, the timber growing smaller and scarcer, until the plains are reached, so that the Black Hills are a cluster separate and distinct from the great range. We gradually approach the upheaval, which is the commencement of the Rocky Mountains.

"No snowy peaks can be seen as you leave the Black Hills, but when nearing the Big Horn the Big Horn mountains appear, and as the march continues their white peaks come out in glit-

"ONE TOO MANY."

tering splendor.  As the mountains are precipitous, abrupt and
of a peculiar formation, and as many stories are told of the
wealth that is in them, western people are of the opinion that
this is the locality to which gold seekers must go if they would
make their fortunes.

"Numerous rivers flow through the cañons out to the plains,
and they are very clear and full of trout.  Wind river flows
through the Big Horn mountains, through a cañon which is
between fifty and one hundred miles long, and it has never been
explored.   Bridger, the famous Indian scout, claimed to have
passed through it, but there is no definite record of its ever having been explored."

Old Jim Bridger, the mountaineer, who has spent forty-five
years in the Rocky Mountains, tells the following story of his
discovery of gold in the Big Horn region :

"In the spring of the year 1859 I was employed by Captain
Reynolds, United States Engineers, as a guide and interpreter to
an exploring expedition of the government, commanded by the
above-named officer, whose purpose was to explore the head-
waters of the Yellowstone and Big Horn rivers, and various other
streams in the Big Horn country.  The party consisted of Captain Reynolds, Lieutenant Lee, and one company of United
States soldiers commanded by Captain Menadier, Dr. Hayden
and several other scientific gentlemen, a number of teamsters
and other employes.

"One day, after having traveled a few days in these regions
known as the Big Horn, I, feeling thirsty, got off my mule and
stooped down at a small brook containing clear and inviting
water from the snow-capped mountains to drink, and while so
doing my attention was attracted by the curious appearance of
the bottom of the stream.  It appeared to me like yellow pebbles
of various sizes, from that of the head of a common pin to a
bean and larger.  Though well acquainted with the appearance
of gold, I was somewhat in doubt of its being the precious metal,
since it had never occurred to me that gold could be found in
that locality; but my curiosity being excited, I scooped up a
handful of the stuff, and rode up to Dr. Hayden and Captain
Reynolds.  Both at once pronounced it pure gold, and asked me
where I had procured it.  After I had told them where I had
found it, Captain Reynolds got very much excited, and insisted

that I should cast it away, and not tell anyone of the party of the matter under any circumstances, he fearing that a knowledge of gold in such abundance and of such easy access would certainly break up his expedition, since every man would desert to hunt for gold. I very reluctantly complied with the officer's request. Since my first discovery of gold I have found the same metal in that country while trading with the Indians, though not in such abundance as the first."

James Bridger is now an old man, but still hale, hearty and active. Nearly his whole life has been spent in the Rocky Mountains and among the Indians. Bridger Pass and Cut-off, on the old emigrant road to California, were named after him many years ago. Mr. Bridger now makes his home in Jackson county, Missouri, near New Santa Fé.

General P. E. Connor, who led an expedition through this region ten years ago, says in a letter to the writer concerning it: " I did not have time to examine its mineral resources, but from information derived from some of my officers and men I am of the opinion that silver and gold will be found in paying quantities on the headwaters of Powder, Tongue and Big Horn rivers and their tributaries."

Frank Grouard, the widely-known chief scout of General Crook's principal expeditions, has frequently told the writer of his knowledge of placer gold in this range, and of his finding it in fine large nuggets. In a letter recently received from him he uses these words: " In the northern portion of the Big Horn mountains there is plenty of gold that I know of myself." Mr. Grouard was for six years a prisoner of Sitting Bull, and in his rambles with the hostiles had ample opportunity to make these discoveries.

Dozens of other reliable authorities could be quoted, but these must suffice, as we wish to take a glimpse at the other resources of this interesting region.

# CHAPTER III.

THE future importance of the Big Horn region rests much less upon the development of rich mines than the average reader can now realize. There is a wealth of farm and grazing lands which alone will soon attract thousands of eager husbandmen and supply the whole northwest with bread and beef. One of the pleasing peculiarities of the country, and one to be considered here, is the water supply. For nearly two hundred miles along the northeastern base of the Big Horn mountains the clearest and most beautiful of streams sweep violently down through their picturesque gorges and course northward 150 miles to the common reservoir — the great Yellowstone. These often occur at intervals of less than five miles, and it is seldom that more than a dozen miles of the unequaled uplands separate them, or that crystal springs do not send pretty laterals bounding over gravel beds to the more pretentious creeks or rivers. These mountain streams and sheltered valleys are more numerous throughout this region than are water-courses in any of the half dozen Rocky Mountain Territories which the writer has had the pleasure of thoroughly viewing. And here he is willing to stake his reputation upon the assertion that none of the Territories can boast a region of similar extent so favored in all the natural elements of fertility, beauty and practical value to producers as is found here along the eastern and northeastern base of the Big Horn mountains.

The soil of the valleys is usually a porous loam, rich, black, bottomless — so far as the needs of the farmer are concerned. Every element of fertility seems to be present and every species of vegetation attests its wonderful nourishment by a most luxuriant growth. Of course rain, out in the lower valleys, "other than the dripping skirts of some mountain shower," are as rare as the average western farmer could wish. But with these numberless dashing streams, bearing with their beauty the impalpable fertilizers of crumbling mountains, irrigation would be a pleasure rather than a task. Vegetable life does not differ very materially from that in Rocky Mountain regions, four hundred miles further south, except that here the same varieties nearly always have a much stronger growth. Wild rye is found in large patches, so tall that a cavalryman could nearly, if not entirely, hide himself in it while mounted. Wild oats, native blue-grass and all the varieties of plains grasses present this same strong testimony of fertility of soil and congenial climate by their heavy carpetings and unusual height. The average altitudes of the valleys being less than 4,000 feet, the region of summer frosts is not reached. Experiments made in the cultivation of the soil at Fort Smith, on the Big Horn, and Fort Kearney, on the Piney, during their occupation ten years ago, proved that all vegetables and cereals commonly grown in temperate climates were thoroughly adapted here. While following the fortunes of General Crook, during the summer of 1876, the writer was furnished a striking example of the possibilities within range in this line even much farther north. When the lamented Custer marched across the Yellowstone region from Fort Lincoln, Dakota, early in the spring, the surface was thoroughly soaked by the more generous rains of that northern country, and his wagon trains cut deep gashes into the black soil. Grains of corn often leaked from the sacks composing these loads and fell into the ruts. When with Crook's gallant division on the terrific march of August following, we crossed Custer's trail, the corn was found growing far above the tops of the highest grasses — some of it as high as our heads — and was evidently in a fair way to mature.

It is the purpose of the writer to prove beyond the shadow of a doubt all claims made in this volume, and where opinions of reliable parties concerning important points are to be obtained, they are inserted. General Luther P. Bradley, of the United States army, spent several years in this region during its occupation by the military, and in response to inquiries made several years ago, put himself on record as follows:

"I respond very cheerfully to your request for information about the climate, soil, grasses, etc., of the country on the east slope of the mountains, from the Big Horn down to the Republican and Smoky Hill, which I prospected or scouted pretty thoroughly in 1867 and 1868. From the Smoky Hill, in about latitude 39 north to latitude 44, the country is very much like that immediately around the Union Pacific railroad, with which you and the traveling public are familiar. The character of all this country is rolling prairie, very well watered, and abounding in good grasses to such an extent that the assertion may be safely made that the supply of grazing is unlimited.

"All of the streams in this range furnish some timber, and many of the tributaries of the Republican, Powder, Tongue, Big Horn and other rivers are covered with heavy forests of hard and soft wood. All of the bottom lands on the streams flowing from the mountains are what would be called east, good, reliable farming lands, fit to produce any of the regular crops, except, perhaps, corn. The only danger to the corn crop would be, I suppose, the shortness of the season, and the frequency of frosts consequent on the extreme altitude of this section.

"North of latitude 44 the country changes materially for the better. It is better watered, having an abundance of pure, clear mountain streams. The soil is richer, the grasses are heavier and stronger, and the climate very much milder than that for several degrees south. I think the valleys of Tongue river, Little Horn, Big Horn and the Yellowstone, will produce corn, and good corn, too. About the other crops, barley, wheat, potatoes, etc., there is no question. This, I take it, shows about the maximum of soil and climate, for there is no question about the value of a country that embraces hundreds of millions of acres, that will produce good crops of cereals and grasses.

"The valley of the Big Horn, five to twenty miles in width, by about one hundred miles in length, I regard as one of the choice spots of the earth. Here the climate, soil, scenery and natural productions combine to make a country I have not seen excelled anywhere from Georgia to Montana, and equaled only by the favorite countries along the Ohio, the Cumberland or the Tennessee. The prevailing winds are westerly, bringing the mild airs of the Pacific to these inland slopes, and tempering the winters of latitude 45° and 46° to about the temperature of the mountain country of Kentucky and Tennessee.

"The value of this country for grazing may be estimated from the fact that good fine grasses grow evenly all over the country, that the air is so fine that the grasses cure on the ground without losing any of their nutriment, and that the climate is so mild and genial that stock can range and feed all the winter and keep in excellent condition without artificial shelter or fodder. The fact of grasses curing on the ground is a well-known peculiarity of all the high country on the east slope of the mountains, and in this is found the great value of this immense range for grazing purposes.

"The difference between grasses which have to be cut and cured and those which are preserved on the ground, is enough to convince the stock-raiser and herder of the value of these immense ranges known as 'The Plains.' I believe that all the flocks and herds in the world could find ample pasturage on these unoccupied plains and the mountain slopes beyond, and the time is not far distant when the largest herds and flocks in the world will be found right here where the grass grows and ripens untouched from one year's end to the other. I believe there is no place in this section of the country, from latitude 47° down, where cattle and sheep will not winter safely with no feed but what they can pick up, and with only the rudest shelter. In the mountains, or in the valleys of the mountain streams, they would find ample shelter from storms in the frequent cañons and ravines.

"The mountain ranges are peculiarly adapted to sheep raising. The range is unlimited, the grasses are fine, and the air is pure and dry— conditions which insure healthier stock and better wool than the climate and soil of the low country.

"I have said that the climate about Big Horn was very mild ; as an indication of this I will state that the average temperature in the valley, latitude 45° 30', was in December, 1867, 32° above ; in January, 1868, 20° above; in February, 40° above, and in March 55° above. In August, 1867, the mercury was as high as 107° above. Coal, iron and fine building stone are plentiful in the mountains of the Big Horn ranges. Fine clay and limestone are found in abundance, and the mountains furnish good pine timber in fair quantity. Nature has provided most liberally for the wants of civilization in this favored region, and when it is opened up to settlement it will attract a large population, and will prove to be a great producing country."

General Raynolds, who had occasion to winter in this region several years ago, uses this language in his official report:

"Through the whole of the season's march the subsistence of our animals had been obtained by grazing after we had reached camp in the afternoon, and for an hour or two between the dawn of day and our time of starting. The consequence was that when we reached our winter quarters there were but few animals in the train that were in a condition to have continued the march without a generous diet. Poorer or more broken down creatures it would be difficult to find. They were at once driven up the valley of Deer creek and herded during the day, and brought to camp and kept in a corral through the night. In the spring all were in as fine condition for commencing another season's work as could be desired. A greater change in their appearance could not have been produced, even if they had been grain-fed and stable-housed all winter. Only one was lost, the furious storm of December coming on before it had gained sufficient strength to endure it. This fact, that seventy exhausted animals, turned out to winter on the plains the first of November, came out in the spring in the best condition, and with the loss of but one of the number, is the most forcible commentary I can make upon the quality of the grass and the character of the winter."

The small rain-fall along the Big Horn mountains is confined to the spring and early summer months. There *is no dew*, and sickness is so rare that, for many days in succession, out of large garrisons of soldiers who were stationed here ten years ago, not one could be found at the hospital. The summer temperature rarely exceeds ninety, the nights always being deliciously cool and refreshing. While the mercury sometimes ranges very low in winter, the cold is far more endurable than in the low eastern sections. The writer has campaigned along these mountains, and far to the north, in midwinter, without tenting and with but scanty bedding, when mercury solidified, and out of five hundred men composing the expeditions not one suffered permanently from frost-bite. Being the chosen winter home of the buffalo and other game, and the choice herding ground for many years of thousands of Indian ponies, this whole region has long since gained the appellation, on the frontier, of the "stockman's future paradise."

The valleys and uplands are totally unlike those of Colorado, or even eastern Wyoming. In those sections it is often difficult to tell where valley ends and upland begins, because the two are

14

so naturally merged by broad stretches of gently-sloping plain. In the Big Horn region the line of demarkation is as plain as the wall of China. The uplands are usually several hundred feet higher than the valleys, and when the visitor descends into the latter he reaches stretches of unmistakable lowlands — but never a slough or marsh, — stretches that may be exquisitely narrowed to almost cañon width or swelled into graceful parks of from two to ten miles wide, and with always the dark valley soil and grateful valley foliage and vegetation. Natural hay lands are really not plentiful, considering the extent of all the valleys, because such an item as overflow of valleys or a permanent swamp is never known. But where stock will not need an ounce of artificially prepared food, as here, there will be little use for extensive hay lands, and enough of the very best quality of hay can be cut for all possible needs. The fall of all the streams is so great that every farmer can have his own system of irrigation, if he desires it, and there is no danger of future quibbles about water-rights in this most bountifully-watered of all regions.

Many of the valleys contain enough cottonwood, ash, box-elder and other timber to supply logs for fuel or building purposes for years to come. But the great mountains overlooking on the one side, and many of the bluffs on the other, are covered with forests of pine, hemlock, spruce, cedar, etc., furnishing building material for all time. We opine that about every other settler will own a coal mine, as the "black diamonds" crop out almost everywhere, and are known to furnish an excellent quality of fuel in numerous localities where tests have been made.

Commencing at the south and naming the more prominent streams in their order northward, we have Powder river, Crazy Woman's Fork of Powder, Clear Fork of Powder, Big and Little Piney, Penoe creek, South and North Forks of Goose creek, Tongue river, Rosebud, Little Big Horn, Grass Lodge creek, Rotten Grass creek, Big Horn river, the latter's numerous tributaries flowing from the northwest, and the Yellowstone. These, in other portions of the west, where moisture is not so abundant, would all be called rivers. Indeed, with their great fall, their wonderfully-swift flow, and their often respectable breadth of channel, they deserve such appellation even here. Then it must be remembered that dozens of large creeks and brooks, drawing their supply from the never-failing snows in the mountains, and from some of the most extensive and beautiful limestone springs on the continent, are not mentioned — they are nameless as they are almost numberless, but in their rambles to the sea play none the less important parts.

In briefly describing some of these prominent streams and valleys we may be frank in commencing by declaring that we have nothing good to say of Powder river, the southern boundary of the Big Horn region. Its waters are darkly mysterious and villainously alkalied; its southern tributaries ditto; and it is far from a fitting gateway to the land of beauty and plenty just outlined. However, the valley soils are among the richest in all the northern region, and the flanking bluffs furnish very fair grazing lands. The stream rises in the Powder River range, flows almost due north to the Yellowstone, and in its tortuous windings has a length of over 300 miles. The valley is from one to three miles wide, is well timbered with cottonwood, and shows the coal formation almost everywhere. Cantonment Reno, garrisoned by United States troops, is located on Powder river near the crossing of the Cheyenne and Big Horn road. It is a general outfitting point for Big Horn miners. The most direct and well-traveled road from Deadwood to the Big Horn region strikes the Cheyenne road near here.

Twenty-six miles north is Crazy Woman's Fork of the Powder. Its waters are clear, flowing over a gravelly bed, and it drains a more desirable region than the parent stream. But not until Clear Fork of Powder, twenty miles north of the last named stream, is reached does the visitor feel thoroughly possessed of that enthusiasm we are endeavoring to inspire. The landscape surrounding is perfect in its loveliness, and the broad valley is very nearly our ideal of a spot for the creation of most inviting homes. The valley is four or five miles wide and seventy miles long, and besides being quite well timbered at the point of crossing possesses greater stretches of hay lands than most others in this section. A ranch and trading post, called Murphy's ranch, the first to be located in the Big Horn region, is found here at the crossing.

Twenty miles travel farther north over grazing lands which are not equaled south of the Platte anywhere, brings the visitor to the forks of the Piney — the road crossing them just above their union. The ruins of old Fort Phil Kearney, near the road, stimulate disagreeable thoughts about the played out peace policy, and lead us to think what a shame it was for a powerful government to lose its grip upon such beautiful domain, and to allow the massacre of its subjects by the hundred. These valleys are about as extensive as that of Clear Fork, are just as beautiful and fertile, and undoubtedly will soon teem with the best life our Yankee enterprise can bequeath. A few miles away lies Lake De Smet, named after the noted missionary. It is about two miles long and nearly a mile wide, and for its shores has a circle of gracefully rounded hills. Myriads of geese, ducks and other water fowl, with evidently little appreciation of danger, float its surface, and in the shallow water of the beaches we noticed innumerable small insects, resembling fish animalculæ. But the water is so wonderfully brackish and charged with alkaline salts that it is doubtful whether fish could exist in it.

In reaching the different forks of Goose creek, tributaries of Tongue river, about twenty miles farther north, we are in the heart of the choicest portion of the Big Horn region. Where the two principal forks of Goose creek unite the valley is nearly ten miles wide, and right here is the garden of the whole northwest. Unequaled ranch sites for either farming or grazing purposes lie up and down the valley for a distance of twenty-five miles. This spot has long been the loved rendezvous for our different savage tribes on fete days or during their grand revelries of hunting and feasting. The streams here furnish fine trout fishing. Hayes and Cloud Peaks overlook the scene and the old Sioux Pass across the Big Horn mountains is close at hand.

A dozen miles or more northward is Tongue river and its many feeders. Tongue river rises in the snow fields of Cloud Peak, and flows out northward two hundred miles to the Yellowstone. The river is extremely crooked and the valley is not often more than two miles wide, its tributaries furnishing more arable land than itself. Shortly after leaving the Big Horn range it is flanked by the Big Panther mountains on the south and by the Wolf and Little Panther mountains on the north. Although these ranges are extremely rough and often well timbered they hardly deserve to be called mountains, as they are generally only from five hundred to one thousand feet in height. The writer does not believe that indications warrant any of the statements recently made that these ranges are mineral-bearing.

Where gold has been found in them, it is our belief that it must have been the wash of deposits far up in the Big Horn range.

Down along Tongue, and other rivers here in the heart of "Indian Ground," are many evidences of savage eccentricity. Many of the cottonwood trees have attained great size, and

GOOSE CREEK RAPIDS, BIG HORN REGION.

numbers which have died are still standing, their bark having all dropped off, leaving a smooth and sometimes almost perfectly white surface. These have often been ornamented by savage artists, the beds of ochre in the vicinity furnishing a pretty fair article of paint for the purpose. One would bear the picture of an Indian horse-race, with the brutes neck and neck, bending

down to their work.  On another would be the scene of a san-
guinary engagement in which white men, pierced with arrows or
bullets, were tumbling from their horses.  But some of these
trees were desecrated by pictures of a still more atrocious and
revolting nature by the hands of these vandal artists, and in
future years, when happy homes take the places of the present
reigning solitude, residents can better judge from some of these
how worthy are our savage wards of the consideration they are
receiving.

Northward still are numerous valleys running out at right
angles from the mountains, and in passing on to the Montana
settlements, a distance of about 300 miles, one is rarely out of
sight of them.  The Big Horn, however, is our limit to the
region we have been describing, and is distant from Tongue river,
by the Cheyenne and Montana route, about seventy-five miles.
The Rosebud, which lies between the Tongue and Big Horn, and
which empties into the Yellowstone, drains a grazing region
which, as a packer who had served all over the trans-Missouri
country said, "beats the world."  From the lowest depth of the
valley to the summits of the highest hills the different varieties
of native grasses grow as though cultivated, and are not only
very thick upon the ground, but attain greater height than elsewhere.  The valley is wide and picturesque, covered with splendid
meadow and possessing numerous large groves of cottonwood.
The soil is deep and practically bottomless, as those of us who
had our horses mired in it in the creek-bed can testify.

The Big Horn and its tributaries probably water more arable
valley lands than any of these streams, the valley of the Big
Horn alone being from three to ten miles wide and over a hundred miles long below its grand cañon.  Large areas of hay lands
here make up for their scarcity elsewhere in the region.  The
Big Horn furnishes choice trouting and is navigable during
early summer months by light-draught steamers to a point some
seventy-five miles above its junction with the Yellowstone.

The belt of land drained by these streams, and to which
reference is made here, lies wholly east or northeast of the Big
Horn mountains, and that portion of it particularly desirable to
the settler lies within twenty-five miles of their base.  West of
the range the region is not generally so fine—although a number
of good valleys are there found—until the valley of the upper

Wind river and its numerous tributaries are reached. These possess the same general characteristics and attractions as the ones on the east side and are already being quite extensively settled.

Bounding this region on the north is the navigable Yellowstone, of which General J. W. Forsythe, of Sheridan's staff, has reported as follows, after one of his visits:

"The Yellowstone river, from the highest point reached by us to the mouth of Powder river, sweeps through the country in long and majestic stretches, with a current of at least four miles an hour. Its bosom is studded with islands by hundreds, some of which are three or more miles in length and covered with cottonwood groves; and many of them are so handsome that they almost make the voyager believe that they are the well-kept grounds pertaining to some English country house. I never saw so fine a growth of cottonwood in my life as on the Yellowstone, twenty-five miles above Tongue river. These trees will run from three to five feet, and some are six feet in diameter. The supply of cottonwood and pine which exists throughout the upper Yellowstone country is ample to meet all the requirements of any settlement of the valley; and the indications are that large beds of coal can be found and worked in the neighborhood of Powder river.

"The mouth of the Big Horn may be regarded as the head of navigation on the Yellowstone river, and for three months of the year this river presents less obstacles to its navigation than the upper Missouri, and, indeed, many other rivers in this and other countries. The channel is unchanging, for it passes over a gravel bed from its head to its mouth, and there are no snags. When this is contrasted with the shifting and unreliable water of the upper Missouri, it ought to make the rates of insurance less on the Yellowstone river than on the upper Missouri.

"We found the greatest abundance of game along our entire route — antelope, bear, black-tail deer, elk, mountain sheep; also herds of buffalo, between Tongue river and the Big Horn, as we went up; but before we returned they had all crossed the river and gone north.

"We steamed up the Big Horn river for a distance of twelve miles, found it quite crooked, with a narrow valley, and were obliged to return on account of the water becoming distributed over so wide a space that the main channel did not afford a sufficient depth of water for us to continue our course. The current of the Big Horn was about as strong as that of the Yellowstone: water muddy, and at the mouth it was about 150 yards wide. Where it joins the Yellowstone the points of land on each side are small prairies with good grass. On the east bank the bluffs run close to the river and are sparsely timbered. On the west bank the valley is mostly filled with cottonwood, and the hills are about 150 feet high, with plateaus on the top. Near the point where we turned back there was a small stretch of prairie about a mile wide and a mile and a half long. The north bank of the Yellowstone, opposite the mouth of the river, is a sandstone bluff, 150 feet high, with rolling plateau on top covered with sage and some bunch grass.

"Where Pryor's river empties into the Yellowstone, sixty-two miles above the Big Horn, is a small stream, twenty-five feet wide, winding through the western part of the prairie, which extends from Pompey's Pillar to it. Very little lumber on it. It is reported to have a fine country near its head-waters.

"After passing above the mouth of the Big Horn the growth of pines is much larger. At a distance of from twenty to thirty miles back from the river, on the south side, a park country exists, as is evidenced by the abundance of game coming from that direction. Miners have found color in prospecting for gold in the different streams in the mountains of this locality. As the tributaries of the Yellowstone have a gravelly bottom of igneous and metamorphic rocks, porphyry, granite and quartz, there is no reason that there should not be gold found, even in considerable quantities, in this formation. The Yellowstone river has its source in the Yellowstone lake, and takes a course a little west of north until it unites with Shields river. At this point it takes a general direction a little north of east to the mouth of Powder river, and thence a due eastern course to the Missouri. In low water the stream is navigable with ease as far up as Pompey's Pillar. The fish of the Yellowstone consist of catfish near its mouth, shiner, catfish and jack salmon between Powder river and the Big Horn west of Powder river. Buffalo, elk, antelope, mountain sheep and beaver are found in great numbers. The Yellowstone valley above the mouth of the Powder river can all, or nearly all, be cultivated, as the soil is rich. The islands, many

YELLOWSTONE LAKE, NATIONAL PARK.

of which are very large, could be cultivated. There is abundance of coal and pine wood that could be taken out with profit. The water is fine. . . . And in the valleys there grow large quantities of wild plums, cherries, crab-apples, grapes, gooseberries, buffalo berries, currants and wild strawberries."

That portion of the Yellowstone valley with which the writer is more particularly conversant lies between the mouths of the Powder and Rosebud, and is one hundred miles long. In this portion we have seen a vast extent of fertile valley and superbly grassed upland. The bottoms often widen to an extent of three or four miles, and occasionally reach a width of ten miles. These are generally ornamented by large groves of cottonwood. The high lands adjacent rise up in picturesque terraces, terminating in broad and wonderfully level plateaus, and covered with a splendid growth of bunch and grama grasses. River, valley and surroundings often blend into the most exquisite landscapes. A stream broad and majestic as the Upper Mississippi; banks gently sloping, or occasionally rising vertically a hundred feet above the water's edge; graceful groves, almost forests, shading and beautifying every bend; and distant mountains with their deep, rich tint of purple, unite to create a picture as pleasing as could be wished.

Why, with cheap river transportation, even these far northern limits of our possessions should not soon be sending cargoes of beef, mutton, wool and grain to lower river marts, it is not easy to see. Then, with our Wyoming and Montana railroad soon to pass along the eastern base of the Big Horn mountains, this proud northwestern empire cannot want for outlets or the most desirable means of communication. Tri-weekly mail service is now furnished by the government from Bozeman and Fort Ellis, Montana, to the mouth of Tongue river, a distance of 350 miles. This is for the accommodation of the military permanently stationed on the Yellowstone, as well as for the benefit of small settlements already clustering near.

# CHAPTER IV.

### FRUITS, FLOWERS, GAME, FISH, ROUTES, ETC.

OF wild fruit there is a great variety in all these northern valleys. Raspberries, strawberries, red currants, plums, cherries and rock grapes are among the number. The settler will certainly not have cause to complain in this respect, and if the growth, so prolific in its native state, gives reliable foretaste of what can be done by cultivation, the production of improved varieties must some day be an important item. During one of our visits some of the valleys were perfect orchards of wild fruits and beds of native flowers. Observing particularly along the Piney, near the site of old Fort Kearney, we found the valley a perfect mass of plum and cherry blossoms, which, with the flowers, fairly charged the air with a delicious fragrance.

Most of the varieties of flowers are those common all along the Rocky Mountains, although a few very lovely varieties seemed entirely new. The rose, blue-ball, butter-cup, daisy, phlox, violet, lily, and dozens of others familiar everywhere as household words, are waiting here to surprise old admirers who may think they are to lose them when they seek such far-off wilds. Nature could not be more extravagant with the gift of flora than that everywhere found inside the Big Horn mountains. In every park, by the side of every stream and lake, and under the shade of either thrifty or ruined groves, we found the same dense masses of scarlet, purple, white, blue and yellow, with all the intermediate shades imaginable. The visitor here in the higher altitude can enjoy the strange sight of blooming strawberries within a few yards of snow-banks, or pluck flowers with one hand and have the other immersed in an all-the-year drift.

As has already been intimated, this is the paradise for hunters, white or red. It was choice ground for the hundreds of Fur Company employes half a century ago, and many were the batteaux, or Mackinaw boats, which floated down the great rivers

from these wilds, freighted with the richest offerings of field,
forest and stream. A pretty good joke — and one with solid
foundation in fact — is told at the expense of one of the prominent officers who led a large expedition through this region
about ten years ago. The column was near the forks of the
Piney, and scouts came back with the report that a large body of
Indians was moving up the valley, with evident intent to attack.
The general hastened forward, took in the terrors of the situation with his field glass, and soon had his forces posted in first-
rate style for defense. The attacking column advanced in very
close order, and kicked up so much dust that little could be seen
of it. But it surged on resistlessly. Men were holding their
breath in the tremor of suspense, and just as they expected the
order to fire a sharp breeze wafted away the dust, disclosing a
herd of a thousand elk — *ten* thousand, our informant says, but
we should prefer not to spoil a good story.

Elk, buffalo, mountain sheep, black and white tailed deer,
antelope, grizzly and other varieties of bear, with all kinds of

small game, find
in this region their
deepest solitudes
and their own
most coveted sur-
roundings. Many
of the streams are
yet full of beaver
and other fur-
bearing animals,
and the region is
literally alive with
several species of
the wolf. From estimates furnished by Indian traders, we are of
the belief that the value of all kinds of furs taken in this region
annually by savages, before the commencement of the Sioux war,
and traded at the agencies, would not fall short of $200,000. The
presence of the prairie chicken here is a fact worthy of note. It
is the first recorded instance of its having attained such an
extreme western range, although its gradual extension westward
in the path of cultivated fields has been known for some time.

The Yellowstone, Big Horn and Tongue rivers, and their thousand tributaries, are plentifully supplied with trout, mountain pike, shiners, catfish, suckers and other varieties. In the rivers and larger creeks the beautiful speckled trout attain a weight of from three to six pounds, while in the brooks a half-pound trout is a very fair average. We have caught these smaller and far more delicate trout, in large quantities, in simple rivulets where there was scarcely room for even such delicate bodies to navigate.

Before passing to the subject of routes, it may be well for us to have a few words on the Indian question. We do not assert that the last American Indian has surrendered his claims to this his loved home, nor do we believe that hostilities are forever at an end. A few small bands of renegades, who do their work under cover of night or from ambush, are yet prowling over the country, and probably will be until they are hunted down. But we have no fears of an extended outbreak so long as the present military management is continued. With officers like General Cook at the helm; and granted all the latitude they need, the question of the early redemption of any frontier is settled. Three thousand determined miners have already crossed Powder river on their way to the Big Horn, while a large battalion of cavalry is kept constantly at work along the base of that range, in endeavors to ferret out the remnants of savage tribes left. Then more than a full regiment of cavalry is stationed permanently along the Yellowstone, to punish depredators from the British possessions. With all this force and a determination upon the part of our people to occupy this region — and the back of the Sioux nation broken — it will be passing strange if the few straggling savages which are left can hold out till the leaves of autumn fall.

*Routes.*—The Cheyenne route from the southeast is the only one which yet furnishes a complete list of camping places and which has been measured by odometer. It is also the only one yet traversed by the writer, and therefore the only one of which he can speak understandingly. It is the old overland Montana route, possesses a splendid road-bed and easy grades from beginning to end, and lies over the country soon to be traversed by the Cheyenne and Montana railway. Following the regular Black Hills road to Hunton's ranch, on the Chugwater, the emigrant then branches off to the northwest upon the old and constantly traveled government highway to Fort Fetterman. Such clear, strong streams as the Laramie river, Horseshoe, Big Cottonwood, Elkhorn and La Bonte creeks are crossed *en route*, affording fine camping places with plenty of wood and pure mountain water. The only unfordable stream, the Laramie river, is spanned by a fine public bridge. At Fort Fetterman an excellent ferry facilitates the crossing of the Platte at seasons of high water. From thence northwest a distance of ninety miles, over choice grazing lands, the traveler will find as fine a road as crosses any portion of our prairies. This stage of the journey completed, Cantonment Reno, on Powder river, is reached. Forty miles distant the grand Big Horn range rises in plain view, and the journey thither is finished easily in a day's ride. At the Powder river crossing a good stock of provisions is always on hand, and that point will be found a most convenient outpost. A weekly mail now goes to that point *via* Cheyenne.

There has been such a wide difference made in distances from different points to the rather indefinite "base of the Big Horn mountains," that we compile all tables to read to the "base of Cloud Peak." Following is an accurate table of distances over the Cheyenne route:

|  | Miles. |
|---|---|
| Cheyenne to Lodge Pole Creek | 16 |
| Lodge Pole Creek to Bear Springs | 20 |
| Bear Springs to Chugwater | 14 |
| Chugwater to Hunton's Ranch | 15 |
| Hunton's Ranch to South Laramie River | 22 |
| Laramie River to Cottonwood Ranch | 20 |
| Cottonwood Ranch to Elkhorn | 25 |
| Elkhorn to Wagon Hound | 15 |
| Wagon Hound to Fort Fetterman | 16 |
| Fort Fetterman to Sage Creek * | 14 |
| Sage Creek to South Fork Cheyenne River | 18 |
| South Fork Cheyenne to Antelope Springs † | 21 |
| Antelope Springs to Dry Fork of Powder River | 23 |
| Dry Fork Powder to Cantonment Reno | 14 |
| Cantonment Reno to Crazy Woman's Fork | 27 |
| Crazy Woman's Fork to Clear Fork | 20 |
| Clear Fork to base of Cloud Peak | 25 |
| Total | 325 |

* No wood.                    † Water poor and scarce.

Rawlins furnishes the shortest routes, but, of course, is yet behind in the way of improving them. There are two roads, as follows:

### FIRST — VIA WHISKY GAP.

|  | Miles. |
|---|---|
| From Rawlins to the Paint Mines | 3 |
| " Paint Mines to Bell Springs | 9 |
| " Bell Springs to Sand Springs | 26 |
| " Sand Springs to Whisky Gap | 15 |
| " Whisky Gap to Sweetwater River | 8 |
| " Sweetwater River to Sunk Creek and junction with Seminole route. | 8 |
| " Sunk Creek to Rattlesnake Range | 8 |
| " Across Range to Poison Springs Creek | 8 |
| " Poison Springs Creek to Cloud Peak | 125 |
| Total | 210 |

### SECOND — VIA SEMINOLE MINES.

|  | Miles. |
|---|---|
| From Rawlins to the Paint Mines | 3 |
| " Paint Mines to Brown's Cañon | 9 |
| " Brown's Cañon to Seminole | 23 |
| " Seminole to Sand Creek | 10 |
| " Sunk Creek to Sweetwater River (bridged over) | 15 |
| " Sweetwater River to Sunk Creek and junction with Whisky Gap Route | 8 |
| " Sunk Creek to Rattlesnake Range | 8 |
| " Across Range to Poison Springs Creek | 8 |
| " Poison Springs Creek to Cloud Peak | 125 |
| Total | 209 |

The roads on these two routes to the Sweetwater river are well defined, easy of travel for teams, and a good down grade all the way from Rawlins. They come together at Sunk creek, sixty-eight miles from Rawlins and eight miles north of the Sweetwater river. Good camping ground can be found at each point where the mileage is given above. The Seminole route has been traveled over more than the Whisky Gap route, it being the road generally used to the Seminole and Ferris mines and mining districts, and also to the Sand Creek settlements; both roads are, however, equally good for ordinary travel. The Sweetwater river is bridged over, but it can be forded nearly all the year.

The Green River route, from Green River City, possesses the advantage of having a daily stage, mail and express, 160 miles of the distance, and of passing through a tolerably well-settled

region and a number of mining towns on the way to Camp
Brown.    Following are the camps:

| | Miles. |
|---|---|
| Green River Station | 9 |
| Alkali Station | 12 |
| McCoy's Ranch | 27 |
| Dry Sandy | 22 |
| Pacific Springs | 13 |
| South Pass City | 12 |
| Atlantic City | 4 |
| Strawberry Diggings | 2 |
| Camp Stambaugh | 5 |
| Miners' Delight | 2 |
| Red Cañon | 9 |
| Eagle Ranch | 9 |
| Lander City | 9 |
| North Fork | 3 |
| Camp Brown | 11 |
| Cloud Peak | 149 |
| Total | 298 |

Fare by the Sweetwater daily stage line is $27 to Camp
Brown; forty pounds of baggage allowed.    Express freight, six
cents per pound.    The Sweetwater line is in excellent trim to
stock the entire route to Cloud Peak whenever the demand
arises for through coaches, as it now possesses first-class equipment and runs one hundred miles nearer than any other.    Running time to Camp Brown, thirty-six hours.    Green River is
well supplied with good outfitting houses.

Evanston, at the extreme western end of Wyoming, offers a
good route to all parties from the west, as indicated by the following:

| | Miles. |
|---|---|
| Evanston to Lander's Cut-off | 20 |
| Lander's Cut-off to Ham's Fork | 25 |
| Ham's Fork to Robinson's Crossing on Green River | 18 |
| Robinson's Crossing to Big Sandy | 28 |
| Big Sandy to Little Sandy | 9 |
| Little Sandy to Dry Sandy | 14 |
| Dry Sandy to Pacific Springs | 10 |
| Pacific Springs to South Pass | 12 |
| South Pass to Camp Stambaugh | 6 |
| Camp Stambaugh to McGraw's Crossing on Beaver Creek | 25 |
| McGraw's Crossing to Cloud Peak | 160 |
| Total | 327 |

15

The Evanston *Age* asserts that "the road from Camp Stambaugh to Sioux Pass passes through a beautiful and fertile valley where there are plenty of springs for water. In fact, the whole route from Evanston to the Big Horn is an old traveled road; plenty of grass, wood and water is found the entire distance, and passes through a country where the Indians never trouble anyone. After leaving Camp Stambaugh the prospector will find color in every pan of dirt he takes up, and when he arrives at Sioux Pass he is only about fifty miles from old Fort Reno, and in the midst of the gold fields."

The distance from Deadwood to Cloud Peak *via* the Pumpkin Butte trail is, as nearly as we can at present ascertain, 200 miles. No route east of the Black Hills and *via* that region is practicable for the Big Horn travel, for the reason that all of them pass over an unsettled and unprotected wilderness from 500 to 700 miles wide. From Virginia City, Montana, to Cloud Peak, the distance is 365 miles, as follows:

|  | Miles. |
|---|---|
| Virginia City to Bozeman | 70 |
| Bozeman to Yellowstone Ferry | 51 |
| Yellowstone Ferry to Clark's Fork | 90 |
| Clark's Fork to Big Horn River | 63 |
| Big Horn river to Cloud Peak | 91 |
| Total | 365 |

The road is an excellent one the entire distance, and numerous good camping places are found between the points above laid down.

# CHAPTER V.

---

## THE BLACK HILLS.

THE Black Hills of Wyoming and Dakota, a section of timber-covered hills, whose dark-blue appearance from a distance gives them their name, are situated between parallels 43½ and 45 north latitude, and the 103d and 105th degrees of longitude west from Greenwich. They are nearly encircled by the north and south forks of the Cheyenne river, have an extent of about one hundred miles north and south and sixty east and west. The boundary line between Wyoming and Dakota runs through them a little west of the center.

This section, lying like a green oasis in the midst of a vast, open, level plain, has a climate peculiar to itself and totally at variance with that of the country immediately surrounding it. While the surrounding plains but a few miles distant are parched with drouth, this section is abundantly supplied with moisture at all seasons. Clear, running streams traverse it in all directions, affording an ample supply of water for mill, mining and domestic purposes and every use which the wants of man require.

The principal streams are the Belle Fourche, with its tributaries, Spearfish, Whitewood, Rapid, Bare Butte and smaller streams on the north and east, and South Cheyenne, with Elk, Box Elder, Spring, French, Castle and Beaver creeks flowing in it on the south and west, with all the small streams feeding them, furnishing a water supply that is unequaled, except, perhaps, in the Big Horn country. Springs of clear, cold water are also abundant.

The elevation is comparatively low, the valleys at the base of the hills being only about 3,000 feet above sea level, and the highest peak only 7,000 feet. The gulches or valleys through which the streams flow are at an elevation of from 3,000 to 4,500 feet, with a fall of from twenty-four to forty-eight inches perpendicular to one hundred feet horizontal distance.

*Early History.*—As there has been a great diversity of opinion regarding the first discovery of gold in the Black Hills, it may not be amiss to give some facts and reports, obtained by diligent research and persistent inquiry, as to whom belongs the honor of having been first to discover gold and mine for it in this region. It is very evident that long before the present excitement gold was found and taken from the streams of the Black Hills. It is well known to many miners and prospectors that there are indications of white men having visited the Hills at some former period, but to whom these traces are due they have been unable to determine. We intend to place such new facts before our readers as we have been able to obtain, believing they will be of general interest.

Mr. H. N. Magnire, of Deadwood, who has been giving considerable attention to this matter, makes the statement, which he believes reliable, that, in the summer of 1852, a party of 300 men left Council Bluffs, Iowa, to cross the plains and mountains in search of the wealth said to lie in the streams of California. They were led by Captain Douglas, of St. Joseph valley, Michigan. After a long, weary march, they reached Fort Laramie, where they rested several days, and while there a company of thirty men left the main party to prospect in the mountains north from that point, and agreed that, if they discovered gold, they would overtake the main party at the Humboldt river and report. Eight of them did overtake the party, as agreed, and reported that they found gold upon two streams (which from the description were undoubtedly Rapid and Spring creeks), but that, owing to the amount of water and depth of the earth, they were unable to reach bed rock. They then moved on to the northern portion of the Hills, where they discovered gold in paying quantities, and sent the party of eight to overtake the main body and induce them to return. This party reached the Humboldt late in the season (November), and the Indians being troublesome it was deemed unsafe to return, and all went on to California.

The twenty-two who remained in the Hills were never heard from, and, without doubt, perished.

Then we have the statement of Jeremiah Proteau, an employe of the American Fur Company, who was stationed at Fort Laramie from 1848 to 1854, giving an account of his experience in northern Wyoming and the Black Hills. The truth of his account is beyond question, as it has been corroborated by contemporary reports. He says: " I left the fur company at Fort Laramie in 1854 and engaged with Sir George Gore as hunter and teamster. James Bridger was employed as guide. We left Fort

PROTEAU'S GOLD MINE.

Laramie early in the fall for the Yellowstone country, taking a route which led us past the Black Hills on the southern and eastern base, and reached the mouth of the Yellowstone late in November. We then marched up the Yellowstone to Tongue river, where we built a fort and remained for the winter, hunting and trapping.

"The following April we started with ten carts and forty

men, crossed the head of the Rosebud and went to the Big Horn
river, where we built flat-boats and floated down the Big Horn
to the Yellowstone, and down that river to its mouth, where we
met Sir George, who had made the trip by land. From there we
came down the Missouri, and ascended that stream to its head,
and then struck across on to the Belle Fourche and down to Bare
Butte, and spent some time on the Swift or Rapid creek and Box
Elder in the Black Hills.

"One Sunday I went out to the falls of Swift or Rapid creek
with Lamourié. The falls were quite high and emptied into a
broad basin. As we were standing by the falls I noticed some
yellow-looking stuff in the water, and I said to Lamourié —

"'By George, there's gold!'

"I took off my shirt and scooped up three double handfuls of
the yellow stuff, and put it in my shirt. Then Lamourié and I
went back to camp. Sir George noticed me as we reached camp,
and asked me what I had in my shirt. I said, 'Gold.' He then
looked at it a little while, when he said, 'O no, Jerry, that's not
gold; that's mica.' I was not very well posted about gold and
thought Sir George was. He took it and put it in two black
bottles, and placed them in his chest. The next day we marched
out of the Black Hills, and two or three days after Bridger told
me that Sir George told him it *was* gold. Sir George also told
Lamourié that if he would prospect on the head of Swift creek
he would find rich gold there. We left the Black Hills on account of the Indians, and when we got back to the Little Missouri we were attacked by about five hundred Indians, who ran
off all our horses."

G. T. Lee, now a merchant, residing at Central City, in the
Black Hills, says: "In 1863 I left my home in Missouri with
twelve others, and started for Montana. We traveled to the
north of the Fort Laramie road and came to the Black Hills,
where we prospected for gold and found sufficient to induce us
to remain. In one locality two of the party, with myself, sawed
and hewed out some boards, and made three sluice boxes with
which we took out in three days $180 in dust. At this time a
fall of snow eighteen inches deep so alarmed us that we left for
Montana, intending to return as early as possible in the spring.

"We reached Montana in December, and succeeded so well that
we did not return. In 1876 I returned to the Hills, intending to

locate where I had mined before, but have not as yet found the spot; but I intend to make further search this summer, and believe I will yet discover it."

The traces left by some of these early gold hunters have excited no little interest. In 1876 some miners prospecting on Battle creek discovered an old shaft about ten feet deep, and thinking it might be an easy place to reach bed-rock, they sank it about ten feet deeper, where, at the depth of twenty feet from the surface, they found an old shovel and a pick. The wooden handles were decayed and the iron badly rusted.

On the same creek some parties unearthed a skull at a depth of three feet, and near by found a pair of silver-bowed spectacles, which looked as if they had lain there a long time. Near by are a number of prospect holes, in some of which are trees growing, the largest about six inches in diameter; also an old oak tree over two feet in diameter, which was chopped down so long ago that the top is entirely decayed. Near Montana, on Whitewood creek, some miners unearthed an old hammer and a small poll-pick at a depth of fifteen feet, badly rusted.

An old hatchet was found below Deadwood, or Whitewood creek, which shows evidence of having been buried for many years. Between Rapid City and Galena there is an old trail, along which are stumps which are so badly decayed that the slightest blow upturns them, showing the ax marks where they were chopped. The bodies of the trees have disappeared.

An oak tree stands in a gulch near French creek which has a hole chopped in the side, plainly indicating the work of an ax. The annular rings of growth overlaying the ax marks show that it was cut over twenty years ago.

With these facts before him the reader can readily see how fallacious is the popular belief that the Eldorado has been unknown and unappreciated until the present. The first mining —during the present excitement—was done on French creek, near the stockade, by Gordon's party, in the winter of 1874-5, though General Custer's party prospected during the summer of 1874, and found gold in French and Spring creeks.

*The Mineral Wealth of the Black Hills*—Consists of gold, both placer and quartz; silver in quartz, carbonates, sulphates and argentiferous galena ores, and perhaps, in some locations, gray copper; copper in small quantities, and iron in the form of hematite, and block iron. Mica has been found in plates large enough to be valuable. Large beds of gypsum are found in the red beds surrounding the Hills. Coal has also been found in large quantities. The mineral bearing belt proper extends about sixty miles north and south, and from five to ten miles in breadth, the richest deposits, as far as known, being in the vicinity of Deadwood and Galena, though some good ore has been found near Custer.

The quartz deposits are mostly in decomposed quartzite and slate, and though not generally extremely rich in gold, are so easily worked in stamp mills that nearly all the rock will pay for milling. The silver deposits have not been worked to any extent as yet. In the vicinity of Bare Butte some mines have been opened and very rich ore taken out, but as it requires smelting to obtain the silver, and there are no smelting works in operation, the actual value of the mines is not yet thoroughly determined.

Gulch or placer mines are found on nearly all the streams in the Hills, but the principal work has been on Deadwood and Whitewood gulches, in the northern portion, and the smaller gulches running into them. About $1,500,000 in dust were taken out of there in 1876. The introduction of improved machinery, however, will make it profitable to work many other gulches and "hill diggings." Not until the deep gravel deposits on Spring, French, Rapid and lower Whitewood creeks are thoroughly developed, will inquirers realize the vast riches of the region. Potato and Nigger gulches have furnished the bulk of the coarse gold, several thousand dollars in nuggets having been brought to Deadwood, the smallest piece of which would weigh twenty-five cents, while some would weigh over $100.

On Rapid creek, near Rapid City, Messrs. Boughton, McIntyre & Co. have a ditch and flume over three miles in length, giving them a head of water along the bars of from twenty-five feet to one hundred and fifty feet. They are working five bars and expect to run from six to twenty hydraulics and employ from one hundred to five hundred men. Their works have cost over $10,000. Other companies are putting in works on Spring and on Whitewood creeks.

A great many reports have been in circulation regarding the amount of gold taken out of Deadwood; some of them so extravagant that we have taken pains to learn the truth in regard to them. It is found, from the best authority, that out of one and a half claims on Deadwood creek, Wheeler and his two partners took about $140,000, their expenses probably being $20,000, leaving about $40,000 for each partner; the claims were then sold for $3,000, and the parties now working them have taken out about $30,000, and are still taking out good pay. These claims are the richest that have been worked. Several others have yielded from $25,000 to $50,000 each.

The quartz lodes which are now being worked extensively on the Hills in the neighborhood of Deadwood gulch and Lead City are destined to make that section the principal milling point. There are at least twenty good mills either finished at present or in course of erection. Pinney's mill, at Central City, was the first stamp mill in the Hills, started the 1st of January, 1877. It is working an excellent grade of ore from the Alpha and Omega mines. Pearson's mill commenced work May 1, 1877, and crushes fifteen tons per day to ten stamp. One run on ore from the Fairview mine — about 150 tons — gave $359\frac{1}{2}$ ounces, worth over $7,000. The Hidden Treasure mill was the first in the Hills to crush quartz; it was started in the fall of 1876 with a pulverizer, but was changed to a twenty-stamp mill in May, 1877, and is taking out large quantities of gold.

The mills at Lead City are also doing well. The cost of mining the ore worked at these mills is about one dollar and a half per ton, and it can be milled at an expense of four dollars. The bulk of the quartz runs from eight to forty dollars per ton.

There are a large number of gold lodes which promise richly, among which are the Father de Smet, Fairview, Hidden Treasure, Deadwood, Aurora, Keats, Luella, Chief, Golden Star, Anchor, Giant and American Flag. Among the promising silver lodes in the vicinity of Galena are Red Jacket, Florence, Treasure, Hart, Red Cloud, Sitting Bull, Il Refugio, Mammoth, Lone Star, Caribou, Monte Christe and Popoagie. Two smelters are in course of erection and the value of these mines will soon be determined.

Among prominent sales of mining property thus far effected are the following: The Golden Terry was sold for $50,000; the Florence for $51,000; one-half of the Keats sold for $50,000; Home Stake, $50,000; and the Dustan for $20,000. A number of others have been sold at nearly as good figures.

The milling of the gold ores in the Black Hills is a simple and not very expensive process. The quartz being "fed" into large iron boxes with small streams of water running through them, where the constant dropping of heavy iron stamps reduces the rock to powder, which is carried by the water through fine screens and dropped upon copper plates coated with quicksilver, which catches the particles of gold and holds them while the rock and other metals are carried away by the water. When the quicksilver has become loaded with gold, it becomes solid enough to scrape from the plates, and is then placed in a piece of buckskin, where, by a strong pressure of the hands, the quicksilver is forced through the pores of the buckskin and the gold is left behind in a solid lump held together by a small quantity of quicksilver which still remains. This is removed by heating in a close retort until the quicksilver becomes vaporized and passes through the tube of the retort into water, where it condenses and is saved; the gold being left in the retort is now ready for market.

The process of saving the gold in gulch-mining is to throw the sand and gravel into long boxes or sluices, through which a constant stream of water is flowing, which washes away everything but the gold and black sand, these being caught by cleats nailed across the bottom of the sluice. Where the gold is fine, quicksilver is placed in the sluices, and catches the gold as in the quartz mills.

The amount of gold taken out in the Hills from April, 1877, to July, 1877, is estimated at $1,500,000, and that a little larger yield will be furnished by the gulches by the time work closes in the fall, which, with that taken from the quartz by mills, will make an aggregate of $4,000,000 for the summer's work. This reaches market about as follows:

Dust and retorts consigned to Cheyenne banks ................. $2,000,000
   "            "      shipped to Denver and the east by individuals...  1,000,000
   "            "      carried out of the Hills by northern routes ......  1,000,000

    Total ............................................. $4,000,000

To extract silver from the ore is a much more expensive process, requiring furnaces to melt the rock and separate the metal, which must then be separated from the baser metals by another process. The smelting and refining works being very expensive, and the cost of running them much greater than in milling free gold ores, requires the silver ores to be much richer than gold ores to make them profitable.

It is estimated that not more than one-third of the present population of the Hills are furnished employment in mining or kindred industries, and that at least 10,000 people are out of work. There are various reasons for this. The country was pretty well overrun by experienced prospectors months before the great stampede which has resulted in such a large population of non-producers, and as the "poor man's mines" are comparatively limited in number they have been rapidly claimed. Many people went to the Hills with a determination to engage in mining and nothing else. Disappointed in their first plans, they have often either given up in despair, a burden upon the settlements, or else have gone home to curse the country. Of the thousands who have flocked to the Hills a very large proportion reached their destination without a dollar or the prospect of getting a meal, and, of course, such had no way of engaging in stock raising, farming or lumbering. even on the smallest scale. But no stampede is without its lesson and advantage to almost every participant, or without its ultimate grand benefit to new sections of country. In the present case the gold hunting furore has led to the peopling of a rich region, which otherwise would have remained a howling wilderness for half a century. It is also resulting in the settlement of the vast Big Horn and Yellowstone regions, which, without the all-powerful incentive of gold, would for ages have failed of redemption from savage sway. However much individual participants may suffer in the start, their necessities will drive them to exertions never dreamed of before, and when, as members of our grand army of producers, they go hand in hand with prosperity, they will thank the influence which held them to a new land and forced them to a new life.

Mechanics and miners who do find employment get from three to five, and in exceptional cases as much as six, dollars per day. Board and lodging at the cheapest houses is from six to eight dollars per week ; at good hotels from ten to fifteen dollars. In the mode of living so commonly called "batching it," where four or five men club together, buy their own provisions and do their own cooking, one can subsist at a cost of anywhere from three to six dollars per week.

The writer does not desire to encourage a further migration of mining prospectors to the region known as the Black Hills proper. It will be noticed from the foregoing data that the country already contains a preponderance of this worthy class. But while turning the adventurous seeker of precious metals to the hundreds of square miles of unprospected territory in the Big Horn and Wind River ranges, attention is especially called to those fields here offering rich reward for development. The judicious investment of capital in the immense deposits of mineral already discovered and the faithful labor of the stock-grower and farmer are invited on every hand, with almost absolute surety of excellent returns. In no region of similar extent in the new west are mineral deposits more abundant and valuable, valleys more numerous and fertile, and pasture lands more extensive and luxuriant, than in the Black Hills.

*Agriculture.*—The fertile soil and abundant rain-fall of the Hills and the luxuriant growth of vegetation is evidence that agriculture can easily become one of the leading industries of this region. Nowhere can wild grasses of even tender varieties be found in greater abundance — a sure indication that cereals will succeed. The rain-fall, averaging five days per week during the growing season, insures against drouth, and the absence of noxious weeds makes husbandry a pleasure. In the high parks potatoes, cabbages, peas, turnips and other hardy vegetables will yield abundant crops, while in the lower valleys the grains will do better. Squashes, cucumbers and melons can be raised among the foot-hills, and the hardier varieties of corn will succeed.

Mr. Ed. Wolfe, at Crook City, commenced farming in the spring of 1876, and raised corn, potatoes, beans, peas, cucumbers, parsnips and carrots, all of which yielded largely. The present season he has planted ten acres in general crops, which are looking well and promise an abundant harvest. There are about one hundred acres of crops planted in the vicinity. Near Custer City crops of all kinds are looking well. Near Deadwood are a number of gardens, which furnish a supply of the finest vegetables. M. G. Tonn has about forty acres in the more important farm products, which are looking well. At Spearfish, in the extreme northern part of the Hills, there are several fields of grain of all kinds and small patches of garden vegetables, all flourishing finely. These successes, so general in all parts of the region, and at all altitudes, dispel every shade of doubt concerning the adaptability of soils and climate to agriculture.

A luxuriant growth of grass spreads over the whole region, even upon the steep hill-sides. The valleys of French, Spring and Rapid creeks are especially adapted to grazing, and between Cold Spring ranche and Jenny's stockade many hundred tons of hay can be cut the present season. The varieties of grass are almost endless; wild oats, wild rye, crowsfoot, chess and grama grass cover the valleys and hill-sides, while along the lower streams blue stem and rushes make excellent food for stock. Many thousand head of cattle and sheep can subsist in the Hills, the timber patches furnishing shelter from winds and storms, and the numerous streams and springs insuring them against thirst. For fine stock the parks and valleys cannot be excelled, sufficient hay can be cut in almost any locality to supply their wants during storms, and that of the very best quality. The cool, equable atmosphere and ice-cold water render this section unrivaled for dairying, and the mining population insure a good market for all dairy products.

With all these advantages it can be but a few years till the agricultural and stock-raising interests will far exceed the importance of the mines. The mining excitement is but a stepping-stone here, as it has been in California and elsewhere. It compels settlement, while agriculture and stock-raising are the industries which bring about thorough development.

*Forests.*—There have been extravagant statements in regard to the extensive forests of heavy timber in the Black Hills, which lead people into the belief that the supply is almost inexhaustible. In all the magnificent stretches of timber land the amount of timber that will furnish merchantable lumber is comparatively small. At least nine-tenths of the pine (which is all that will do for sawing) is young and too small for lumber. Good judges estimate that the total amount of merchantable saw timber in the Hills will not exceed 50,000.000 feet. Of this, about 15,000,-000 feet has been sawed and used, and it will require 10,000,000 more to finish the improvements in progress at present and in contemplation, thus exhausting nearly one-half the supply that is in the Hills. Now, allowing an equal amount of smaller timber that can be used for lumber, the amount is not enough to justify the assertions which have been made, that there was enough to supply the whole prairie country lying south and east. Those regions will be compelled to look toward the Powder river and Big Horn ranges for their timber.  Of smaller timber there is an abundant supply, unless it is destroyed by fires; but with the reckless waste which is generally found in newly settled countries, a few years will make good timber a scarce article in the mining districts.  Boughton & Beary, who are among the most extensive manufacturers of building material, have been compelled to move their mill from Deadwood to False Bottom, over twelve miles, on account of this scarcity, and they say that in less than a year they will have to move twenty or thirty miles to find logs to saw, and other mills will be compelled to do likewise.

The principal varieties of timber in the Black Hills are Norway pine, scattered over the whole extent of the Hills; black and white spruce, found on the north hill-sides of a large area of the country; burr-oak, along the foot-hills of the eastern slope; white elm along the streams in the foot-hills; cottonwood and box-elder along the streams; white birch, aspen, ash and mulberry are found in some sections, but with the exception of a small quantity of oak, the pine and spruce are all that are of any merchantable value.

The oak, which in some sections attains a good size, is often brittle and decayed, and unfit for anything but firewood.  The spruce is seldom larger than fifteen inches in diameter, the greater portion being less than ten inches, and will be found valuable for all purposes where strength and lightness are required, it being very light and elastic when seasoned.  The pine which is too small for lumber is well adapted for piling, ties, timbering mines, building small bridges, etc.  Lumber of the different grades sells at from $30 to $50 per thousand feet at Deadwood.

The wild fruits growing in the Black Hills are evidence that this can be made the fruit country of the northwest.  Large quantities of red raspberries, gooseberries, currants, service berries, bear berries, strawberries, plums, cherries and grapes are found in different sections of the Hills and along the streams. Hazel nuts and hops are also found, the hops making a growth that is scarcely equaled in the rich bottoms of the Mississippi and Missouri.

The flora of the Hills is extensive; many plants which are carefully propagated in the eastern States grow here in profusion.

Besides the flowers of the fruit-bearing plants, are roses, larkspur, wild geranium, asters, phlox, several varieties of lilies, pinks, and many others in wonderful abundance and of most brilliant hues.

## CITIES AND CAMPS.

*Deadwood.*—Deadwood, the present metropolis and grand objective point of all who journey to the Black Hills, is a noisy, bustling city of six or seven thousand souls. It is located in a narrow valley, at the junction of Deadwood and Whitewood gulches, near the northern extremity of the Hills. It was organized temporarily in April, 1876, and laid off into twenty-two lots, 100 feet by 50 feet, and building commenced. As hundreds of new comers crowded in, the gulch was laid out for a mile in length, and every lot occupied. On September 11, 1876, an election was held, and E. B. Farnum elected mayor; Sol. Star, Dr. Carter, J. Miller, — Philbreck, K. Kurtz and Judge Whitehead, councilmen; Con. Stapleton, marshal; and J. A. Swift, clerk and recorder. At the time of the location the county had not been open to settlement by the whites, and Indian "scares" and depredations were common. But the thirst for gold overcame all difficulties, brought thousands to these wilds, and in less than one year Deadwood grew from a few small log cabins to a city of seven thousand people, with buildings and improvements that are estimated to have cost a million dollars, and with business almost incalculable. It supports three daily newspapers and three weeklies; over two hundred shops and mercantile houses have been opened, up to this writing (July 15, 1877), some of them doing an enormous business; two large saw-mills are kept running night and day to furnish lumber, which is taken as fast as sawed and at once put into buildings. Three large banking houses, over thirty hotels and eating houses, with over seventy saloons and gambling houses are crowded with business, and everything is at a fever heat. Gold dust being the principal medium of exchange, everybody carried a sack or bottle to hold their change, and every place of business keeps gold scales to weigh out the change required. Everything has two prices, one for gold and the other for greenbacks, the currency price being ten per cent. less than gold prices. Two variety theatres are crowded every night, and Sunday as a day of rest is unknown.

These, of course, are flush times for Deadwood. The lower part of the city, called Elizabethtown, in honor of Miss Elizabeth Card, the first woman in the place, is devoted to manufacturing and to the business of small tradesmen. It also embraces the French settlement and Chinese quarters. A large saw-mill, a planing-mill, brewery, and other manufacturing establishments are in this part of the town.

Some idea of the amount of business transacted in Deadwood can be formed from the following facts. The banking house of Stebbins, Wood & Post was opened April 8, and in two months had purchased $150,000 worth of gold dust and $50,000 worth of retorted gold, their business amounting to $25,000 per day, and some days as high as $75,000. They have one of Mosler's 6,000 pound time-lock safes, and the only bank vault in the Hills. Graves & Curtis have sold over $50,000 worth of furniture, carpets, etc. Bent & Deetkin, druggists, do a business of $5,000 per month. The sales of clothing during the past year foots up over $75,000. Browning & Co., grocers, in less than thirty days sold goods amounting to $7,703.21, and bought goods to the amount of $15,364. Vandaniker & McHugh, proprietors of the IXL hotel, fed, in one day, over 1,000 people.

Deadwood has two churches, several large halls, a good bath-house, a fine system of water-works, and an efficient fire department. There are at present 1,500 buildings of all classes upon the ground.

The distances to various points in the Hills from Deadwood are as follows: Gay City, 1½ miles; Central City, 2; Lead City, 3; Crook City, 8½; False Bottom, 9; Galena, 12; Spearfish, 15; Rapid City, 40; Haywood, 55; Custer, 52; Greenley's Ranch, 10; Pine Grove, 20; Cold Springs, 30.

*Gay City and Central City.*—About two miles above Deadwood, on Deadwood creek, are the towns which claim to be the richest in the Black Hills, Gay City and Central City. Located as they are in a narrow gulch, with high hills on either side, they make a closely built business street over two miles in length. The mining (both quartz and gulch) gives employment to hundreds of men, and the large sums taken out makes money plentiful and wages very fair.

There are found the principal quartz mills, quartz mines and placers at present worked in the Hills. There are five quartz mills already at work, with several new ones nearly ready to commence operations, and the towns are insured a permanency which few other points can claim. The population numbers about 3,000.

*Crook City.*—Crook City, located in a beautiful park on Whitewood creek, eight and a half miles from Deadwood, was named in honor of General George Crook, whose successful campaigns against the hostile Sioux and Cheyennes have enabled the settlers to hold their homes. It was located March 15, 1876, and John Frazer elected recorder, and P. Grant, R. Low and C. Steele, trustees, and by the 1st of May had a population of 200. Its continued steady growth has increased it to a town of over 500 permanent residents.

Crook City is the natural outlet from Deadwood to the east and south, has very extensive mining interests, and, being situated in a fine agricultural region, must naturally become a prominent trading point.

Its business is far above the average of the towns of like size. There are twelve business houses which do an aggregate business of $400,000 per year. H. A. Douglas & Co., formerly of Perham, Minn., publish the Black Hills *Tribune*, the first issue of which was dated June 9, 1876.

Two saw-mills furnish scarcely enough lumber to supply the demand for building and mining purposes. There are three commodious hotels, the Headquarters, kept by Mr. Hazen, the Merchants and the European.

A good public school, with facilities for divine worship, add to the town's attractions for families. There are large quantities of fossils and petrefactions found in the vicinity, and the most extensive caves that have been discovered in the Hills are only a few miles distant.

*Rapid City*, forty miles south of Deadwood, was located on the 28th day of February, 1876, by a party from Spring Creek, consisting of J. R. Breman, J. Allen, W. Marsten, and others. It was named after the river which flows through it. It now has a population of about six hundred, with one hundred and fifty buildings completed, and a number in course of erection. Brennan & Nicholson are building the largest hotel in the Hills, and several large stores are also in progress.

Rapid river, which flows through the town, has a fall of sixty-

16

five feet to the mile, and an abundant supply of water for all purposes. The location being at the very verge of the plains will probably make it necessary to irrigate for agriculture, but the abundant supply of water in the river, and the amount of fall will render this an easy task. The low altitude will probably enable farmers to raise some crops which would not mature in the Hills. The climate is much warmer than at points farther up the river, and but little snow lays on the ground in winter.

*Hayward*, the county seat of Custer county, is situated on Battle creek, about fifteen miles from Rapid, and about the same distance from Custer; has three hundred inhabitants, three hotels, ten business houses, and about twenty saloons. David Young, of Youngstown, runs a local stage line from Rapid to Custer through the town.

The transaction of county business and sessions of court give the place considerable standing. The mines on Iron creek, Foster's gulch, Rosebud and Battle creek are tributary, and lend the town additional importance.

*Custer.*—The pioneer settlement in Black Hills, having the finest location and grandest scenery, is Custer city, situated in a broad, level valley on French creek, in the southern portion of the Hills, it is surrounded by low, grassy hills dotted with pines, with high peaks in the distance, forming a background to one of the finest landscapes in the county. It was laid out in the early part of July, 1875, and called Stonewall. But little was done in the way of building until August, when it was reorganized, and the name changed to Custer City. A plat of the town was then made on birch bark, there being no paper in the camp.

The latter part of August, pursuant to an order of the general government, the citizens were removed by troops to Fort Laramie, leaving six of their company, by permission, at the stockade to guard their interests. Late in the fall some of the settlers returned, and other parties coming in, the town commenced growing rapidly, and the 1st of May following it consisted of about eight hundred buildings, many of them being built of lumber. At this time the town contained over two thousand inhabitants, and all kinds of business enterprises were represented. However, the rich discoveries reported from Deadwood and Whitewood gulches caused a stampede that nearly depopulated the town, and from which it has never recovered.

CUSTER CITY 1876

STREET SCENE DEADWOOD

BEAR ROCK FRENCH CREEK

Its beautiful location and the large extent of mining country must in time bring in a large permanent population, and the fine grazing and agricultural lands insure its wealth and future prosperity.

S. M. Booth, proprietor of the leading hotel, and doing a large mercantile business, estimates the amount of gold taken out of the gulches near Custer at $30,000 per month, and increasing very rapidly. The whole population is at present about five hundred. The city boasts a printing office and thirty business houses, all doing a good business.

*Galena.*—Galena is the principal town of the Bare Butte silver mining region. It has a population of about 300, with 150 buildings. There are two assay offices, four stores, two saw-mills, and a smelter in course of erection. A large number of discoveries of silver mines have been made in the vicinity. There are fine areas of timber for fuel adjacent, and should the silver deposits prove as rich as they are now believed to be, Galena will soon rank among the prominent Black Hills cities.

*Spearfish.*—Situated on Centennial prairie, in the fertile Spearfish valley, about fifteen miles from Deadwood. The finest stretches of farming and grazing lands in the Hills are found here. Spearfish river affords the principal supply of fish for the mining towns.

*Society.*—The natural consequence of the indiscriminate rush of emigration from all parts of the Union into a region really unknown and scarcely redeemed from its original barbarism would seem to be social disorder of the worst kind. But instead of this a genuine disposition to maintain the morality which true manhood moulds has from the first been manifest. A broad generosity and a strict adherence to the equitable code of "miners' rights" were features especially noticed in our visit in the fall of 1876, and are scarcely less marked today. In the absence of law or adequate protection, the miners met and adopted such simple rules as gave the offender no chance for misunderstanding. If a petty theft was exposed, the criminal was drummed out of camp so quickly and unmercifully that a second example was rarely needed. In nearly all the diggings an organization was effected and the usual regulations adopted almost as quickly as the claims were staked off. The privileges then arising were considered settled and sacred rights, which were as universally respected as are the local laws in any portion of our land.

To fully appreciate this condition of affairs, the reader must remember that here was an utter wilderness, covering over 6,000 square miles, but two years ago the jealously guarded rendezvous of the most powerful tribes of Indians on the continent, without the slightest semblance of protection or regulation by the federal government.  In all our observations among the mines we have yet to witness the first dispute or misunderstanding that was not amicably settled.  A walk through the gulches at any time might reveal numerous prospect holes with the absent miner's pick and shovel at the bottom.  Asking about one of them the visitor would probably be answered, " Oh, that belongs to Jim Jones. Jim's gone over to Nigger Gulch, about twenty-five miles north o' here.  But that don't make any difference.  Here's where he makes his grub stake, and we all look out for his claim."  Walking into a new camp after the arrival of a mail and asking whether anything had arrived for yourself, the general result would be: " Look in that cracker-box over there, its got all the mail for the camp!"  Sure enough, every Tom, Dick and Harry would dive into that box among hundreds of letters, con them all over and honestly pick out his own.  It was freedom without rapacity; justice without excessive restraint.  It cannot be said of these people that in their prosperity they are avaricious.  We would sooner risk the chance of universal hearty welcome and unstinted hospitality in the rude huts of the miner than in a similar number of prosperous homes anywhere in the States. From the man who was cleaning up $500 in glittering dust per day to he who had made but his simple " grub stake " of flour and bacon, we have met with the same unvarying kindness.

In the towns where all classes of society can be found, and where it might be supposed that lawlessness would abound, there is a wonderful degree of good-fellowship shown.  The deeds of violence which sensational writers pronounce the rule, are, on the contrary, the rare exceptions.

The variety theatres, though crowded with all classes, are as free from objectionable features as the average variety theatre of the States.  In Deadwood there are two churches and a Sabbath school, well attended.  Crook City also has regular preaching. The Masonic fraternity have a lodge in Deadwood, established the latter part of June, 1877, and occupy a hall in connection with a lodge of Odd-fellows.

*Naturally Identified with Wyoming.*—The interests of Wyoming and the Black Hills region are so thoroughly alike and harmonious that it is simply folly to talk of their being wholly sundered by any such action as the creation of a separate Territory. But as interested parties are at work to destroy so much of this natural identity as they can, it may be well to give Wyoming's status in the case more publicity. Cheyenne and Wyoming have, with work, money and influence, done more to bring about the settlement and development of the Hills than all adjacent States and Territories combined. Our public men have secured legislation; our capital and energy have built roads and telegraph lines; have opened mines and constructed mills, and have, from the first, furnished more swift and reliable means of communication and more hearty support to all Black Hills enterprises than all other commonwealths together. And why? Simply because our interests have been one, and our commercial relations are as natural as the law of gravitation.

Separating the Black Hills from Dakota or Nebraska settlements are hundreds of miles of unsettled, and probably never to be settled, territory. The chasm will at least not be bridged until nearly all other lands in the west are taken, because it is made up largely of treeless, waterless, alkali plains, and when the newest settlements in those directions, generally 400 miles distant, are reached they have no interest, no law and no fellowship in common with this region, for the reason that their pursuits are confined wholly to agriculture or stock-raising, while these are so largely in the development of mines. Their nearest capital, Yankton, is 480 miles distant. Wyoming settlements unite with those of the Black Hills on the south; her industries, her enterprises and her needs are the same, and her capital city, Cheyenne, is only 250 miles distant. Neither can the Black Hills afford a separate territorial government. A summing up of this matter by one of our prominent writers* is so pertinent that we introduce it here:

"Let us suppose that you carve a new Territory out of the southeast part of Montana, northeast part of Wyoming and the southwest part of Dakota, what is gained in substantial advantage? Your young Territory becomes at once a bone of contention among the hungry and clamorous office-seekers of the east,

* Stephen W. Downey.

who, failing to secure positions elsewhere, will struggle to be saddled by the administration upon you. You are cut off at once from all railway revenues. The prospects of statehood will be distant and dubious. What right, what privilege, what security or what encouragement would be subserved by such separate organization, that would not be better subserved by union with Wyoming? The interests, demands and requirements of a large and populous Territory, full of resources and fast approaching admission as a State, receive respectful attention both from the executive and legislative branches of the general government; while those of the small and weak Territories are treated with comparative indifference. That such *should be* the case is not maintained; that such *is* the case will scarcely be denied; and be it remembered that we must deal with things as they *are*, not as they should be.

"The settlement of central and northern Wyoming by a mining population, consequent upon the removal or repression of hostile Indians, will increase the population of the Territory, if left intact, so that admission as a State may be looked for at no distant day.

"The southern part of Wyoming seeks, and will seek, by all honorable means in her power, to preserve unsevered the Territory as now organized. By such preservation we believe the highest interests of the whole region will be subserved. The whole, as now organized, is destined, ultimately, to be a great mineral and pastoral region, with sufficient agricultural belts, probably, to supply the home market. These interests can be better defended and fostered by united than by divided action. All parts will be easily accessible by the Union Pacific railroad and its projected branches.

"We extend a warm welcome to those that have recently crossed our borders to engage in mining enterprise. Now, in view of the common resources, interests, hopes and perils pervading the length and breadth of our Territory, we ask you to join us, to be part of us and to make common cause with us in warding off disruption. For the same or similar reasons we invite those of you whose fortunes have led you to locate east of our boundaries, to seek a separation from a Territory which, apart from this vicinity, has nothing in common with you, and to attach yourselves to a Territory which has everything in common, and whose legislative policy, as Territory or State, will constantly foster by all reasonable means the industry in which you are engaged, because it is the industry by which, if at all, must come the future wealth and greatness of our State.

"First, we have a unity of geographic, climatic and geologic characteristics, binding us to the same labors, purposes and ends, by a law of nature stronger than the law of political government, forcing to legislation for the common interest regardless of party predilections.

"Second, by union we have *one strong* Territory, able to command attention to our necessities and our rights, instead of *two weak* and *inefficient* organizations.

"Third, by union the north shares with the south in the benefits of $125,000 annually paid in taxes by the Union Pacific Railroad Company, which by a severance the north foregoes.

"Fourth, by union the extension of railway facilities will be fostered, whereas by severance it will be retarded; and

"Fifth, by union we can look forward to a much nearer statehood, with the high privileges of independence which it brings.

"Having followed the course of empire thus far westward, let us unitedly work out here the destiny of the second great State sitting astride the crowning ridge of the American continent."

*Routes, Outfitting Points, etc.*—After traversing two of the principal routes to the Hills, and much of the region crossed by two others, the writer unhesitatingly pronounces the Cheyenne route incomparable; and, what is of little less importance, can state emphatically that no city aspiring to such trade has half the facilities for outfitting miners and settlers, or for forwarding them and their freights, as Cheyenne. All the local papers regularly publish tables of distances, with every minutia of camping places, eating stations, etc., and we need not indulge in such details. It need only be said that the Cheyenne route for the first hundred miles north of the city passes through the best settled portion of Wyoming, where for years our finest herds have roamed and where now nearly every occupied homestead will compare favorably for the value and style of its improvements with those of any western State. The remaining one hundred and fifty miles of road is being rapidly redeemed from the original solitude by ranches located on every stream.

Our home stage line is simply perfect, and the telegraph,

stretched along the entire route, is another advantage and facility offered only by the Cheyenne road. In the matter of freighting no city can hope to compete with Cheyenne. There are over twenty large and reliable firms, running two hundred wagons, regularly engaged in this business, and a great number of smaller freighters who aggregate as many wagons more. The entire number give employment to over four hundred men, and can easily move two million pounds of freight at one loading. Freight rates to Deadwood are from three to five dollars per hundred pounds, the price first named being the lowest for ox-team freights, and the higher price being the average for fast horses and mule trains.

The following comparative table of distances is compiled from official reports of odometer measurements, where they could be obtained. In other cases the statements of the best informed and most reliable citizens of the Black Hills are made a basis for estimates. It will be seen that Cheyenne is nearer Deadwood by forty miles than any other point on the Union Pacific railroad, and seventy-five miles nearer than Bismarck, the terminus of the Northern Pacific:

|  | Miles. |
|---|---|
| Cheyenne, Wyoming, to Deadwood | 250 |
| Sidney, Nebraska, to Deadwood | 290 |
| Kearney, Nebraska, to Deadwood | 358 |
| Bismarck, Dakota, to Deadwood | 325 |
| Yankton, Dakota, to Deadwood | 480 |
| North Platte, Nebraska, to Deadwood | 373 |
| Fort Pierre, Dakota, to Deadwood | 230 |
| Grand Island, Nebraska, to Deadwood | 450 |
| Bozeman, Montana, to Deadwood | 490 |
| Cloud Peak, Big Horn Mountains, to Deadwood | 200 |

# CHAPTER VI.

WHAT would a book of this character be, in this runaway age, without a chapter of Reminiscences? Nothing in the west, or east either, for that matter, is so young, or old, or "middle-aged," that it doesn't date back to a period when it deserved immortalization in gossip. For instance, when the Union Pacific railway company, in the very early history of Cheyenne, offered a town lot to the first boy born there, Mr. William Wise, without any particular parade or fuss, one bright morning in December, 1867, stepped around to the company's headquarters, and informed them of the very recent birth and immediate christening of "George Cheyenne Wise." To be more particular about dates, that the boy may be enabled to get a good title to his property, we will state that this happened on December 6, 1867. But many bouncing Wyoming boys immediately followed, and the first little pioneer was soon lost sight of by the general public.

November 13, 1867, the Union Pacific railroad track reached Cheyenne, and we are told that music, enthusiasm and bunting celebrated the event as was never such an event celebrated before in a Rocky Mountain town. On Sunday, August 4, 1867, the first sermon was preached to a Cheyenne congregation by a Baptist minister, whose name deserves the publicity we are unable to give it. In September, 1867, Thomas E. McLeland, as the first postmaster of Cheyenne, commenced his official duties in a 10 by 15 shanty. He handled nearly 3,000 letters per day, and received the gratifying salary of one dollar per month. The first paper, the *Leader*, was issued by Mr. N. A. Baker, on the 19th of September, 1867. In the first few months of its publication it told of the arrival of the first theatrical company. "The Julesburg Theatrical Troupe;" of the Wells, Fargo & Co.'s coaches leaving for Denver three times per week, and the Union

Pacific track approaching Cheyenne at the rate of two to four miles per day; also, of the completion of telegraphic connection with Denver. The advent of a velocipede, on January 23, 1868, among the cow-boys, "bull-whackers" and western riff-raff generally, was the occasion of no little talk and merriment. About that time occurred a rather primitive wedding, and it was primitively announced in this wise: "On the east half of the north-west quarter of section twenty-two (22), township twenty-one (21) north, of range eleven (11), east, in an open sleigh, and under an open and unclouded canopy, by the Rev. J. F. Mason, James B., only son of John Cox, of Colorado, and Ellen C., eldest daughter of Major O. Harrington, of Nebraska."

March 22, the arrival of W. C. Erwin from the Sweetwater mines, with sixty-five pounds of gold dust, excited new interest in those diggings, and not a few of the Cheyenne people went to the scene of the rich strikes. Then, on that memorable day in April, 1869, when appointments of officials were announced for the new Territory of Wyoming, there was a wonderful flutter of office-seeking hearts. There is a standing joke to the effect that a large delegation of patriotic citizens who had long suffered in Washington, that their beloved Territory might be honored by their appointment, were compelled to walk home across the States and plains, while the successful aspirants from other lands came in the usually dignified and fitting manner, by rail. Cheyenne boasted a school as early as the 9th of February, 1868, Mr. M. A. Arnold and wife being the teachers. The first church building was completed early in September, 1871, by the Methodist Episcopal society. Masonic and Odd-Fellows lodges were organized in the early months of 1868.

Black Hills reminiscences, although dating back only three years, are in a fair way to be lost sight of, unless soon placed in enduring shape. The first building of any kind in the Hills was that erected by Gordon's party on French creek, in the fall of 1874. It was really a stockade, eighty-six feet square and ten feet high, with six cabins ranged around the inside. The party numbered twenty-six persons, and included Mrs. Talent and her infant child,—the first white woman and child to enter the Black Hills. Gordon's party mined near the stockade during that winter. The first town was Custer City, laid out in July, 1875, and the first frame building in the Hills was built at Custer, by

J. W. Lytle, in February, 1876. The pioneer saw-mill commenced turning out lumber in the vicinity of Custer in January, 1876, and was started by Daniel Durett. Printing offices were among the earliest enterprises, the first to reach the Hills being that of Merrick & Laughlin, of Denver. Its entry was at Custer, in May, 1876, but it was moved to Deadwood during the following month, where the *Black Hills Weekly Pioneer* was soon flung to the breeze. They came to the conclusion that it was not good to live alone in those northern wilds at a very early date, for James Hines and Miss Mattie Douglas consummated the first marriage in March, 1876, when mail and telegraph were unknown, and folks had hardly thought of building anything but log houses. Ethel Arnold was the first babe born in the Hills, and was announced at Custer on May 25, 1876. Rev. H. W. Smith, who preached the first sermons ever listened to by Black Hills congregations at Deadwood and Custer, in the early spring of 1876, was killed by Indians in ambush while he was *en route* to Crook City one Sunday morning to fill an engagement there.

Gold was taken out of Deadwood gulch for the first time during the present stampede by a miner named Nuckles, in September, 1875. To Mr. W. H. Hibbard, of Cheyenne, belongs the honor of first extending the electric wire to Custer, Deadwood and other Black Hills cities. His telegraph line was completed to Custer October 19, 1876, and to Deadwood December 1st of the same year. Crook City boasts a newspaper, the *Tribune*, published first on June 9, 1876. Following the *Pioneer*, at Deadwood, were the *Times* and *Champion*. The three last named now publish large daily and weekly editions, where two years ago the amiable savage was reading his title clear and swearing that he would have $80,000,000 for the country or die in the last ditch,— all of which disappeared in smoke. J. J. Williams built the first log cabin on the present site of Deadwood in November, 1875, and his modest effort of twenty months ago is now overshadowed by fifteen hundred good frame houses. The "Bella Union" variety theatre was first to give public entertainment of that kind at Deadwood, and opened with a grand flourish of trumpets and cool toilets early in the summer of 1876. But the inimitable Jack Langrishe and his accomplished wife soon appeared on the scene, with a good legitimate theatrical troupe, and gave amusement-seekers a chaste and high-class character of entertainments. When business grew dull Mr. Langrishe wielded a graceful editorial pen on the *Pioneer* staff, or else worked his gulch claims. From the latter he made good pay in the depth of winter, when he was compelled to boil water to thaw out the frozen ground. Black Hillers who thought they wanted a new Territory called their first meeting on April 7, 1877. It was proposed to call the Territory "Lincoln," and numerous meetings were held, which resulted in the sending of delegate Myers to Washington to push the matter there. But the storm has subsided.

Post-trader Adair, at Cantonment Reno, on Powder river, furnished an item for this chapter by building the first bridge which ever spanned the turbid Powder, in February, 1877. Its building was contracted to a young German miner, who was wintering at the cantonment with the intention of going into the Big Horn mountains in the spring. The contractor took the job very low, but employed a dozen companions and paid them very fair wages. When the bridge was half finished it had cost more than the contractor was to receive, and in order to make the matter square the employes voted enough of their wages back to their employer to finish up the structure, and then agreed to go ahead and complete it. This was finally done, but a day or two afterward the stream exhibited its ugliness by piling up a terrific ice gorge and sweeping the heavy logs downward to the Yellowstone. Captain Pollock, in command at the cantonment, then built a beautiful and massive structure, 160 feet long, near the ruins of the old one. But this, too, was destined to early destruction, and in the month of May the floods swept it down as though it was mere cob-web. Murphey's ranch, on Clear Fork of Powder, established in July of the present year, is the first trading post in the Big Horn region. It is located within fifty miles of the scenes of several of the hardest-fought Indian battles of the past few years, and we hope will cluster around it fitting monuments to the skill of General Crook and other officers, and the bravery of our frontier troops. A good story has been going the rounds at the expense of Perry Cheen, who is at present, and has been for many years, interpreter at the Crow Agency. During the visit of the Earl of Dunraven to Montana, in 1874, he called at the Crow Agency, and after giving a sumptuous "feast" and having a little "medicine talk" with the chiefs, he commenced making inquiries in regard to the business professions, etc., of the white men present, and, turning to Perry, inquired of him his occupation. Mr. Cheen stretched himself up to the full dignity of his profession and delivered himself thusly: " I am interrupter to the Crow Indian-ey and dis-tri-buter of the India-new-ities."

The story of the first steam-whistle on the Missouri river, as told by a Kansas paper, is amusing, if it is old. Its introduction dates back to 1844. At that time the settlers on the Missouri river were in the habit of making regular yearly visits to St. Louis to do their trading for themselves and friends. They were not provided with daily intercourse with the outside world, and many who lived back from the river seldom, if ever, saw a steamboat more than once a year. It happened that during the fall of 1844 the new steamboat Lexington started up the Missouri river loaded down to the guards with freight. Among the passengers were Theodore Warner, Ben Holiday and a planter named George Yocum.

The steamer Lexington was provided with a steam-whistle — the first used on the Missouri river — and, as it happened, no one knew about it except Warner, who was a wag and a lover of a joke. The night after leaving St. Louis the passengers were collected together, playing cards (for fun) in the cabin, when the talk turned upon steamboat explosions, then very common.

" I feel perfectly safe on this boat," said Warner, as he dealt the cards.

" Why?" inquired Yocum, the planter.

" Why?" echoed the rest of the company.

" I will tell you why," said the wag, carefully studying his cards. "This boat is provided with a new patent safety-valve, which notifies the passengers on board when it is about to blow up. It is a concern which makes a most unearthly noise, and when you hear it it is time to get back aft or jump overboard."

Notwithstanding the fact that Warner told his story with the most solemn and earnest countenance, some were skeptical. Not so, however, with the planter. Next morning, when the Lexington was steaming up the long, straight stretch of river just below Washington, Missouri, the passengers were at breakfast. The meal had been called and all were busily engaged in

doing justice to the kind of meals they were accustomed to serve
on steamboats in those days. Suddenly the whistle commenced
to blow — the first time on the trip. The passengers looked at
each other a moment, and horror and dismay spread itself over
their faces. The first man to realize the situation and act was
Yocum, the planter, who, with hair erect and blanched face,
jumped up, crying, as he pulled over one after another of the
passengers :

"Run, run for your lives! the d— thing's going to bust!
Follow me and let's save ourselves!"

Of course there was a stampede for the rear of the boat, and
it was only by the exertions of some of the crew that the more
excited were restrained from jumping into the river.

But the best of all incidents and remembrances, and those
fraught with most direct import to the people of the great northwest, are the records of the creation of our great trans-continental railway. Commencing in 1865, forty miles of track were
laid westward from the Missouri river. In 1866 the rails had
reached out three hundred miles into the wilderness of plains
which their influence is now so rapidly changing into a land of
beautiful homes. By January 1, 1868, five hundred and forty
miles had been completed and the backbone of the continent
surmounted, and by May 10, 1869, the oceans were united by
continuous bands of iron. In a little over three years this
mighty western continent was spanned, the foundation for half
a dozen grand States laid, and a region believed to be irredeem-
able turned into one vast mine of production reaching from one
end to the other. A force of from 20,000 to 25,000 men were
engaged on this gigantic project, and from 5,000 to 6,000 teams
were kept in constant employ during its progress. No summing
up could be more fitting and striking than those already given
so much publicity by Hon. Henry T. Williams: "Think of the
wonderful results accomplished in a few years by the opening of
the Pacific railroad. In 1850 the Far West was unknown and unexplored. In 1860 its total population was but 619,000, most of
whom were residents of the Pacific coast. In 1870 the population had *doubled*. In 1876, seven years after the opening of the
Pacific railroad, see how wonderful the change. The population
of the far western States and Territories had again increased forty
per cent, and the Far West now includes this immense field reached

only by this railroad. Population in 1875, 1,524,703; area of square miles, 1,445,332; area of square acres, 1,332,744,755. The entire capital now invested in railroad enterprises in this vast region now exceeds $750,000,000. Over three hundred towns and stations have arisen on the great trans-continental route and its branches. The annual receipts exceed $30,000,000 a year, and the number of passengers, both through and local, exceeds 1,000,-000. The tide of pleasure travel has turned westward, and Europe clasps hands with China and Japan across our continent. Thus have seven short years turned the travel of the world."

17

251

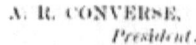
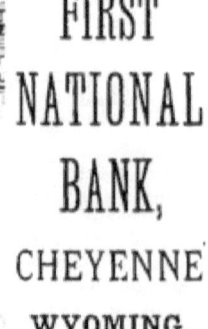

# EDITORIAL BRIEFS.

*Sportsmen's Outfits.*—Parties outfitting for the mines, or preparing for a hunting and fishing tour in the mountains, are reminded that Cheyenne boasts an armory in keeping with its other extensive establishments. The Messrs. Freund Bros. have an endless supply of breech-loading rifles, fishing-tackle, etc., and the very best manufacturers are represented with goods and prices which defy competition in the West.

*The Chicago, Burlington & Quincy.*—In this time of improved railroading facilities it is difficult to discriminate between rival lines, but we are of the belief that the Chicago, Burlington & Quincy is simply perfection. Few of the routes leading to our region pretend to compete with it. Take this old, reliable, magnificently equipped and splendidly managed line from Chicago to Omaha, and enjoy the benefits of palace hotel cars, Pullman drawing-room and sleeping cars and first-class equipment generally.

*The Cheyenne Daily Sun.*—One of the brightest, newsiest and most reliable of all Western papers, is the Cheyenne *Daily Sun,* as conducted by E. A. Slack, Esq. Its editorial corps comprises thoroughly representative Western men; its correspondents are scattered in every city and camp, and its management spares no pains or expense to furnish a journal really in advance of every other interest. A weekly edition furnished the desideratum so often asked by Eastern readers — a perfect resume of frontier news and frontier interests, and is published at the low price of $2.50 per annum.

256

257

# STEBBINS, WOOD & POST

# BANKERS,

## Deadwood, - Dakota,

## DO A GENERAL BANKING BUSINESS

### Buy and Sell Gold Dust, Coin and Bullion,

MAKE ADVANCES ON BULLION AND ORES FOR SHIPMENT ON
ACCOUNT OF PRODUCERS.

*Drafts on All Parts of the United States and Europe for Sale.*

**Telegraph Transfers on All Parts of the United States.**

## SPECIAL ATTENTION GIVEN TO COLLECTIONS.

# GRAVES & CURTIS,

# FURNITURE, CROCKERY

Glassware, Chandeliers, Window Glass,

**CARPETS AND BEDDING,**

**METALLIC BURIAL CASES.**

Main Street, - Deadwood, Dakota.

---

# BENT & DEETKIN,

WHOLESALE AND RETAIL DEALERS IN

## Drugs, Medicines, Paints, Oils, Chemicals

Toilet Articles, Books, Stationery and Pocket Cutlery,

**DEADWOOD, DAKOTA TER.**

---

J. B. VANDANIKER.                                    P. McHUGH.

# IXL

# HOTEL AND RESTAURANT

## DEADWOOD,

**The Largest and Finest Hotel in the Black Hills,**

LOCATED ONE BLOCK FROM STAGE OFFICE.

*The Tables always supplied with the Best the Market Affords.*

C. M. CLARK. CHIEF CLERK.                 VANDANIKER & McHUGH, PROPS.

262

# TO OR FROM

# CHICAGO AND DEADWOOD

## VIA

## OMAHA OR YANKTON,

### OR VIA

## FORT PIERRE OR BISMARK.

◆•◉•◆

## THE

# CHICAGO & NORTH-WESTERN

## RAILWAY

Is by all odds the best line for all persons to take going to or coming from the BLACK HILLS. It owns the SHORTEST and BEST ROUTES, and can offer choice over all other routes.

All Railroad and Ticket Agents can sell you Through Tickets by this route.

Insist that your Tickets between Chicago and Council Bluffs read over the CHICAGO & NORTHWESTERN RAILWAY, and refuse all others.

Pullman Hotel Cars are run on this line.

No other road runs Pullman or any other kind of Hotel Cars between Chicago and Council Bluffs.

The trains are made up of elegant new PULLMAN PALACE HOTEL and SLEEPING COACHES, luxurious, well lighted and well ventilated DAY COACHES, and pleasant lounging and Smoking Cars. The Cars are all equipped with celebrated Miller Safety Platform and Patent Cuffers and Couplings, Westinghouse Safety Air Brakes, and every other appliance that has been devised for the safety of Passenger Trains. In a word, this

# Great Through Line

has the Best and Smoothest Track, and the most elegant and comfortable equipment of any road in the West, and has no competitor in the country.

Remember you ask for your Tickets via the CHICAGO & NORTH-WESTERN RAILWAY, and take no other.

MARVIN HUGHITT,
    General Manager.

W. H. STENNETT,
    Gen'l Passenger Ag't.

# KANSAS PACIFIC RAILWAY.

## *SHORTEST AND MOST DIRECT ROUTE*

### BETWEEN

## COLORADO AND THE EAST.

## 114 MILES THE SHORTEST LINE FROM DENVER TO KANSAS CITY.

## 26 HOURS QUICKER THAN ANY OTHER ROUTE FROM DENVER TO KANSAS CITY AND POINTS EAST.

**THE ONLY LINE** running through trains, with Pullman Palace Cars attached, between Denver and Kansas City, making close connections in Union Depot, Kansas City, with through trains for the East, North and South.

### Baggage Checked Through to Destination.

# The Great Through Freight Line.

Unrivaled facilities offered for direct and prompt dispatch of freight.

ITS "FAST FREIGHT EXPRESS" CONNECTS CLOSELY WITH ALL WESTERN CONNECTIONS.

## THROUGH BILLS OF LADING

Given from Seaboard and intermediate points to

**DENVER, CHEYENNE, COLORADO SPRINGS, PUEBLO, CANON CITY, LA VETA AND EL MORO.**

## The Popular Route to New Mexico, Arizona and San Juan.

The only route west of the Mississippi River equipped with the

CELEBRATED WESTINGHOUSE IMPROVED AUTOMATIC AIR BRAKES.

☞ On all East-bound shipments we offer special inducements. The favorite ore, wool and hide line. Through bills of lading issued and every advantage offered.

### Mark and Consign "Care Kansas Pacific Railway."

| | |
|---|---|
| D. E. CORNELL, | JOHN MUIR, |
| Gen'l Passenger Agent. Kansas City. | Gen'l Freight Agent. Kansas City. |

T. F. OAKES,
Gen'l Superintendent, Kansas City.

# SHORTEST, BEST AND ONLY

## STAGE LINE TO THE

# WIND RIVER AND BIG HORN REGIONS

### FROM THE UNION PACIFIC RAILWAY.

— —

## COACHES OF THE

# SWEETWATER DAILY STAGE LINE

Make Direct Connections with Union Pacific Trains at
Green River City for

# PACIFIC SPRINGS, SOUTH PASS CITY, ATLANTIC CITY,

# CAMP STAMBAUGH, MINERS' DELIGHT,

# LANDER CITY AND CAMP BROWN,

Carrying United States Mails and Express.

— — —

This Line also offers to Tourists the nearest practicable
Route to the

# YELLOWSTONE NATIONAL PARK

The Park is only 300 miles from Green River City, and Coaches
on the SWEETWATER LINE run over half the Route, making the
distance to be traveled by coach or private conveyance 200 miles
shorter than by any other.

A. E. BRADBURY,                              S. S. HUNTLEY,

*Supt., Green River, W. T.*                      *General Manager.*

THE OLD RELIABLE

# CHEYENNE AND BLACK HILLS STAGE LINE.

## Six Horse Concord Coaches

**LEAVING DAILY FOR**

# Deadwood, Custer, Battle Creek,

## RAPID CITY, GOLDEN, GAYVILLE,

*AND ALL OTHER MINING CAMPS IN THE HILLS.*

Close Connections with Union Pacific Trains at Cheyenne.

This Line carries the United States Mails and Express Matter, and passes over the Shortest, Best Settled and Best Protected Route.

First-class Eating Stations and attentive Division Agents add to render the Pioneer Line unequaled for Safety, Comfort and Speed.

J. T. GILMER.                              M. T. PATRICK.

  M. SALISBURY.                              L. VOORHEES.

# THE QUICKEST ROUTE

## TO THE

# BLACK HILLS

### IS VIA THE

# UNION PACIFIC RAILROAD

### AND

# CHEYENNE OR SIDNEY.

If you are going direct to Deadwood, via rail and stage, the Union Pacific routes, via CHEYENNE or SIDNEY, are the quickest, safest and cheapest. If you desire to make your own arrangements for transportation after leaving the railroad, Cheyenne or Sidney are still your best points of departure, since they are conceded by all to be the

## BEST OUTFITTING POINTS

on any route. The many merchants who have located at these points with large stocks of goods in all lines, make the price of supplies as reasonable as in Eastern cities. These points, being located within easy reach of the

## CELEBRATED GRAZING DISTRICTS OF WYOMING

afford special facilities for the purchase of horses, mules and oxen. It may be relied upon that to outfit at either of these points will be attended with less cost than at any other points advertised as outfitting posts.

☞ RATES ALWAYS AS LOW AS THE LOWEST.

# Special Notice to Gold Seekers.

In addition to the advantages of quick time and short and comfortable stage journeys via the UNION PACIFIC ROUTE, the following LOW RATES of fare and arrangements for ticketing have been made for your accommodation:

|  | 1st Class. | 2d Class. | 3d Class. |
|---|---|---|---|
| Chicago to Custer City, | $29 25 | $33 00 | $28 00 |
| Chicago to Deadwood, | 49 25 | 38 00 | 28 00 |
| St. Louis to Custer City, | 39 25 | 33 00 | 28 00 |
| St. Louis to Deadwood, | 49 25 | 38 00 | 28 00 |

One hundred and fifty pounds baggage free by rail, and twenty-five to one hundred pounds free overland, according to route and class.

As the THROUGH RATES from Omaha to Deadwood, Custer City, and all other points in the Black Hills, are considerably less than the LOCAL RATES by rail and stage, money will be saved by purchasing THROUGH TICKETS.

Holders of tickets to Sidney, Cheyenne, etc., can exchange them for through tickets to any point in the Black Hills at the Omaha depot.

☞ All Black Hills tickets sold by connecting roads over the Union Pacific MUST BE EXCHANGED at the U. P. depot before passengers take the train.

Special arrangements made for large parties.

272